MY SECRET
VALENTINE

By Julie Cannon

Come and Get Me

Heart 2 Heart

Heartland

Uncharted Passage

Just Business

Power Play

Descent

Breakers Passion

I Remember

Rescue Me

Because of You

Smoke and Fire

Countdown

Capsized

Wishing on a Dream

Take Me There

The Boss of Her

Fore Play

Shut Up and Kiss Me

The Last First Kiss

Summer Lovin'

By Erin Dutton

Sequestered Hearts

Fully Involved

A Place to Rest

Designed for Love

Point of Ignition

A Perfect Match

Reluctant Hope

More than Friends

For the Love of Cake

Officer Down

Capturing Forever

Planning for Love

Landing Zone

Wavering Convictions

Three Alarm Response

By Anne Shade

Femme Tales

Masquerade

Love and Lotus Blossoms

Her Heart's Desire

In Our Words:
Queer Stories from Black, Indigenous and People of Color
Stories Selected by Anne Shade
Edited by Victoria Villaseñor

Visit us at www.boldstrokesbooks.com

MY SECRET VALENTINE

by

Julie Cannon, Erin Dutton, and Anne Shade

2022

MY SECRET VALENTINE

ISBN 13: 978-1-63679-071-8

THIS TRADE PAPERBACK ORIGINAL IS PUBLISHED BY
BOLD STROKES BOOKS, INC.
P.O. BOX 249
VALLEY FALLS, NY 12185

FIRST EDITION: FEBRUARY 2022

CREDITS
EDITOR: SHELLEY THRASHER
PRODUCTION DESIGN: STACIA SEAMAN
COVER DESIGN BY TAMMY SEIDICK

CONTENTS

I MET SOMEONE
    Julie Cannon   9

TAKING A RISK
    Erin Dutton   85

BOUQUET OF LOVE
    Anne Shade   167

I Met Someone

Julie Cannon

Valentine's Day 1992

The table was set, the room decorated with red and white balloons, an expensive arrangement of flowers sat in the middle of the fancy set table, dinner was warming in the oven, and the video camera was focused on the front door. I paced back and forth looking at my Timex at least a dozen times, waiting for my Valentine to arrive. It was the first of what turned out to be twenty-nine Valentine's Days with my (now) wife Laura. Two weeks earlier I had told her I loved her, and I wanted this evening to be special—duh.

My BFF, who I will call T, was dating M, Laura's BFF, and we had hatched a plan to surprise our girls. T had told M that I was planning a special, romantic dinner at my place for Laura and it was her job to get her to my house. I had told Laura that T was planning a surprise romantic dinner for M and it was her job to get M there. We often did things together, so this wasn't an odd request.

Confusing? Not really. T and I were both surprising our valentines with a special dinner at my house, then dancing at our favorite bar—the Cash Inn.

We had hatched this plan a month or so earlier and had planned every detail. We weren't creeps, the video camera—yes, it was an 8mm Sony—was poised to capture our girls' expressions when they realized what we had done and that the evening was all about them.

Way back then we were all pretty much living paycheck to paycheck, and I had no money to buy the place mats, napkins, flowers, and assorted other romantic accessories to make the evening perfect. This was before ATM cards and credit cards were in everyone's wallet, so I went to the store knowing I'd have to pay the exorbitant $10.00 insufficient-funds charge, in addition to the amount of the check. But my girl was worth it.

I don't cook. I heat things, even today, thirty years later, so I left the chef duties to T. We planned the menu, while T did the cutting, chopping, stirring, and baking for our evening meal. As T toiled away in my kitchen, I set the table with military precision. Everything was in perfect placement, all the corners lined up and each cloth napkin rolled tightly into its holder.

The theme was black and white, and T and I looked fabulous in our rented white tuxedo jackets, black shirts, and jeans and shined boots. I was so afraid I'd get something on my jacket, I put it on only when the headlights of Laura's truck passed across the front window.

"T, they're here!" I shouted, but not loud enough for our girls to hear. We had gone through several practice sessions with the video to know exactly where we needed to stand, and T hurried over to her spot.

It took FOREVER for the doorbell to ring. My hands were shaking, my heart pounding, and I was nervous as hell. I took a deep breath and reached for the knob.

Thirty years later we still talk about that special evening.

Julie Cannon

CHAPTER ONE

How do you tell your best friend that you've met someone? That you've met the woman you want to have by your side, for better or worse, richer or poorer, in sickness and in health, forsaking all others until death do us part.

The forsaking all others was always my biggest hang-up, until I met my "someone." I'd also want to die first because I wouldn't want to live without her. Just thinking about that is enough to send me into a panic attack.

Should be pretty simple, right? Your best friend loves you, wants what's best for you, and wants you to be happy. The complication here is that "my someone" is said best friend, and she has no idea how I feel about her. But today is February 14, and tonight is the night. The night when I'm going to tell Claire I am madly in love with her. Okay, maybe not the full-on "I'm in love with you so much I can hardly breathe" disclosure, but more along the lines of I want to be more than just your friend—a lot more.

It started six months ago when I met Clarice. She hates that name, by the way. She says it reminds her of Jodie Foster's character in *Silence of the Lambs*. I like it because it's her name. Every time I watch the movie, I'm not thinking about Jodie. I'm thinking about Claire.

We met in grad school, when a tall, leggy redhead sat in the vacant chair beside me. We were in a cramped classroom waiting for the instructor of the dreaded Statistics in Economics course to arrive. I had trepidation about this class, and judging by the number of people who had found seats in the room, they, like me, did not want to take the course online.

I was getting my MBA because I had always dreamed of being one of the most successful businesswomen in the country. Okay, maybe not the country, maybe the state, and on some days maybe only as much as my company. Claire, on the other hand, was an architect and wanted to open her own firm. She thought the MBA would help her be successful. Personally, I thought we could find better things to do with our time besides having our heads in a book every evening studying algorithms or whatever else we were going to learn in this stupid class. I will admit I was selfishly glad she had come to this class. What was it that Humphrey Bogart said… "Of all the gin joints in all the towns in all the world, she walks into mine"? I can echo that sentiment. "Of all the statistics classes in all the universities in all the world, and she sits down next to me."

She was older than me by a few years, which made her in her mid-thirties. As we sat chatting, waiting for the instructor to grace us with his presence, we hit it off. I don't make friends easily. I live by myself. The only roommates I ever had were during the two disastrous years I spent in a dorm for my undergrad courses. Other than roommates from hell, I had a great time, met a lot of people, partied with some, slept with more than I probably should have, and barely remembered most of them. I'm at a different university now, far away from home and talking to the most beautiful woman in the classroom. How I got so lucky, I don't know. I think I'll stop and buy some lottery tickets on the way home.

The instructor finally arrived, coming in all pompous, thinking he's all that in his tweed jacket and tortoise-rim glasses. It was August 12, and we were in Phoenix, Arizona, for crying out loud. The outside temp when class started was still over a hundred and ten degrees. What was with the jacket? Did he think we were at Harvard? Did he get off at the wrong stop? Was it wishful thinking on his part, or was he just a deranged, nutty professor? I shot a glance at Claire, and her expression said she was thinking the same thing. Did I mention she had a smattering of freckles across her nose, a breathtaking smile, and the greenest eyes I had ever seen?

The guy was old school, passing out paper copies of the course syllabus. Yes, that's correct, paper copies. Glancing around, I saw some people in the room that had probably never held a piece of paper. We were older than most in the room, the ink still wet on their undergrad diplomas. I'd been working for almost ten years and, at the ripe old age of thirty-two, had realized that to get anywhere else, I needed that ridiculous MBA at the end of my name. At least in my company, I did. I don't mean to insult anyone that has it, but I say ridiculous because I have real experience, which, in my mind, is much more valuable and practical than the degree. This, I thought, was evidenced by my six-figure salary, 40 percent annual bonus, my paid-for, two-year-old truck in the parking lot, my spacious apartment in one of the newer buildings in the city, and my almost-paid-for cabin in the pine woods up north.

Anyway, back to Claire…

CHAPTER TWO

I'm Claire Wheeler," she said, extending her hand. Her voice was smooth, like honey on a warm, sunny day.

"Hayes Martin," I said, barely able to pronounce my own name. From the moment she walked into the room, she had my complete attention. I'm not terribly religious, but I prayed she would sit next to me. Fate, or a higher being listening, had just made my day.

Claire's hand was soft and warm, and I didn't want to let go. Actually, I wanted to put her hand in one of my suddenly very sensitive girl parts, but I have some sense of what's appropriate in a room filled to capacity. It was six thirty p.m., and this was not the time to make that level of my interest known.

She made notes on her syllabus, using an interesting-looking pen, and I imagined her hand traveling over me. Her handwriting was bold, containing harsh lines like the ones in an architect's drawing. I wondered if she learned to write like that as a child or later in life.

I had a hard time concentrating on what Prof Pompous was saying, my attention shifting between the scent of Claire's perfume and erotic thoughts of her fingers writing naughty words on my naked skin. Claire didn't seem to be having any trouble, and an image of her tutoring me in how 69 is not a prime number flashed in my mind.

Claire moved her head close to me. For a heart-stopping moment, I thought she might kiss me.

"Are you okay?" she asked, her question deflating my lust balloon.

I looked at her, then glanced around the room. Everyone was either taking verbatim notes or writing the great American novel. My notebook was completely blank. The heat of embarrassment at getting caught crawled up my neck like a bad rash.

"Yeah. Just taking it all in," I mumbled. Or was it some other stupid response? I wasn't sure. But I did know I'd better start paying attention to the gray-haired guy in the front of the room instead of the captivating redhead to my left, or I'd be taking this class a second time. God strike me down now.

"Do you believe this guy?" Claire asked as Professor Tweed Jacket droned on.

She had a soft Southern drawl that drew me in like a warm bath. Her eyes were the color of fresh-cut grass, and her right ear was pierced four times. I have two holes in each ear, and I know from experience that the higher up you go, the more stars you see when the needle jabs through.

"I can honestly say I've never had a teacher quite like him. He's exactly what I expected an econ professor to look like. All buttoned up and wearing horned-rimmed glasses. The jacket is a bit much though."

Claire stifled a laugh. "I'm sweating just looking at him."

The guy in front of me turned around and glared at us. We both forced back a giggle. Finally, after seventy-five brutal minutes, our instructor pranced out the door, followed by everyone in the room except Claire and me. She looked about as shell-shocked as I felt.

"So, did you get all that?" she asked, almost deadpan.

I must have said something witty because she started laughing. It sounds corny, but her giggles were like my favorite song to my ears. I got warm all over—certain areas much hotter than others.

"Do you want to grab a coffee or something?" Claire asked. "Maybe we can compare notes."

I certainly knew what "or something" I'd pick, and it didn't come out of an espresso machine, but it would definitely keep me up all night.

"Sure," I managed to say through the erotic haze between my ears.

We made small talk on our way downstairs to the small coffee shop on the first floor. Claire bought her coffee and said she'd get us a table. The guy behind me in line nudged me, my attention on Claire's ass she walked away instead of the barista asking for my order.

We chatted over coffee, and that's how I found out Claire was, in fact, an architect, had a two-hundred-gallon fish tank, and lived not far from me in one of the new high-rises downtown. She never mentioned a boy or girlfriend, and the opportunity to ask never came up. My gaydar had been on the fritz lately, and I was not going to make that embarrassing mistake again.

The coffee shop catered to the requisite flavors and concoctions of coffees. Tables for two were scattered around the cozy dining area, with overstuffed, comfy-looking chairs by the windows. A dozen tables for four were covered by laptops and papers. A couple in the corner was on a first date, their body language a dead giveaway. The place smelled wonderful but was a complete waste on me. I took my coffee plain, black, no sugar, preferably Peets or Dunkin Donuts.

I tried not to stare at Claire when she talked, but she was mesmerizing. Her eyes danced when she spoke about something exciting, sparkled with intelligence, and twinkled with laughter at a funny story. She was expressive, using her hands to make a point, and she drew me in to the point that I could barely breathe. What in the hell had happened to me?

She was like a sorceress, casting her spell over me. Corny but true. If I believed in love at first sight, I'd have chirping birds and butterflies floating above my head. Jesus, I had it bad. Now if I could only get rid of what "it" was, I'd be in good shape.

I must have been able to carry on a somewhat coherent conversation because Claire gave me her complete attention. As I said earlier, my gaydar needed a tune-up, so I wasn't sure if she was flirting with me or just being friendly. She didn't hesitate to lean close when she looked at my class notes, and our arms brushed when she pointed to something specific on the page. Goose bumps jumped to attention, as did my libido. That too had been on hiatus for a while but roared back when Claire had entered the classroom. It felt like I'd known her forever, and I definitely wanted forever to be, well, forever.

"Wow. I kept you out way too long on a school night."

She winked at me, and schoolgirl thoughts did not pass through my mind.

Out on the sidewalk, the temperature was hovering in the upper nineties, a typical late-summer Phoenix evening.

"That was fun," Claire said, almost shyly. It surprised me because she had done most of the talking and hadn't seemed the least bit nervous.

"Yes, it was." I agreed. "Let's consider it a reward for sitting through that class."

"Great idea. You can pick the place next time," Claire said, and my heart leapt at the thought of a next time.

"You're on," I said, trying to keep my schoolgirl giddiness to myself.

"See you next week, Hayes," she said before turning to walk down the sidewalk.

It might have been the heat, might have been the way she said my name, but I melted nonetheless.

CHAPTER THREE

For the next six days, I thought of Claire constantly. A flash of red hair out of the corner of my eye at a luncheon honoring the Phoenix Woman of the Year sent my heart skittering and my feet shuffling through the crowd on a search-and-find mission. My effort was fruitless, and I was the last person to sit at the table sponsored by my employer. I tried not to look too obvious as I continued to scan the people at the tables around me. When it was over, a woman whom I had met earlier cornered me, preventing my escape and the continuation of my safari for the redhead.

Tuesday couldn't come soon enough, and I'd tossed half of my closet onto my unmade bed, much to the chagrin of Keo, the cat I rescued from the garbage dumpster a few months ago. For much longer than I want to admit, Keo has been the only other female to lie in my warm, tumbled sheets. As a result, I was cranky and had a tough time focusing.

Tonight was class, and I'd see Claire again. At least I hoped I did. In previous courses, attendance had dropped off in the second class and steadily went downhill as the weeks crawled by. I prayed she was persistent and goal oriented.

Anyway, back to my wardrobe dilemma. I had a late meeting and would have no time to come home and change from my stuffy business suit to something a little more attractive. Not that a killer, don't-fuck-with-me suit ever went out of style, but I wanted to look fun and interesting, not buttoned up and totally professional. I supposed I could stop and change on my way out of the building, but that would entail hauling everything in from my car to my office to ensure nothing got wrinkled or, God forbid, I forgot some key wardrobe element like my belt or my socks. I could change in my car in the parking garage, but with my luck, I'd get arrested for indecent exposure. My driver's license photo was bad enough that I can only imagine what my mug shot would look like. No way was I going to get half naked in a gas-station bathroom.

Keo grumbled, cat-speak for "just pick something. It's a class, not your nomination speech for the president of the US. You're there to learn something, not score, even if she is the most beautiful woman you've ever seen." The alarm on my watch told me I'd better get moving or not only would I be late, but I'd probably spill my coffee all over myself in my haste to maneuver through later-than-normal morning traffic.

Finally pulling myself together, I gathered up the work I had tried and failed to complete last night, shoved my sleeping laptop into my briefcase, took my suit jacket and To Go coffee in hand, and reached for my keys. I had a moment of panic when I couldn't find them but located them with my handy-dandy Find My Key app. They were under a stack of mail I'd tossed onto the table last night. I had better calm down and replace my giddy-can't-wait-to-see-her-again face with my cool, confident, professional persona. The one I had worked my ass off to learn and master.

"Wish me luck," I shouted to Keo as I headed out the door into the garage.

"Fuck." I hit the button again with the same result—nothing but a groan from the garage-door opener hanging from the ceiling. I did not need this complication this morning. The solution was simple. Grab the red handle hanging from a red-and-white string attached to the opener and pull. If I got a speck of dirt on myself heaving the door up and over my head, I'd be seriously pissed. Not to mention how Keo would feel having her queendom throne on my bed disrupted again.

Somehow, I made it to work without a mishap. A few people were in, and I passed several empty cubes to the last office on the left. I grabbed a stack of papers off the community printer when I saw the top sheet was the cover page of a proposal I was working on. I always sent something to the printer, then promptly forgot about it. Several months ago, they removed all our individual printers in our offices under the auspice of "cost efficiency" and installed mega all-in-one machines in strategically placed locations on the floor. Strategic to the offices closest to them, but not to me. Personally, I think they did it as a way to get us off our butts and walking a few dozen of our suggested ten thousand steps a day to drive down our health-care costs. The lights in my office flicked on as I entered, another recent efficiency improvement that made me nuts when they shut off while I was sitting at my desk, because I wasn't moving enough for the blinking green light to sense I was still there.

"Wanna grab a pizza tonight?" Barb, the woman in the next office, stuck her head in my office after lunch. We weren't dating, just two single, unattached ladies who needed to eat. Barb was as straight as a ruler but could have been a stand-up comedian if she gave up her day gig. We occasionally hung out together, commiserating about our love lives and talking smack about our latest disaster date over a few beers.

"Can't. I have class tonight."

"That's right," she said, shaking her head. "How do you do it? I would pull my hair out strand by strand if I had to sit through a math class for two and a half hours."

"Surprisingly, it kept my attention for the entire class." No need to tell Barb exactly why.

"You're a better woman than me. That's why you'll have the big office in the corner, and I'll still be in that one." She waved her thumb like a hitchhiker in the direction of hers.

Barb had the hottest office on the floor, and no number of visits by Oscar, the cute maintenance guy, could fix the problem. Personally, I think she sabotages the thermostat so he will visit her.

"It's my last class for my MBA, and I have to get an A or B, or our tuition-reimbursement program won't reimburse anything." That was a mouthful. "That, and I just want to be done. It feels like I've been at it *forever*."

"Well, you have fun," Barb said before disappearing out of my doorway.

"I completely expect to," I said with confidence.

♥

I took my same seat and waited anxiously for Claire to arrive. I swear, the second hand sounded like a ticking time bomb waiting to detonate if Claire was a no-show. When I'd looked in the mirror this morning, I imagined Claire beside me. She was a little taller than my own five foot seven, and I carried more than a few extra pounds than she did. My dark hair was a nice contrast to her red. I had caught our reflection in the window of the coffee shop and thought we made a very striking couple. In my dreams.

Finally, at two minutes till the hour, she hurried in. Her gaze went straight to mine, and she frowned when she saw the books on the table next to me. I quickly moved them and indicated that the spot was hers.

"Thanks for saving me a seat," she said, sitting down beside me, out of breath. "An accident was blocking the intersection, and it took forever to get here."

"No problem," I said, trying not to watch her breasts move up and down as she caught her breath.

For the next few weeks after each class, Claire and I found a quiet place where we could review our notes. We met for dinner a few times before class and quizzed each other on an upcoming test. We were a good team. Claire got the theory that escaped me, and I excelled in the practical application. I told her so one night after class.

"I agree," she said. "I don't know if I would be doing as well as I am if not for you."

She laid her hand on top of mine, and my mouth was suddenly very dry. Her smile rocked my pitiful world.

"Right back atcha," I said stupidly. I didn't move my hand, not wanting to break our connection. With my luck, I was the only one feeling like we were something other than classmates. In four weeks, Claire hadn't given me any clue if she was interested in being more than study buddies or even if she was a lesbian. I didn't know if I was barking up the wrong tree, driving in the wrong lane, swimming upstream, or any other stupid analogy for a lesbian falling for a very straight girl. No way was I going to spill the beans or show my hand. If I was wrong, I'd probably lose her. It wasn't worth the risk.

Chapter Four

H ayes?"
I sat up in bed so fast, I got a little dizzy. Claire's ringtone woke me from a sound sleep. "Claire? Is that you?" We'd talked on the phone many times, but she didn't sound like herself. "Are you okay? Has something happened?"

"No."

I tamped down my panic. No, she was not okay, or no, something didn't happen?

"Claire, what's wrong?" I threw back the covers, dashed across my bedroom, and flicked on the light. I grabbed a pair of shorts from my drawer and the first T-shirt in my closet. I was scrambling for my shoes. I needed to be where she was, and now.

"I'm sick."

"I'm on my way."

"No. You…" She coughed, an awful, raspy sound. "You don't need to come over."

"Too bad. I'm on my way. Do you need anything?"

"No. Just you." The last two words were more than a whisper.

I broke all kinds of traffic laws, which didn't matter, because no one was on the road at two a.m. I cut the normal time of fifteen minutes to get to her place in half. I jumped out of my truck almost before the engine shut down and ran to her front door. I knocked several times.

"Claire. Claire, it's me. Claire, honey, come open the door." I was looking around for where she might hide a spare key when I heard the deadbolt turn. I didn't wait for her to open the door. I just went in.

She was wearing a pair of sleep shorts and a thin T-shirt, and she looked awful. Her eyes were puffy, her hair askew, and she was really pale.

"Jesus, Claire," I said putting my arm around her and leading her back to her bedroom. Her steps were slow, and it felt like she'd lost at least ten pounds. "How long have you been sick?"

"A few days." She coughed again, this time doubling over in her attempt to breathe. When we'd gone to a Halloween party a few days ago, she'd seemed fine.

"Jesus. Let's get you into bed." I stopped when we reached her bedroom. Even from the doorway, the air was stale and smelled like sickness. It was my first time in her bedroom, and I found the light switch on the wall. I didn't take time to register the decor, too busy taking care of her.

"Come on," I said, leading her to the bed. "Can you stand up by yourself?" The bedding was a mess and needed straightening. She nodded, which was good. Talking would probably start her coughing again.

Finished tugging on sheets and pulling on blankets, I said, "Okay. Let's get you tucked in." She didn't need any encouragement but almost fell into the bed. I lifted her legs onto it and covered her with the sheet and blanket. Her forehead was warm, and I made a side trip to her bathroom, where I found the Tylenol in the medicine cabinet. I'd seen a bottle of water on her nightstand, but even if she'd taken a dose of the fever-reducing meds recently, a couple more probably wouldn't hurt.

I had to cajole her to swallow the pills, then tucked the blanket under her chin. I started to bend down and kiss her forehead but stopped when I realized she was probably contagious. "I'll be back to check on you in a minute."

Her fridge was completely stocked with everything from mayonnaise to several neatly stacked Tupperware containers on the second shelf. She had two quarts of milk in the door and a six-pack of beer on the top shelf. But I didn't see any 7 Up or Ginger ale or anything that resembled what a sick person should drink to stay hydrated. No saltine crackers or chicken soup in her pantry either. After clicking on my Amazon order, I grabbed a chair from the kitchen and went back to the bedroom.

She was sleeping, her breathing a little ragged. I planned to stay awake and keep a close eye on her, and if she got any worse…do what? Blessed with good genes, I was rarely sick and had never taken care of someone that was. Would I know what to do?

I checked on her every fifteen minutes. At four, she was burning up, the recent dose of meds apparently not working. She was drenched in sweat, her sheets damp. How long had she been like this and I hadn't noticed? Shit. What should I do now? Every solution known to mankind was in Google, so I grabbed my phone and GTS—Googled that shit.

Somehow, I managed to get her into a cool bath and was sitting on the edge of the tub when she started to slide dangerously close to complete submersion. Not knowing what else to do, I stripped and climbed in behind her. Cradling her against me, I couldn't help but think how good she felt in my arms, cool water be damned. I reacted as I always did with a naked woman in my arms but pushed those thoughts away. This was not the time. Twenty-five minutes later, Claire back in bed with fresh sheets I'd found in the closet, I took a hot shower, my shivers almost uncontrollable.

It was another full day before her fever broke. I'd sat beside her bed, sometimes holding her hand, infection be damned. I was so worried. I changed her sheets and pj's three times to keep her comfortable. I was just finishing putting the clean sheets away when I heard her call my name. I raced into her bedroom.

"You're here," she said, her voice weak but clear.

I sat on the bed beside her. Her forehead was cool, her eyes clear. "Where else would I be?" I was so relieved she was getting better.

"I didn't know if I was dreaming or not."

"Nope. I'm here in the flesh. How are you feeling?"

"I'm thirsty."

I reached for the glass of water I had infused with electrolytes. "Here. Just a few sips."

Her hand shook as she reached for the straw, so I covered it with mine, steadying it.

"How long have you been here?" she asked after lying back down.

"Two days."

"Two days," she said and tried to get up.

"Hey. Lie back down. You were really sick. You still need to rest."

"But—"

"No buts allowed. I called your work and told them you wouldn't be in for the rest of the week. They sent a beautiful bouquet of flowers, by the way."

"How, why did you get here?"

"Don't you remember? You called me Saturday night, or, actually, it was early Sunday morning, and I came right over."

"I called you?"

"Yes, and I'm so glad you did. You were really sick, Claire. I was worried. If you hadn't turned the corner today, I was going to take you to the hospital."

"Wow. I'm sorry."

"For what? For thinking of me when you needed help? I feel really special," I said, trying to cheer her up. "I even got to see you naked."

Her eyes opened wide.

"Yep. Kind of hard to change your jammies without that happening. I swear, though, I didn't look." This time she smiled. "You get some rest. We'll talk more later."

"Hey," Claire said two hours later. She was standing in the doorway leading to her bedroom. I jumped up off the couch and went to her. She looked a hundred times better than when I first arrived.

"How are you feeling?" She took my arm for support as we walked to the couch.

"I think I'll live. Better yet, I think I want to live. For a while there it was touch-and-go." She chuckled.

"Are you hungry?"

"Starved. I feel like I haven't eaten in days," she said, pulling her feet up under her.

"That's because you haven't. We'll start easy. Let me get you some soup."

Her color and the sparkle in her eyes were returning, and my hand shook as I stirred the soup. The worry and adrenaline rush I'd had over feeling completely helpless while she was sick were leaving, and I was crashing. I had to hold it together for a little while longer.

"I need a shower," she stated about thirty minutes after she finished eating. She started to get up, but I was there first.

"Take it easy. You're still not up to speed. Let me help you."

I helped her into the bathroom, and she insisted she would be fine. "Seeing me naked in a therapeutic way is different than seeing me naked in the shower," she said, her eyes twinkling.

"I don't know. You could slip and fall," I said, teasing. I couldn't describe how good it felt to have her back.

"You're fired, Florence Nightingale."

She shut the bathroom door, her laughter drifting through it.

Chapter Five

Do you want to go camping?"

"Camping? Like 'sleep on the ground and pee in the woods' camping?" Claire asked, sounding skeptical.

"Well, we could, but I was thinking more along the lines of a cabin, roaring fire, comfortable beds, and indoor plumbing. In other words, my cabin." We would be on Thanksgiving break next week, and a long weekend away was exactly what I needed.

"Oh, thank God. I thought you were serious." Her relief was apparent. "You have a cabin?"

"Yeah. It kind of fell into my lap. One of my coworkers was getting divorced, and his wife had just found out about his little love nest. He had to sell it fast, so he offered me the proverbial deal I couldn't pass up. It's a remodeling work in progress, but the important, comfortable things I did first."

My cabin was on three acres of wooded pine, my backyard nestled against a national forest with my nearest neighbor almost a mile away. I try to get up there every other weekend to escape the rat race and the unrelenting heat in the summer. It is my space, my go-to place for solitude and to recharge my batteries.

Over the past two years, I'd put on a new roof, increased the insulation, replaced the windows, and upgraded the kitchen and bathroom. The place wasn't big—only two bedrooms, one bath, and a kitchen/great room. I'd done all the work myself, often limping into work on Monday mornings. I had just installed a new generator so the place would be warm or cool, as the weather dictated. The next project was to refinish the wood floors.

I had never invited a woman to the cabin, not even my friends.

Even though Claire was a friend, I wanted her to be more—much more. I had almost blurted out my wish more than a few times, but somehow, I was able to keep my feelings to myself. I had debated inviting Claire for several weeks, the opportunity to be with her far more appealing than spending another weekend alone.

Ten days later we were pulling into the driveway. It didn't take long for us to unpack and settle in front of a warm fire on the back deck.

"It's so beautiful here. I can see why you've kept it a secret."

We'd left late Thursday afternoon, and on the drive up, I'd told Claire she'd be the first person to use the guest bedroom. As a matter of fact I'd had to buy furniture and make a quick trip up here to set up the room before we arrived.

"It's not so much that I keep it a secret. It's just that I have no family here, and I enjoy the peace and quiet and solitude." Until I met Claire, that is.

"So why did you invite me?"

"Excuse me?" I knew exactly what she was asking but played dumb to give me a few minutes to come up with an answer other than "I want to share my special place with you, and one of these days, I'll get up the nerve to kiss you."

"You said you like being alone here. Why did you invite me?"

"Actually, I like not having to entertain anyone. I like to do the legendary 'chill out and not play tour guide or entertainment director,' and you seem to fill that bill." Other than class stuff, we'd gone out a few times to dinner and an occasional movie. We even went to the home-and-garden show, which was a first for me—going with someone. I'm more of a loner when it comes to stuff like that, preferring to look at the things I'm interested in and passing up all the things I'm not.

"You're taking a big chance. We're here for four days. That could be three more than forever." She was the one teasing now.

"I'll risk it," I replied, actually thinking that getting to know Claire better was worth the risk.

"Thank you again for taking care of me when I was so sick."

It was at least the third time she'd thanked me. "I would say it was my pleasure, but that just doesn't sound right." Yet it had been a pleasure in an odd way. The fact that Claire trusted me enough to turn to me when she needed help blew my mind. She had other friends that she'd known longer than me—we had all played cards a couple of times—but she'd called me. I was able to take care of her, which meant everything to me.

"I think I know what you mean."

Several minutes later Claire leaned her head back and sighed. "The stars are so bright."

"We're several thousand feet higher than Phoenix, plus there's no light pollution."

"Light pollution?"

"When the streetlights and all the lights in the surrounding area fill the sky."

"I wish I'd paid more attention in astronomy class," Claire commented.

I stood and picked up our glasses. "I'll get us a refill while you find the Big Dipper."

After making a quick stop at the bathroom to brush my teeth and then refilling our wineglasses, I returned outside. Claire had taken the blankets off the chairs, lowered the back on the double chaise lounge, and tossed two throw pillows from the couch onto it.

"We'll get a kink in our neck looking up all night. This way," she patted the cushion beside her, "we can just open our eyes, and everything's right in front of us."

I couldn't find fault with her logic, so I settled in beside her. I tried hard not to think about the fact that I was lying next to her, inches separating us. She radiated heat, and I itched to reach for her.

"Is that it?" Claire pointed to the sky.

"What?" My mind was a little fuzzy from being this close to her, so I didn't remember what we'd been talking about.

"The Big Dipper. I think that's it right there."

"Where?" I didn't tell her I had no idea where it was. All I knew was that it was a group of bright stars that formed a…well…a dipper.

She rolled over and leaned against me. "It's right there. Follow my finger and go straight out."

Her perfume was intoxicating, her face inches from mine, her breath caressing my cheek. If I turned my head just a bit, I could kiss her. My mind went to places it hadn't gone in a while, and my body liked the trip.

"Do you see it?" Claire asked, seeming oblivious to what her nearness was doing to me.

"Yes, I do." I needed to move before I did something stupid, like kiss her. She rolled away from me and onto her back. Disappointment overshadowed relief.

"I could lie here and look at this forever."

"I could lie here like this forever too," I said honestly, changing the words to fit my thoughts.

As my body raged with ideas of its own, I was eerily at peace. Maybe content was a better word. Every time I was with Claire I was exactly where I wanted to be. It just felt right.

I hadn't paid much attention to another woman since the day Claire sat down beside me. I had absolutely no desire to, yet I tried, really tried. I had gone out several times with my friends and even had a few dates, but I kept comparing everyone to Claire. They all came up way short.

"When did you realize you were a lesbian?"

My heart thumped, but not from passion. I was very cautious. I had disclosed my sexual preference to Claire one evening after class over a cup of coffee. She took the news in stride, as if I'd just said today was Tuesday. She didn't blink or sit back in her chair to create more distance from the lesbian at the table.

"That was a stupid question." Her voice betrayed that she also felt stupid.

"No. Not at all. It's a reasonable question. I guess I was in my teens when I realized that I wanted my girlfriends to be my *girlfriends*. Some lesbians realize it early on and others not until later."

"I was just wondering."

What else was Claire curious about? I quenched any further thoughts that would only result in heartbreak. With a blanket of stars overhead and Claire lying beside me, I closed my eyes.

When I woke, the air was crisp, and even without opening my eyes I knew the sun was peeking over the horizon. It would be another hour before it cleared the treetops. We'd slept out here all night, the pain in my back confirming that fact. I came instantly awake when I realized she was curled against me in a typical lovers' embrace. Her leg was over my thigh, her head on my chest, and her hand lay warmly on my stomach. My arm was around her, holding her close.

How many times had I dreamed of this moment? Well, not exactly this scenario, but waking up in a rumpled bed with her warm and close to me the morning after.

Claire rolled over to her other side, pulling me with her into the proverbial spoon. I covered us with one of the blankets, the early morning air chilly. She found my hand and moved it between her breasts and held it there. I didn't even try to go back to sleep. Not only was I wide-awake all over, but I also wanted to imprint this moment in my memory bank.

Claire fit perfectly against me. Her cute butt was snug against my crotch, like a puzzle piece. I let my mind go places I had tried to stay away from. Falling asleep every night sated from making love. Waking every morning wrapped around her like this. The everything in between was just as sweet. The mundane of everyday life would never be boring with Claire, the routine never growing old. The intimate moments where our eyes would meet over coffee or we'd laugh together at something funny on TV would always be fresh and new. I pushed away what would never be and focused on the here and now. I was Claire's friend, nothing more.

"What are you thinking about?"

Claire's question surprised me. I had no idea she was awake. "What are you thinking?"

Best way to deflect the question is with another question.

"That this is a wonderful way to wake up."

She shifted even closer, if that was physically possible. What did she mean? Waking up to a crisp cool morning or here, with me, like this?

"Yes. It is."

"But I'm freezing."

"Me too. Let's go inside," I said reluctantly.

Claire stood and held out her hand to help me up. I stood and stepped so close to her our breath mingled. She looked at my lips. "Kiss me," my mental telepathy screamed.

She gazed at my lips for a long time and then stepped back. "I need a hot shower."

I need a cold one.

After our showers, mine cold and involving a little self-satisfaction, we headed into town for breakfast. Claire had commented earlier that, by the looks of my pantry, we'd starve to death if we got snowed in. So, after splitting an enormous omelet and two cups of coffee each, we made our way back to my truck.

"Didn't you say you went to NAU?" Claire asked suddenly after we had passed a sign that pointed in the direction of my alma mater, Northern Arizona University.

"Yes. I did."

"At the risk of wearing out my welcome on the first day, will you take me on a tour?"

"Really?"

"Yes. I want to see where you went to college. But I really want to hear about your escapades." She raised and lowered her eyebrows several times, emphasizing her point.

"I don't think I had any escapades."

Claire chuckled. "Hayes, honey. We all had escapades in college. I'll tell you mine if you tell me yours."

I'll show you mine if you show me yours. That's what I really wanted to say. Instead, I said, "Deal."

I loved hearing Claire laugh, so I may have exaggerated or enhanced a few stories. I showed her my dorm, and she made us stop at the bookstore. She bought a T-shirt, and I snagged a hoodie on sale.

Back at the cabin, after putting away a few groceries we'd stopped for, we went for a walk on one of the many trails in the area. We talked about everything and nothing and often didn't say anything at all. After a light lunch we were exhausted from the hike in the thin air and relaxed in the lounge chairs. I felt completely comfortable having Claire in my space. She didn't force a conversation or seem to have the need to fill the silence. She appeared to be as content as I was just enjoying the company, the quiet, and the view.

"I'll be right back," she said. She went inside and came back a few minutes later holding a book. "May I read this?" She held up a paperback written by an author famous for her hot sex scenes.

"Um," I stammered. "Sure, but it's a lesbian novel."

"I know. I read the blurb on the back."

"That author writes some pretty hot sex scenes," I said in warning.

"So does that mean I can't read it?"

"No. Not at all. It's a great story. One of my favorites. Just buyer beware," I said, reinforcing my caution.

"Duly noted."

I remembered the book opened with a steamy sex scene that lasted at least a dozen pages. I'd read somewhere that authors needed to grab the reader's attention in the first few pages, and that book had certainly grabbed mine.

I watched Claire out of the corner of my eye as she turned the pages one by one. Her expression never changed, but I noticed the time between pages grew longer. Typically, if you're not interested in a particular scene, you skim over it and get on to something more interesting. She was taking her time on every page. A couple of times she raised her eyebrows and nodded, as if saying, "well, that's interesting," or some other enlightened thought. Her face was flushed, and I thought I saw her hand shake slightly when she turned the page.

The sun was sliding behind the trees, the air getting chilly fast. She, however, didn't seem to notice. I got up and retrieved a light blanket and laid it over her legs. She mumbled her thanks, or at least I think she did. I wasn't sure because she was still riveted to the book.

"Didn't your mother tell you you'll ruin your eyes reading in the dark?" I said, swinging my legs off my chair. The sky was now almost completely dark.

She looked up and around at her surroundings. "Oh, my God. How long have I been reading?"

"You tell me," I said, grinning.

"At least a dozen sex scenes and three code blues," she said, laying the book in her lap.

"What do you think?" I asked, indicating the book.

"This woman." She pointed to the photo on the back of the book. "She sure knows how to write a scene."

Was she referring to the sex scenes or the medical ones?

"God. If I could have the sex Adrianne has, I'd be one happy lady."

"If you had the sex Adrianne has, you'd be a lesbian."

"Well, there is that," Claire said, then paused. "Do you...I mean is that what..." She didn't finish her question. "Never mind. It's none of my business."

"Are you asking if that's what I do or a more general question?" Her question solidified my belief that she was straight, and I crashed with disappointment. If she wanted to know how I had sex, I'd let her know exactly what she was missing.

"Nothing. Forget I asked," she said, flushed again.

Interesting, I said to myself. I'll have to keep that physical reaction in mind.

We bumped elbows making dinner and laughed about silly things. I wasn't much of a cook, so I hated people in the kitchen when I tried to prepare a meal. I felt embarrassed that I was thirty-two and could barely boil an egg. Claire did most of the work, and I followed directions—cut these up, grate that, and stir the sauce. I had never felt so comfortable having someone in my space. It was like she'd always been there.

After the dishes were done and put away, I filled our wineglasses and brought the bottle outside with us. The night was cooler, and each of us bundled up on our lounge chair.

After quite some time, Claire broke the silence. "Are you cold?"

"Freezing," I admitted, but with Claire sitting beside me, I had no desire to go inside.

"Me too, but I want to stay out here. It's so beautiful, and we leave the day after tomorrow."

"You must be reading my mind," I said.

"Come over here," Claire said, scooting over in her chair. She lifted her blanket in invitation.

If she could read my mind, I'm sure she would rescind the invitation.

"Come on. We can keep each other warm and stay outside longer."

I wasn't sure if she was telling me something or if it was my imagination, but I was never one to pass up an invitation to be in the arms of a beautiful woman. Especially if that woman was Claire.

I slid in beside her, and she covered us both. We were cocooned, so our combined body heat would do its job. Actually, I was on fire, and the chilling air was doing nothing to douse it.

"Thank you for bringing me here." Her voice seemed inches from my neck.

"My pleasure." No two words were truer.

We must've fallen asleep like that because when I woke, the fire was out, and the temperature had dropped considerably. Reluctantly I moved out of Claire's arms.

"Claire, we've got to go in. Claire, sweetie," I said, gently nudging her awake.

"What?"

"It's too cold to stay out here. We have to go in."

"But I was sleeping so good. I love sleeping with you," she said drowsily.

"I'd like to not sleep with you more," I mumbled, then raised my voice. "I do too, but the sooner we get up and into warm beds, the better. Come on."

I took her hands and pulled her to her feet. Sleepily, she swayed a little, and I wrapped my arm around her shoulders and led her inside.

I double-checked to make sure all the doors were locked, then went to my room. Claire's light was on, and I imagined what she was doing to get ready for bed. Why is it the more you try not to think about something, the more you do? I closed my eyes and tried not to imagine Claire in the middle of the bed across the hall.

CHAPTER SIX

We had a leisurely breakfast the next morning and took a long walk on one of the trails that crisscrossed through the forest. It was warmer today, and Claire was wearing a long-sleeve T-shirt and black running tights with a bold stripe of color accentuating her curves that made me trip over my own two feet. Her hair was pulled through the hole in the back of a white cap. Given my chivalrous nature, I let her go first when the trail was too narrow for us to be side by side. Actually, I did it so I could watch her ass without getting caught.

After lunch, we sat on the deck just enjoying each other's company. We talked about politics, our favorite music, and our most embarrassing moments in high school. Claire made me laugh, her storytelling enchanting. Other than her question about me coming out, we stayed away from the topic of boyfriends or girlfriends. We cackled about our instructor and speculated about our classmates.

"That was certainly a page-turner," Claire said an hour later, closing the book she'd been reading yesterday.

"I'm glad you enjoyed it."

"That's one way to describe it," she said, more to herself than to me.

"I have a few others by that same author, if you want to read more."

"I'm not sure how much more of that I can handle."

"They are a bit…uh…intense," I commented.

"Intense isn't the word I'd use to describe it."

I looked at her, waiting for her to expand.

"Hot is a more appropriate word," she said, fanning herself with her hand. "I wonder," she said, "does she write what she knows or how she wants it to be?"

"Does it matter?"

"Lucky for her if it's autobiography versus fiction."

That was an interesting comment.

An hour later, I asked, "How about we go fishing?"

"Fishing?" Claire asked, sounding skeptical.

"Yes. Do you know how to fish?"

"Yes, but I don't usually catch anything. Certainly not enough for a meal."

"Not a problem. I only catch and release. How about it?"

"Not if it means I have to get up before dawn. We're supposed to be relaxing, and tomorrow is our last day."

I laughed at her humor, which was one of the many things I liked about her. "No. We can go later this afternoon. Right before the sun goes down."

Claire studied me like I'd lost my mind. Maybe I had—over her.

"Okay, but don't expect me to bait your hook."

Two fishing licenses, one boat rental, and a cooler of beer and snacks later, we were in the middle of one of the prettiest lakes in the state. Tall pines surrounded it, with a scattering of picnic tables along the shore. The water was dark blue but clear enough to see a few feet down. The sun was low in the afternoon sky.

True to her word, Claire didn't bait my hook, and she had hers in the water first. She was also the first to get her line caught in the rocks and almost turned over the boat in her excitement over catching the first fish.

I paid more attention to her than to my own line. She concentrated on her bobber floating on top of the water, often talking to the fish, encouraging them to come along and bite the yummy worm. When it got too dark to see, we returned to the boat launch. It was then, when she stepped out, that the shallow boat tipped, and I ended up in the drink.

I came up gasping, the cold water taking my breath away. I immediately looked around for her. Had she fallen in as well? Did she know how to swim? Was she hurt? None of the above. She was standing on the dock laughing.

"Hey, it's not funny," I said, trying to catch my breath. I was more embarrassed than angry.

"I'm afraid it was. The look on your face when you realized you were going in was priceless."

"Lucky for you I have a great sense of humor. And a towel behind the back seat in my truck."

She approached the dock and extended her hand to help me out. I grabbed it.

"Don't you dare," she said when she realized my intent.

I thought for a minute about pulling her in, then thought better of it. Both of us didn't need to be soaking wet and freezing.

My teeth were chattering by the time we got back to the cabin. Claire shooed me into the bathroom with specific instructions to take a long, hot shower. My hands were numb from the cold and shaking so bad, I couldn't get the buttons of my shirt open. Claire came in a few minutes later to get my wet clothes.

"Why aren't you showering?"

"I can't unbutton my shirt," I managed to say between chatters.

"Jesus, Hayes. Why didn't you tell me you were that cold? Here," she said, batting my hands away. "Let me get it."

If I wasn't so cold and desperate to warm up, I'd have enjoyed the sight of her undressing me. Her hands made quick work of the stubborn buttons on my shirt, and I shivered when the cool air hit my exposed skin. It was almost impossible to get my wet bra over my head, and my nipples were rock hard from the cold. Or was it from Claire's hands on me? She hesitated for an instant at my breasts as she dropped to her knees to unzip my pants.

Her hands were shaking as she unbuckled my belt and unfastened the top button. I had to fight the urge to shift my pelvis into her hand that was moving my zipper down. Was she taking her time, or was it just hard to lower? I shimmied, helping her get my jeans down and over my feet. Next came my wet socks and finally my briefs. I thanked the underwear goddess that I had on my best pair.

Claire pulled open the shower curtain. "In," she commanded, but her voice was a little husky.

I wanted her to join me but was too cold to do anything about it if she had.

Twenty minutes later, wrapped in a large, fluffy towel, I stepped out of the bathroom. Claire was sitting on the couch and looked up when I opened the door. I heated where her eyes raked over me. My skin, already flushed from the water, burned hotter as her gaze traveled across my bare shoulders, over my body, down my bare legs, and back up to my face.

Something remarkably looking like desire burned in her eyes, but before I had a chance to drop my towel, cross the room, and kiss her, she spoke.

"You better get dressed. You'll catch another chill."

Effectively dismissed, I did just that.

Over dinner we laughed about what Claire called "my little spill" and then binge-watched three James Bond movies—the Sean Connery versions—before calling it a night.

The weekend ended way too soon, and after an early dinner in Flagstaff, we packed up and headed back down the mountain.

It was quiet in the car, both of us lost in our own thoughts. I couldn't put my finger on it, but she was different—quiet, more reserved than I'd ever seen her. She had a faraway look in her eyes, her hands clasped tightly in her lap.

"You okay?" I asked, not sure if I wanted to hear the answer.

"Yes. Why?"

"You look nervous or unhappy or something." I didn't mention her white-knuckle grip. "You looked a million miles away."

Her smile appeared forced.

"Just sad about leaving and going back to the real world."

I knew something about her was different, but I didn't press it. If she needed my help, my ear, or my shoulder, she'd let me know. She had several times before. Whatever was bothering her, as much as I wanted to fix it, was really none of my business.

"My firm is having their annual holiday party in two weeks," she said, breaking the silence.

"Is it one of those 'must go to' events?" I'd been to enough of those that I'd vowed never to attend another one unless I wanted to.

"Actually, they're a lot of fun. No drunks making career-ending passes at coworkers. Just good music and great food."

"Lucky you," I said and proceeded to tell Claire about one such event that was a complete fiasco.

"It's on the fifteenth at the Wrigley Center." Claire named one of the area's swankier resorts.

"Very nice," I commented. I'd been to a few events at the center, and the place was nothing but class.

"Will you go with me?"

"To your work party?" Why was I suddenly struck dumb?

"Yes, silly, to the party. You can be my plus-one."

Did I tell you how my stomach tickled every time she called me "silly"?

I took my eyes off the road for a moment and stared at her. "You want me to be your plus-one at your work Christmas party? With the people you work with?" Phrased that way, it sounded pretty revealing.

"Yes."

One simple word, and I had absolutely no idea what it meant. Was I her date? Her escort? A friend she brought along so she had someone to talk to? They all had very different connotations. Either way, I was in. All in.

I dropped her off at her front door after getting a hug that was definitely not a straight-woman hug and far too long to be friendly.

"Thanks for a great weekend" were her parting words, along with "I'd love to do it again sometime."

I almost asked what she was doing the following weekend. What the fuck?

Chapter Seven

The party wasn't formal, but I bought a new outfit anyway. No way could I show up as Claire's plus-one in anything other than the best. It was important to me that I give her nothing to be sorry about in inviting me.

The valet exchanged my keys for a card with a number on it while another held the door open for Claire. She was dressed in a form-fitting, dark-green dress that was both sexy and appropriate for a work function. The neckline was modest—no cleavage showing, and her hemline fell just above her knees. The man looked at her legs for more than what I thought was acceptable, and jealousy surged through me. The thought of anyone else looking at her and thinking the thoughts I did about her made me nuts. I had to get over this serious crush.

Side by side we stepped inside, and a middle-aged man with Albert Einstein hair, baggy dark pants, and an open-collared, long-sleeve white shirt approached. "Claire, I'm glad you could make it." He gave her an appropriate work hug.

"Thank you, Gerard. I wouldn't miss it." She put her hand on my elbow. "This is Hayes Martin. Hayes, Gerard Formula, the owner of the firm."

He extended his hand. "Hayes, welcome. I'm glad you could make it."

"Thank you, Gerard," I said, returning his firm grip. "I'm happy to be here."

"Please, eat, drink, and enjoy yourselves. The food is in the next room, and the bar is over there." He indicated it with a nod. "If you need anything, please come find me. Claire, you look lovely, by the way."

I saw nothing sleazy about the way he complimented Claire, and I had a good feeling this party would be just what Claire had said it would be.

"Thank you, Gerard, and thank you for hosting. I know we'll have a good time."

Claire steered me toward the bar as her boss greeted other arriving guests.

"Gerard is a bit eccentric," she said, smiling. "But everyone loves him and would do anything for him."

Drinks in hand, we stood at the outer edges of the room as Claire gave me the lowdown on her coworkers. With few exceptions it was all positive. It was apparent she liked being at the firm, but I could understand why she wanted to leave and start her own.

"You should probably mingle," I said, encouraging her. On the way over she had told me that, however enjoyable the event was, she hated making small talk at parties, even with her coworkers.

"This is why I brought you along," she said. "I'd probably be standing here for most of the evening, otherwise."

"So, I'm your…what…air cover?" I wasn't angry, just disappointed that she didn't want me to be her date.

"No, silly," she said, smiling at me. "You're my courage."

My heart did a major flip-flop. *Holy fuck, that came out of nowhere and almost knocked me over. I was her courage? This confident, successful woman needed me?*

Claire took a deep breath. "Okay. Let's do this."

She was a natural, moving from person to person, small groups and large, seeming to melt into the conversation like she'd been there from the beginning. She was charming and witty and included me in the chitchat as much as possible. She was polite and refused to talk shop, saying it was rude to do so at a party. I have no idea why she said she wasn't good at this. She was fabulous.

"Claire, you look amazing." An older woman in a well-tailored Anne Klein suit stopped in front of us. She had shoulder-length dark hair and couldn't take her eyes off Claire. I'd seen her several times this evening looking at Claire like she was on the dessert tray. Funny that Claire had never mentioned there was at least one lesbian in the office.

"Pamela, hello," Claire said, her voice far less friendly that when she'd greeted everyone else. Something was up here.

"That dress is perfect for you. It brings out the color of your eyes." The woman was practically undressing Claire with her gaze. I placed my hand on Claire's lower back for support. She was tense, but I felt her relax.

"Thank you. Hayes, this is Pamela Forier."

I stepped forward, inserting myself into the space between Claire and the woman. "Ms. Forier. Pleased to meet you." I extended my hand, and she had no choice but to step back and shake it. It was obvious she did not like my intrusion.

"Hayes, is it?" She practically glowered at me.

"Yes," I said, looking directly at her, my message clear—back off.

"I worked on the plans for Pamela's house last year," Claire said, putting the relationship in context.

She looked at Claire again. "And she did an outstanding job. She was a challenge, but eventually Claire gave me everything I asked for. And a few things I didn't," she added, intimating more than a professional relationship between them.

Claire shifted beside me. "I'm sure Claire was the consummate professional, as she always is," I said, letting her know that I realized her insinuation was full of smoke.

"Is Claire working on something for you?" she asked. "She has a wonderful imagination."

"Yes, she does," I said, floating my own intimation out there. "But no. I don't mix business with pleasure, and I know Claire doesn't either."

Pamela looked back and forth between Clair and me. "Yes, well, I see someone I need to chat with. Good to see you again, Claire." She said nothing to me as she walked away, which didn't bother me in the slightest.

I turned to Claire, who appeared angry, her jaws clenched. "I'm sorry, Claire, if I overstepped. I'll apologize to her. I don't want you to get into trouble." I was not sorry for the way I reacted, my protective claws extended, but I would apologize to the woman.

"No. It's fine." Her voice was flat.

"Did she try something with you?" I knew Claire would never have a relationship with a client.

"Only every time we spoke. That woman would not take no for an answer."

"Do you want me to go over there and punch her?" I asked, joking, yet completely serious. It was obvious Claire was uncomfortable around her.

"Yes, but that might be a career-limiting move."

Claire surprised the hell out of me when she leaned in and kissed my cheek. Her breath was warm on my face, her eyes bold.

"Thank you for defending my honor."

"Well, I am your wingman," I said, the safest thing that came to mind. Claire looked at my lips for a long, long time before she turned away.

"I need to use the ladies' room. I'll be right back. Will you be okay?" She handed me her glass.

"Sure. I'll scope out the buffet. Always lots of good conversation around the hors d'oeuvres and dessert."

I was in the middle of a conversation about baseball when Claire returned. I reached for her hand but pulled back. What was I thinking? Wishful, that was what I was thinking.

"Claire, where have you been hiding this woman?" one of the men asked. "She's a baseball-statistics savant. She knows every stat we threw at her."

Okay, savant was probably a bit much, but I loved the game and was all over those numbers.

"Why haven't you told me this interesting tidbit of information about yourself?" she asked in a teasing tone. I wasn't sure if she was impressed or simply being agreeable. She was much more comfortable around these guys than she had been around Pamela.

"Guess it just never came up in conversation," I said. "It's not a big deal."

Claire excused us and found the exit to the patio. The evening was cool but not uncomfortable. Gotta love Phoenix in the winter. Claire nodded to several other people enjoying the fresh air and didn't stop until we were on the far side, out of earshot of everyone.

"Baseball savant?" Her eyes were sparkling with mischief.

"His words, not mine." I held up both hands in front of me, defending myself.

"Marv doesn't extend compliments lightly."

I shrugged, not sure what else I could say.

"I suppose you have season tickets to the Diamondbacks?" she asked, referring to our hometown professional baseball team.

"Absolutely."

"Is that why you went to the World Series games in October?"

I had paid through the nose to get tickets to the most sought-after games of the year. It didn't matter who was playing. At least in my mind it didn't.

"Guilty." I had gone to class one night jet-lagged from a red-eye coming back from game three. No way was I going to miss sitting close to Claire again.

Claire looked at me, her lips tight, her brows together. "What else do I not know about you?"

"A bunch of things, I suppose." Like how I love the color of your hair, the way you confidently walk into a room, the way you treat the waitresses, how your forehead scrunches up when you're concentrating, that the way you look at me takes my breath away. I could go on for days.

"Tell me one of them."

A light breeze blew the scent of her perfume over me. It took a moment for me to regain my thoughts. "Well, let's see," I said, rifling through my mental file cabinet for something unusual. "I can break down and reassemble a Glock 17 handgun with my eyes closed. I have a concealed-carry permit and can shoot ten arrows in the center ring at one hundred yards. Or at least I once could. Not sure about now. I'm a little out of practice. Oh, and I have a first edition of one of Edgar Allan Poe's books."

The expression on her face was priceless. She wasn't sure if I was pulling her leg or telling the truth.

"You're kidding, right?" she asked skeptically.

"About which one?"

"Poe."

Interesting that out of all of those, that was the one she doubted. "Dead serious. It's in my safety-deposit box. I'll show it to you if you'd like."

She laughed, and my heart skittered across the patio. "Is that like 'would you like to come up and see my etchings'?" she asked. The phrase was an old euphemism for would you like to come in and have sex?

My heart beat faster. "You would absolutely have no doubt if I wanted you to see my etchings. And if I wanted to see yours," I added.

Something hot flashed in her eyes, and I wasn't sure if it had actually been there, or if it was wishful thinking on my part. She was staring at my lips, and time seemed to stand still. The sounds of the party drifted away, replaced by the soft sound of her breathing. She leaned closer, and I knew she was going to kiss me. I lifted my chin to meet her halfway.

"Claire."

I jumped back at the voice calling her name. The interruption was so jarring, it sounded like whoever spoke was right behind us. I looked at Claire, and she couldn't meet my eyes. Her breasts, however, were rising and falling rapidly, as if she was trying to catch her breath.

"Claire," someone said again, someone coming into my peripheral vision.

"Gerard is looking for you," the man said. "He's over by the bar."

"Okay. Thanks, Kyle." Her voice quivered a little, and she darted her gaze everywhere but to me.

"Will you excuse me?" She looked at me, then immediately looked away.

"Sure. Go ahead." That must have been the permission she needed to hustle off the patio and back inside.

I spent the next ten minutes trying to figure out what had just happened. Well, I knew what had almost happened. I just wasn't sure why. In addition to being completely turned on, and confused, I felt stupid. I'd known Claire for almost four months, and I still wasn't sure if she was a lesbian, bi, or straight. She'd never said, and I never asked. I know, stupid of me, but in the beginning it didn't matter. Later, when it did, I had no idea how to broach the subject. For a college-educated, successful woman, I was in a laughable position. You don't just out of the blue ask someone who they like to sleep with. But then again, Claire was about to kiss me. Or was she? I had my head wrapped around myself so bad, I wasn't sure what day it was.

I went back inside and saw her talking to a beautiful woman. Gerard was nowhere in sight. The woman reached out and touched Claire's arm, and it was not a *friendly* gesture. Even from where I was standing, I saw Claire's shoulders tense. I saw red. Was every woman but me hitting on Claire? Even though the woman wasn't looking at me, I gave her dagger eyes nonetheless.

"That's Roberta, Gerard's wife." One of the men I was discussing baseball with appeared beside me. "She's after everyone that wears a skirt."

I tore my attention away from Claire and looked at the man, stunned he would say such a thing about his boss's wife to someone he'd just met.

"I like Claire, and you had better go rescue her. Roberta doesn't give up."

"Claire can handle herself," I said and watched as she did just that. She must have excused herself, because she turned and started walking away. She looked around the room and, when she saw me, headed directly toward me. The man beside me disappeared.

"I'm ready to go. I've had all the holiday cheer and schmoozing I can handle for one night."

I looked at her, trying to detect any sign she was upset from her conversation with Roberta. All I saw was relief and fatigue.

"Absolutely. Let's go."

Claire stood close as we waited for the valet to bring around my truck. "Well, that's my firm. What did you think?"

"Other than Pamela and your boss's wife hitting on you, it was great."

Claire looked at me, apparently surprised that I mentioned it.

"Yes. I saw her. One of your coworkers told me who she was."

"What? Who?" Claire asked, clearly alarmed.

"I think his name is Donald, one of the guys in the group that was talking baseball."

"What did he say?"

"Nothing specific. He just told me who she was and that she didn't give up. Said she chased anything in a skirt."

"Fuck." Claire shook her head.

"Is that what happened?" She found something fascinating on the ground. "Claire?" I tried to prompt her.

"I handled it."

"Your boss's wife hit on you?" I asked, incredulous that someone would do that. Then again, people surprise me every day.

"I handled it," she said again, a little more forceful this time.

"What are you going to do?" I asked as the valet pulled up with my truck.

I repeated my question when I pulled out of the circle drive.

"Nothing."

"Nothing?"

"I don't know, all right? What am I supposed to do? Go into Gerard's office on Monday and tell him his wife propositioned me?"

"She propositioned you?" I was now more than angry.

"I said I handled it."

"But what about next time?"

"I said I handled it, Hayes, so drop it," she barked.

I was stunned. Claire had never been angry at me.

"I'm sorry," I said. "I overstepped. Of course, you know what's best."

After a few minutes of silence, she reached over and took my hand and put it in her lap. "No, I'm sorry. I shouldn't have jumped down your throat like that. I guess I'm still a little rattled. Something like this has never happened to me before."

"Was she there last year?"

"Yes, and she was the perfect hostess. Never any hint of what she said tonight. That's what caught me off guard. I've known her for years."

I didn't dare mention my suspicion that, because I was Claire's plus-one, she thought Claire was a lesbian and would be interested in a…what? An affair? A dalliance? A quickie in the coat closet? My anger returned full force, but I kept it to myself. She had enough shit to deal with.

"How about we stop for something to eat?" I asked, hoping to take her mind off the woman. "There was food everywhere, but it was just finger food, and I'm starved." That made Claire laugh, and my anger slipped away.

"You're always hungry."

CHAPTER EIGHT

I was more than a little nervous as I walked up to Claire's front door. I'd made this trip dozens of times before, but this time was different. I was her escort to her family's New Year's Eve party, and to me, that was a big deal. Or at least I thought it was. I had to play it cool and take my cues from her.

The week after we went to Claire's office party she asked if I would be her date to this annual party. I wasn't sure if she had actually used the word *date* or if it was my imagination. She probably just asked if I'd like to go with her. According to her, it was the social event of the year for her parents' crowd.

"It's New Year's Eve," I said. "Don't you want to take a real date?"

"I want to take you," she said simply.

"What will your parents think, you showing up with a lesbian?"

"My mother will probably have a stroke; my dad won't care, and my brother will tease me unmercifully. You up for it?" Her gaze was probing and confident.

"Absolutely."

The event was black-tie, so I had dressed in the best tuxedo I could afford. My rented shoes pinched my left pinkie toe, but when I stepped in front of the full-length mirror in my closet, I thought I looked pretty damn good. I had a fresh haircut, spent a few days beside the pool to get a little sun, and felt like the queen of the world that Claire had asked me.

My hand was shaking when I pushed her doorbell. I focused on my breathing as I waited for her to answer. When she opened the door, I almost passed out.

No words could adequately describe the vision of Claire standing in her doorway. Stunning, beautiful, gorgeous, and classy came to mind, but one word—hot—quickly displaced all of them.

She was wearing a royal-blue suit jacket long enough to cover her hoo-ha and not much else. She didn't have a blouse or anything on underneath, exposing a lot of smooth skin, and my mouth watered. Her legs looked a mile long in a pair of strappy three-inch black heels. Her hair was swept up into a beautiful French braid, exposing her long, smooth neck. My mouth gaped open and closed as I looked for the right word.

She smiled, obviously knowing exactly the effect she was having on me. She took my hand and pulled me inside.

"Come in, silly."

"Um, is that dress legal?" I asked when she closed the door behind us. She smelled like dangerous seduction.

"In some states, yes."

"Lucky me that we're in one of them. You are absolutely breathtaking." I couldn't possibly hide my reaction to her, and at this moment, I didn't care.

"Thank you. Just let me get my bag."

I think my tongue fell out of my mouth when she turned and walked away. The sway of her hips begged me to follow, but somehow, I managed to keep it together.

"Stop staring. You're making me uncomfortable," she said without turning around.

Uncomfortable was not how she was making me feel. "The way you look in that dress, everybody will be looking at you. By the way, is that a dress or a jacket?" I asked, pointing to her outfit.

"I'm not sure. But it does have a certain impact, doesn't it?"

"I'll say." That was about all I could manage as she glided back to me. *How does she do that in those heels?* I was about to ask but lost all thinking ability when she stopped inches from me and adjusted my tie.

"Every lesbian at the party will be staring at you. Maybe even a few straight women. You look," she finally said, "very butch and very hot."

Hot? She thinks I'm hot? Wait. What? Lesbians will be at the party?

"If lesbians *are* at the party, they'll all be looking at you, not me."

"I doubt that," she replied. "Let's go. We don't want to be too late."

She had to take my hand again to get my legs moving.

I hustled around her and opened the passenger door of the car. I'd spent two hours washing and waxing it, and its black clear-coat gleamed under the streetlight.

"Is this yours?" she asked, pointing to the BMW.

"No. It's my brother's. I can't pick up a beautiful woman in my truck."

"But I love your truck. It's so you."

She loves my truck?

My mouth gaped open again as I watched her dress slide up her legs even farther when she sat down in the front seat.

"Hayes?"

"Huh, ugh, yes?" Huh? What was I, a Neanderthal? The way I was reacting to Claire, I sure felt like one.

She quirked her finger, indicating that I come closer. Leaning into the car, I took advantage of the perfect view down the front of her dress. Oh my God.

"Hayes?" she said again. "Up here." Her manicured finger under my chin lifted my head, and I dragged myself from her teasing cleavage. Her eyes were sparkling. I was so busted.

"Thank you. But you better pull yourself together before we get there, or your champagne will dribble down your chin."

"Yeah, right. Easy for you to say."

"Hardly."

I was so close I could see the flecks of green in her eyes, the spattering of freckles across her nose, and the shine of her lip gloss. If I dropped my head a few more inches, I could kiss her. She gazed at my lips.

"Hayes?" Her breath caressed my name.

"Yes?"

"We'd better go."

"Oh, yeah, right," I said, gathering my composure, and stood. I took another look at her legs before I closed the door.

"Are you all right?" Claire asked a few minutes later as we pulled into traffic.

"Yes." Other than trying to keep my eyes off her legs and on the road.

"You have a death grip on the steering wheel."

"I'm trying to remember to breathe," I said foolishly. "You're killing me in that dress."

She didn't say anything for a few minutes, and I began to think I'd gone too far.

"We're friends, right?"

I wasn't sure if that was a statement, a question, or a warning.

"Of course we are. But I am a lesbian, and I'm not blind." I didn't dare chance a glance at her, lest I lock my attention on her bare thighs and kill us both.

"Are lesbians attracted to straight women?"

Oh, God, don't go there.

"Some, but I certainly don't speak for all lesbians."

"Are you?"

Fuck. She went there.

"Not usually," I answered honestly. I've never been attracted to straight women until Claire. She was definitely a bunch of firsts for me.

"Do I make you nervous?"

"No." Nervous was not what she was making me.

"You seem, I don't know, different," she said thoughtfully.

That's because I've never been this turned on before and can't do anything about it. I'm trying to keep my head, and other parts, from exploding.

"Well, maybe I am a little nervous. It's your family party. I don't want to embarrass you or anything."

She put her hand on my thigh. My muscles jumped at the contact.

"You have nothing to worry about. Everyone will love you."

She didn't move her hand from there for the remainder of the drive. *Jesus, give me strength.*

CHAPTER NINE

The party was in full swing when we walked through the door. I was still sweating after catching a glimpse of Claire's inner thigh as I helped her out of the car. Her warm hand resting in the crook of my arm made me feel ten feet tall. This was another of many moments to memorize, knowing I'd probably never experience it again.

She introduced me around, never leaving my side. I'd never seen so much glitter and sparkle in one place.

A man who had to be her twin brother joined us. "Holy shit, sis. All the men can't take their eyes off you." He kissed her cheek, took her hand, and spun her around. "And the women want to either kill you or be you. You look hot in that outfit. Jesus, girl. Talk about making a statement."

"Thank you, and you look very handsome yourself. You always did clean up pretty good."

Claire turned toward me, took my hand, and pulled me to her side. I had stepped back a bit to give them some space. "Hayes, this is my favorite baby brother, Maxwell, aka Max. Max, Hayes Martin."

He looked back and forth between Claire and me, then broke into a big grin. "Well, I'll be," he said, pumping my hand. "My big sister—"

"It's not what you're thinking," Claire said.

Confusion replaced Max's smile, followed by, what? Disappointment maybe?

"Damn. That's too bad. You two are a hot-looking couple."

"Max, stop, and mind your manners." Claire scolded him like a parent would.

"Party pooper."

He turned his attention to me.

"Pleased to meet you, Hayes. Sorry about that. I got carried away with the idea that my sister…" He looked at Claire, who gave him a warning glare. "Found someone that made her happy." He looked back at her as if for approval of his words.

Her frown was gone, but she wasn't smiling either.

"Nice to meet you, Max. I can see you get your charm from your big sister. And her smile."

"I'm glad my ego is big enough to be okay with a woman who looks better in a tuxedo than I do," he said after giving me the once-over.

"Well, I agree with Claire. You are the most handsome man here."

"She's a keeper," he said to Claire.

"Don't worry, Max. I'm not going anywhere."

Max was far too observant, and I had to remind myself to be careful. I didn't want Claire to become uncomfortable and call a halt to our friendship.

A tall woman who had to be Claire's mother approached, a not very authentic smile plastered on her face. She looked me up and down, and I know she didn't like what she saw.

"Clarice, I heard you had finally arrived."

I detected more than a little disapproval in her statement. Claire's hand tightened on my arm. I wasn't sure, but I think she stepped a little closer to me.

"Hello, Mother. I looked for you when we got here, but you were deep in conversation with the mayor."

"Yes, well, are you going to introduce me to your, uh, friend?"

The last word was clearly a struggle for the woman to eke out. She was not subtle in her disapproval of either my tuxedo, my short, spiky, dark hair, or the fact that I was obviously with her daughter.

"Of course. Mother, this is Hayes Martin. Hayes, my mother, Diedre Wheeler."

Claire's mother's eyes narrowed noticeably. I noted that Claire had not used any word to describe me. Not friend, acquaintance, escort, nothing—leaving it up to her mother to draw her own conclusions. I extended my hand.

"Mrs. Wheeler. It's a pleasure to meet you. Claire has told me so much about how this is the party of the season."

Her hand was clammy, and she had one of those weak, girly handshakes, the kind that make you want to rub your palm on the side of your leg to get the ick off. I have better manners than that.

"Thank you, Ms. Martin. I'm afraid Clarice hasn't mentioned you at all," she said, sending Claire a scolding glare.

Ouch. That was a rude dig. I felt Claire stiffen beside me.

"Mother," Claire said, but I jumped in.

"That's perfectly understandable. I don't tell my mother a lot of things either. Especially when they're none of her business."

Max stifled a snort with a fake cough.

"Have you seen Dad?" Claire asked her brother.

"Last I saw him he was on the patio smoking a cigar with Fred Harvey," Max said. "Let's go find him. See you later, Mother."

"Nice meeting you, Mrs. Wheeler. I hope to see you again."

She blanched at my last comment.

"God, what a bitch," Max growled when we were out of earshot. "Do you think she could have been ruder?"

"It's more rude, and did you expect otherwise?" Claire asked.

"I'm sorry. What am I missing here except you deflecting your mother's verbal assault she launched your way?" I was furious for Claire.

"Our mother is a bitch," Max repeated. "Nothing Claire ever does is good enough for her."

"Max," Claire said in warning tone. "It's a party. Let's not air our family's dirty laundry tonight." She turned toward me.

"I apologize that you had to see that. She usually has better manners in public."

"It's because Hayes is your 'date.'" Max used air quotes.

"Nothing to be sorry about," I said in an attempt to ease Claire's obvious embarrassment. "We all have some type of family drama."

After a few moments, Claire asked, "What things do you not tell your mother?" She looked more relaxed.

"Everything. I haven't spoken to my mother in seventeen years," I said with as much emotion as I had for my bigoted, homophobic mother. I turned away from Claire's shocked expression to Max.

"You said something about finding your father?" I said, gearing up for another duel.

"Dad is great," Max said, beaming. "Nothing like our mother. I have no idea what they ever saw in each other or why he's still with her. Opposites most definitely do attract in that relationship, but yuck!" Max twisted his mouth.

Claire laughed, the tension leaving her face.

Johnathon Wheeler was a joy. Charming and engaging, he

obviously loved his children. Claire practically beamed when he asked about her job and plans for starting her own firm. My stomach tickled when she called him Daddy.

Johnathon excused himself to resume his host duties, and Max left a few minutes later.

"I apologize again for my mother."

I waved off her words. "No need. You didn't do anything wrong."

"But."

"But nothing. It's fine," I reiterated. "Mother-daughter relationships can be tough." I could personally vouch for that fact.

"My mother thinks I should have a more ladylike profession."

I didn't know people still used the word *ladylike*. "There is absolutely nothing wrong with being an architect," I said, even though Claire didn't need my approval. "What does she think you should do? Let me guess. Pediatrician, teacher, choir director?" Even those occupations probably weren't ladylike enough for her mother.

Claire chuckled, and not in a happy way. "Like a nurse or, better yet, a stay-at-home mom taking care of babies and doing volunteer work. In other words, follow in her footsteps. For crying out loud, I'm old enough to know what I want. I'd rather join a convent than be my mother," she added.

"Well, that would be a damn shame," I said, and Claire finally smiled.

A few more people came up and talked with Claire for a few minutes and then moved on.

"It's almost midnight, and I have to go to the ladies' room," Claire said. "Will you be okay?"

"Absolutely. I'm wearing my best party manners tonight." I indicated my tux.

Claire ran her fingers under the thin lapels of my jacket, the backs of her fingers a caress against my breasts. My heart started pounding.

"In case I didn't tell you, you look fabulous in Armani."

I'd rather have you see me in nothing.

I watched her walk away and got caught staring when she looked over her shoulder at me.

"What exactly are you to my daughter?" Diedre asked, coming up behind me a few seconds later. It was like she'd been lying in wait to pounce on me.

"Excuse me?" I can honestly say no one has ever asked me that question, especially in such an accusatory tone.

"I asked exactly what you are to my daughter."

"I think that's between Claire and me."

"Are you two lovers?"

I had expected her to be rude, but that question surprised even me.

"With all due respect, Mrs. Wheeler, though I'm not sure you deserve it at this point, but if we are, that's none of your business."

Her face turned red. "How dare you."

"There is no dare to it, Mrs. Wheeler. Claire is a wonderful woman with a mind of her own, and we enjoy spending time together. Now if you'll excuse me," I said, effectively dismissing her. I had to put some space between us, or I'd tell her exactly what I thought. And that would probably mean more trouble for Claire in the long run.

A tall, blond woman with a gorgeous tan and killer red heels intercepted my search for Claire. She was attractive if you liked the predatory look. *Jeez, what next?*

"I don't think I've ever seen you at one of these parties. I know I would have remembered you," she said, checking me out from top to bottom. "Ruth Blackwell." She extended a slim hand, the multiple bangles on her wrist clinking against each other.

"Hayes Martin."

She held my hand much longer than was polite.

"Well, Hayes Martin, may I say you are the most handsome woman in the room?"

It was obvious Ms. Blackwell was imagining what was under my tux. "Thank you."

"Are you here alone?"

"No. I'm here with Claire Wheeler."

Ruth's eyes widened. "Dierdre's Claire?"

"Diedre is her mother, yes."

"Well, I'll be damned. I never thought Claire—"

"Never thought Claire what?" she asked, stopping beside me and putting her hand back in the crook of my arm, where it was whenever she was beside me. Was I her shield, or was she sending me and everyone else a message? Either way, it felt good there.

"Never thought you'd step over to the wild side."

The way Ruth said it made it sound scandalous.

"I bet your mother blew a gasket," she added gleefully.

"Did you want something, Ruth?" Claire asked and moved possessively closer. Interesting.

"Yes. I did," Ruth said. "Until Hayes said she was with you. Rest assured, Claire, I don't poach."

"I trust Hayes completely."

My eyes felt like a tennis ball lobbing back and forth between these two. What was going on? Claire hadn't denied any of Ruth's assumptions.

"Lucky you." Ruth turned toward me. "If you—"

"I won't."

Ruth took one more look between us and sauntered off.

"You told her we were together?" Claire asked when Ruth was out of earshot.

"No. I told her I was *here* with you. Big difference in the lesbian world."

I detected something in Claire's question but wasn't sure what. First her brother, then her mother, and now Ruth. She was probably tired of being thought queer.

"Ruth goes after only the best-looking women."

"I'll take that as a compliment from you, but not from her."

"Why not? You're single, and she was obviously into you."

"Because I'm here with you." *And because I want to be* with *you in the lesbian sense.*

Claire's gaze drilled into mine as if she were searching for something. I let her find whatever she was looking for.

"All right, partygoers. Grab your special someone." Claire's father's voice boomed over the crowd. "It's three minutes until we ring in the new year."

Johnathon's voice broke the connection between Claire and me. She blinked a few times, as if realigning herself to where she was.

I took a step backward to give her some space as the people in the room started counting down from ten. I didn't know what to expect at the stroke of midnight. Were we supposed to have the traditional kiss? A hug? Shake hands? At five, Claire closed the distance between us. At three, she grabbed the lapels on my jacket and pulled me to her. At one, she kissed me, and my world tilted off its axis.

CHAPTER TEN

I didn't know which was louder—the cheers coming from the hundred guests or the roaring in my head. Claire's lips were as soft as I imagined, and she knew exactly what to do with them. I was about to reach for her when she broke the kiss.

She was breathing hard, her eyes glazed and face flushed. I couldn't quite read her expression. I opened my mouth to say something, I had no idea what, but Claire beat me to it.

"Happy New Year, Hayes."

"Happy New Year." That wasn't what I wanted to say, but it would have to do for now. "So far it's fabulous," I added.

Max kept anything else from happening between us and put a glass of champagne in our hands. He clinked the glasses.

"Cheers and Happy New Year," he said, seeming oblivious to what he'd interrupted. But what did he interrupt? I tried to get my head around the fact that Claire had kissed me. On the lips. Intentionally. And it wasn't a friendly peck.

"Was that Ruth I saw sniffing around earlier?"

I took a couple of deep breaths so I could think clearly. It would take more than that before I would get back to somewhere close to normal.

"Yes, and I told her to get lost."

"Meow, sis," Max said.

"Damn right."

Claire turned to me. "Dance with me?"

"Excuse me?" Couples had been on the dance floor all evening.

"I asked you to dance with me."

"Here? Now?" I croaked like a schoolboy whose voice was changing.

"Well, yes."

"Your mother," I said, giving Claire a gracious out if she hadn't realized what she'd asked.

"Can watch or leave the room. Her choice."

"You're sexy as hell when you get your back up," Max said before leaving us alone.

"I have no idea what that saying has to do with anything. Are you going to dance with me or not?"

"I thought you'd never ask."

"You lead," she said.

The thought of Claire surrendering to me on the dance floor, or any place for that matter, made my head spin.

I extended my hand to her, and we headed toward the crowd that filled the dance floor. She stepped into my arms like she'd done it thousand times before, and my world rocked again. She was a great dancer, light on her feet and smooth. She molded her body to mine, and I tried not to stumble. My heart was pounding so hard as we moved around the floor, Claire had to have noticed. No one had ever felt this good in my arms. Her hand on my shoulder was electrifying, and the one in my hand felt like it had always belonged there. Whatever emotional distance I'd managed to keep closed in like the petals on a soft flower. This time I did stumble.

Claire leaned away just far enough to ask, "Are you okay?"

"I have no idea," I said honestly.

She smiled at me knowingly and pulled me closer.

I lost track of how many songs we danced to but thanked the DJ gods for the opportunity to hold Claire in my arms. She smelled like sunshine and happiness—corny but true. We didn't talk. I don't think I could have held a coherent conversation with the lascivious thoughts swirling around in my head and echoing in my nether regions. The more we danced, the more she relaxed, her body fitting mine perfectly. This was not the way a straight woman danced. Now I was completely confused.

"I don't mean to cut in, but your mother is about to have a stroke watching you two. As much as she might deserve it, I'll never hear the end of it. Have pity on your old dad and dance with me?"

Claire's father's hand on my shoulder didn't feel threatening. I really liked Johnathon, and I wished that…forget about wishes and back to reality.

"You don't mind, do you, Hayes?" he asked, turning to me.

"Of course not. Dads, especially good dads, always trump friends."

Claire stepped out of my arms, and I could still feel where she'd touched me. When I started to walk off the dance floor, Max came up beside me.

"Let's dance, but I insist on leading," he said, taking my hand. "I never learned how to dance backward."

"I think I can manage," I replied, laughing. "At least I'm not in those heels your sister is wearing. I don't know how she does it."

"Speaking of my sister."

"We met in statistics class, and we're just friends."

Max laughed. "That's about as much BS as my mother. Who are you trying to convince, you or Claire?"

"There is…"

"Save your breath. You'll need it for when my sister kisses you again."

He had obviously seen Claire kiss me. "There is…" I stopped denying something that was so obvious.

"I know, just friends," he said. "But friends don't look at each other the way you two have all evening and not want more than friendship."

"Max," I said in my most persuasive voice, "I appreciate your compliment, but you're a bit off base." The base was that Claire was interested in me.

"Okay. I'll stop talking about it. At least I will until I get Claire alone. You don't know me from the man in the moon, but I can tell you that I have never seen Claire look at someone the way she looks at you. The chemistry between you two is off the charts. And I'd know because I teach chemistry. You two could spontaneously combust."

I glanced over Claire, who was laughing at something her father had said. Then he said something else, and her expression turned serious. I caught her looking at me. Oh, to be a fly on her shoulder.

CHAPTER ELEVEN

R eady?" Claire asked twenty minutes later. The party showed no signs of breaking up, and she looked tired.

"Whenever you are."

"My feet are killing me," she said, and I let my gaze drift down her legs to her shoes.

"How do you wear those?"

"I hate them. They obviously hurt my feet, but they make my legs and ass look fabulous. So, wearing them is worth it."

"No argument from me." My clit throbbed as I imagined me on my knees taking off her shoes, then running my hands up her legs and sliding the silk stockings down those fabulous legs.

"I need to say my good-byes to my mother. You can get our coats. I'll only be a few minutes."

"Not a chance of my leaving you to face her alone. There's strength in numbers." I straightened my tie and my jacket and held out my arm. "Let's do this." Her smile lit up my world.

"Come on, silly," Claire said, then gave me quick kiss on the cheek. *What were we talking about again?* "Let's get it over with." As we approached, Diedre obviously noticed Claire's hand in the crook of my arm. An unpleasant expression crossed her face, like she had a bad taste in her mouth.

"We're leaving, Mother. Great party, as usual. I heard several compliments on the food and the music."

"Are you two going home?" She looked at both of us when she said "you two," her insinuation very clear. We were going home and fucking—a lot.

"Yes. It's late."

"Ms. Martin, I'd like to speak with my daughter. Privately." The tone of Diedre's last word was more a command than a request.

I looked to Claire for my answer, and she nodded. "Why don't you get our coats? I'll just be a minute."

"Mrs. Wheeler, again, a pleasure to meet you, and thank you for extending the invitation. Good night."

Diedre barely waited until I was out of earshot before saying something to Claire. I couldn't hear what it was, but by the tone, it told me it wasn't that she liked me.

One of the party staff handed me Claire's coat, her perfume drifting up and igniting my memory. The coat covered more of her legs than her dress did, yet she had made no attempt to use it to cover her legs when she was in the car.

Other than our interactions with Claire's mother, it was a great party. Lots of stimulating conversation with interesting people. I really liked Max and was looking forward to seeing him again. The same with Claire's father. It was obvious he loved and supported his children. Oh, and did I mention that CLAIRE KISSED ME!

I felt Claire's hand on my shoulder. She used me for balance as she took off one shoe, then the other. For some reason, that was just plain sexy.

"God, that feels better." She moaned.

I held out her coat and slid it up onto her shoulders, hesitating just a moment to savor the feel of her under my hands. Tension lines bracketed her mouth and eyes.

"I shouldn't have left you alone with her," I said, one of the biggest regrets of my life.

"No. It's all right. Nothing I haven't heard before."

I raised my eyebrows, my expression saying "really"?

"No. Not the lesbian part, but she did take the opportunity to tell me exactly how being with you would ruin my life and, of course, hers too."

"But we're not together," I said, stating the obvious.

"It's fine. I just want to forget about it. Just please take me home."

Claire did not agree or even acknowledge my comment about us not being together.

As I drove her home, her mood at the end of this evening was the opposite of when it began. Gone was the confident, smiling, sexy woman who was Claire Wheeler. She was quiet, and this time when I looked at her, it wasn't to stare at her legs but at her facial expression. How priorities change.

I pulled into her drive and turned off the ignition, the click and clack of the powerful engine the only noise in the car. I wanted to take her in my arms and tell her it would be okay. Hell. I wanted to make it okay. But with the whole lesbian thing, I didn't do anything but sit there and clench my fists. How could a mother be so hurtful to such a wonderful woman? I almost laughed at myself when I thought about mine. Jesus, this world was fucked up sometimes.

"Would you like to come in?" Claire's voice was quiet.

"Only if you want me to," I replied.

"Yes, please."

This time when I helped her out of the car, I drew her into my arms and hugged her. Nothing sexual, just comfort. She hung on tightly. I don't know how long we stood there before she took a deep breath and exhaled.

"Thanks. I needed that. Come on. It's freezing out here."

"I can't believe how she still has that effect on me," Claire said after we settled on opposite sides of her couch, each holding a glass of wine. "I mean, my God, I'm a grown woman with a successful career, and she still digs at me whenever she can. What kind of mother does that? And why me? Not that I want Max to experience any of this, but still?"

"Do you think she's jealous of you?" I asked.

Claire looked at me, obviously puzzled. "What? Why?"

"I don't know. Maybe because you're happy and she's not. I'm no expert on mother/daughter relationships, but I'm sure they can be difficult."

"I suppose that's as good reason as any. You know she actually told me that she would disown me if I was a lesbian."

I muttered several four-letter words under my breath.

"I agree."

Okay, not so under my breath.

"My dad liked you." She seemed to perk up. "He thinks you're good for me."

I slowly turned toward her, afraid of what her expression might say about his observation.

"He said you brought me out of my shell. I didn't even know I was in a shell," she said reflectively.

"He was great, and Max is a kick. He really loves you, you know."

"What did he say?" she asked cautiously.

"Nothing," I said, hiding my grin behind my wineglass.

"You better tell me," she said, but the twinkle in her eyes said she wasn't serious.

"Nope. My lips are sealed." I loved bantering with her. Her spunk was coming back.

"You better tell me."

"Or what?"

She sat her glass on the table beside her and started crawling over toward me. SLOWLY. She was still wearing the jacket-dress thing, and every time she moved, she exposed a little more flesh. Little did she know that I was physically incapable of talking. I swear to all things good that I stopped breathing when she straddled my lap. I could feel the warmth of her on my thighs. My heart was now beating in my head, which started to swim. She put her hands on the couch behind my shoulders and leaned forward. The world spun, and my senses sizzled with attention. Holy fuck, she was going to kiss me. Holy fuck, in that position I was going to do more than kiss her.

"I have ways of making you talk."

At this point, I'd say anything.

"What did he tell you?"

Her breath was like a caress across my ear. I swallowed, hard. Then she started tickling me.

To say I was shocked was an understatement. I was slow to react, my senses totally focused on the pounding between my legs. Finally, I was giving as good as I was getting, and she eventually scooted off my lap and collapsed against my side, her legs under her.

"I guess I need to change my interrogation technique." She lifted my arm and draped it around her shoulders, cuddling closer.

Her head was just under my chin, the familiar fragrance of her shampoo filling my senses. "If I told you I'd sing like a canary, will you do it again?"

She didn't answer, and after a few moments, her slow, rhythmic breathing told me she had fallen asleep. I didn't dare move for fear she'd wake and this moment, this wonderful, magical moment would end.

The front of her jacket-dress thing gaped open, revealing more smooth flesh, which I could not take my eyes off. I reached out to touch her but stopped. Not because my hand was shaking so badly, not because she would wake up and throw me out, but because I could not take advantage of this situation.

I managed to kick off my shoes and raise my feet onto the table in front of us. Claire snuggled closer, putting her hand in my lap. Holy Christ! How many times had I dreamed of her hand between my legs? I tamped down those thoughts, leaned my head back, and closed my eyes.

I woke with a start, not quite sure where I was. It all flooded back when I recognized Claire next to me. I had a crick in my neck, and Claire would feel even worse in the morning. I carefully disengaged her arms from around me and slid off the couch.

"Come on, sleepyhead. Let's get you to bed."

She didn't respond, just stretched out on the dark-green fabric, more skin than not exposed.

I left her for a minute and rummaged through her dresser looking for something she could wear to sleep in. I spent far too long in her panty drawer, and not finding anything appropriate, I moved to her bed. After striking out again, I moved to the nightstand and congratulated myself when I saw an old T-shirt and boxers in the drawer. I lifted them out.

"Oh, fuck," I said out loud. Underneath Claire's jammies was a vibrator, and it was not new. All kinds of images flashed through my head, all of them X-rated. I closed the drawer, my hand shaking so badly the lamp almost fell over.

I took a moment to simply look at Claire asleep on the couch. She was beautiful, the lines of tension gone from her face. I stepped toward her. Her shoes were history, so the next logical and uncomfortable looking piece of clothing was her stockings.

I reached up, expecting to find the panty part of her pantyhose, and found warm, soft skin instead. Checking to see if she was still sleeping, I raised the bottom of her dress-jacket thing. Oh, fuck. Nothing but a thong and a lacy garter belt. I sat down on the coffee table, my breath ragged. I ran my shaking hands over my face and through my hair. Everything I had dreamed of was right in front of me, and I could do nothing about it. I had to stop myself from touching her. I had it bad.

I could sit here all night and just watch her breathe, watch the pulse beat in her neck. What would it feel like under my tongue as it pulsed with desire? How would she respond as my hands and fingers danced across her skin? I had to take a few deep breaths to banish those thoughts and concentrate on what I needed to do.

As I had imagined, her nylons were silk, and I unhooked them, then slid them easily down her firm thighs and off her legs. The garter belt followed. The dress-jacket thing was a bit more troublesome. I was able to get it off, some sort of sticky tape on her chest holding it all in place. Her breasts were perfect, her nipples begging for my mouth. I pulled her T-shirt on her before I did anything really stupid. Then I covered her with the blanket that was folded neatly across the back of the couch, grabbed my shoes and jacket, and locked the front door behind me.

Cool January air cooled my heated skin but did nothing for the thoughts racing through my head.

CHAPTER TWELVE

"**M**ax was right. You are a keeper."

I was sitting on my patio when Claire called, doing nothing but reliving every minute of the night before. Especially the parts where Claire was naked. "I'll remember you said that when you want to kick my ass to the curb."

Claire chuckled. "I may kick your ass, but never to the curb."

"Good to know. How are you feeling today?"

"A little hungover and a whole lot embarrassed."

"No need. I was just glad I was there to help."

"Well, thank you anyway. I guess I was so exhausted I just passed out."

"We were out late."

"Is that a polite way of referencing my mother?"

"Well, that too."

"You're so kind not to mention her."

She hesitated, and I could picture her biting her lower lip like she always did when she was nervous. Would she thank me for not mentioning what I saw in her bedside table? She had to know I saw it.

"You took my clothes off," she said hesitantly.

"What you were wearing, however hot, did not look at all comfortable to sleep in." The image of the contents of a bedside drawer sailed into my head. Who was I kidding? They never left my head, nor did her garter belt, stockings, and her thong.

Claire didn't say anything, and the silence grew uncomfortable.

"I did it with my eyes closed." I quickly realized what that would mean. "Sorry. How about I didn't look? Jeez. That didn't sound any better, did it?"

Claire chuckled. "You're crazy."

Crazy for you, I thought.

"Well, that's one way to get through it." I turned serious. "I hope last night doesn't make you uncomfortable…to be around me." God, I sounded so pathetic.

"No, no, not at all. I appreciate it."

"In that case, you're welcome."

After another long silence Claire asked, "Will you take me dancing?"

Not at all what I expected. "Dancing?"

"Yes. Dancing."

I didn't know if I could stomach watching her dance with a guy. See her put her hand on his shoulder, his hands on her. But at that point I'd do just about anything that made Claire happy.

"You're a wonderful dancer," she said. "Where do you go?"

"To a lesbian bar."

"Then take me to a lesbian bar."

My heart started racing. "Why would you want to go to a lesbian bar?"

"Because I'm tired of guys hitting on me. I just want to dance."

"If you go to a lesbian bar, I can guarantee you, women will hit on you." *And it would kill me if you accepted, worse than if it were a man.*

"What if we pretend to be together?"

I wouldn't be pretending. "You really want to go to a lesbian bar?"

"If that's where I can dance with you, yes."

I wasn't sure I could keep my hands to myself and my desires in check if I spent another night with Claire pressed against me. But again, I wasn't stupid enough to miss the opportunity.

"What should I wear?" she asked, a week or so later. We were going dancing at Crystals on Saturday night. Crystals was a country bar that had somehow managed to stay in business for as long as I could remember. It was, and had always been, my go-to place.

"Certainly not that dress-jacket thing you wore the last time we danced. I'd have to beat the women away with the pool cue if you did." There was that jealous thing again. "I think you wore it to get a rise out of your mother." Over the last few months, Claire had told me many stories of the disagreements between the two of them.

"No, silly. I wore it just for you," she said calmly.

But there was nothing calm about the way my pulse started racing, and the room had suddenly tilted. Somehow, I managed to pull myself together and think of something other than the way Claire looked in that outfit, and out of it.

"I'm wearing jeans, boots, and a collared shirt. You can wear whatever you want."

"Then I guess we need to go shopping."

I hate shopping. But I love being with Claire, so there we were sitting across from each other in hard plastic chairs in the food court.

We hit a couple of big department stores and walked out with a garment bag of two suits for what Claire called her pain-in-the-ass clients. Another stop at a Western store, and I was carrying a box of Tony Lama boots under my arm.

"I need some new undies," she said, pulling me into Victoria's Secret. This was the last place I wanted to be with her. I had a variety of X-rated thoughts as I watched her pick up lacy things and barely-there other things, feeling like a blob in my boxer briefs and functional bra. I could barely speak when she asked me if I liked the black or red of something she was holding up made of very little fabric.

"Well?" Claire asked, fully expecting my opinion.

"Red is sexy, and black is seductive and powerful."

"Hmm," she said, mulling over her choices. "I'll get both. Never know what mood I'll be in. Best to keep my options open."

The idea of her in a sexy mood was enough to make me crazy, but the thought of her seducing someone would definitely kill me. Thank God she didn't come out of the fitting room and ask me what I thought, or I might have melted right where I sat. I sighed in relief when we walked out, the trademark pink bag swinging from Claire's hand.

A Coke and a cookie later, we were on the other side of the mall when Claire pointed and said, "Waterworks. I've wanted to go in there since it opened."

I trailed behind her as she crossed the threshold of the newest swimwear store. I didn't know how much more of this torture my heart could handle.

I volunteered to hold Claire's packages while she took the maximum number of suits into the fitting room. If I were lucky, she wouldn't come out and show me. While I waited, I peeked into the pretty pink bag. I didn't touch anything but felt like a voyeur, nonetheless.

"What do you think of this one?"

I dropped the bag at my feet, feeling like she had caught me peeking into her lingerie drawer—or her nightstand.

"Hayes?"

I vaguely heard my name through the pounding in my ears. I couldn't tear my eyes off her beautiful body, and my face heated. She didn't have a perfect figure, since she was in her late thirties, but she definitely had all the right curves in all the right places. Even though I had seen her in almost nothing, I was certain my mouth dropped open at the sight of her standing in front of me. The important parts were covered, but not by much. The items in the Victoria's Secret bag may have covered more than that suit. I'd never seen Claire in a swimsuit, because if I had, my heart would've stopped.

"Hayes?" she asked again, with an expectant look.

"Oh, yeah. It's nice."

She studied me for a minute. "Nice? That's all? Nice?"

"It's a great color?"

Claire looked at me like I was crazy. "Uh-huh," she said.

She came out next in a pair of board shorts and a bikini top. Her abs were firm, her breasts perfect, and her skin smooth and soft. My attention shifted to her hands tying the string at the waistband. The turquoise shorts hung low on her hips, and I wanted to lick the flesh between her navel and the bow. In a word, she was hot. Cute was the second word that came easily to my rattled brain.

"I like it," I managed to croak out. "But I have a preference for board shorts," I added.

"Okay. One other one and that's it," she said, turning around and heading back into the changing room.

I was sure I was sweating, but my shaking hand came back from my forehead dry. While I pulled myself together, two girls that had been standing nearby giggled—at me, I was pretty sure. I shot them a glance, and they gave me a thumbs-up. Great. Just what I needed—an audience.

"What about this one?"

I completely lost my sense of reality and anything else remotely related to normal everyday reality when Claire stepped out in front of me wearing a bright-yellow bikini. I couldn't decide if I was more interested in the flesh I was seeing or what the thin triangle of materials was concealing. Either way, I had no idea what I said, how I reacted, or how I managed not to crawl after Claire on my hands and knees, following her into the changing room. I returned to reality when one of the girls that had been watching came over to me and put her hand on my shoulder.

"Breathe."

CHAPTER THIRTEEN

Claire had settled on tight jeans that made her ass look fabulous and a long-sleeve green Henley shirt when I picked her up three nights later. I was a nervous wreck, but she appeared to be pretty calm. Shouldn't it have been the other way around? I'm the lesbian, and we were going to a lesbian bar—where women kiss and touch each other.

I remember the first time I went to one. It just felt right. I felt at home, like I'd never been anywhere else. What would Claire think? Would she be appalled? Disgusted by what she saw? She wouldn't have asked if she was afraid of what she'd see. The women didn't actually fuck on the dance floor, but I have walked in on some serious hanky-panky in the ladies' room.

I was petrified that one of the women I'd slept with would come over and started talking to me. What would Claire think? She had to know I had sex. Even though it had been a while, no one had come knocking on my door wanting my lesbian card back.

I held the door open, the pounding of the music escaping the confines of the small building. I nodded to the bouncer as I paid the cover charge, and we stepped inside. Heads turned when we walked in, and eyes immediately zeroed in on Claire.

She took my hand as she surveyed the room. I wondered what she saw. Pool tables were in a small area to the right, the dinging of the dart machine mixing with the crack of the balls. The bar was to the left, the dance floor straight ahead. High-top tables with stools tucked neatly under a few formed a natural separation of the areas.

"Would you like a beer?" I asked, stepping close to be heard over the music. She nodded, and we made our way through the crowd to the bar. She had a death grip on my hand, the only sign that she was nervous.

Cold beers paid for, I led us to an empty table on the other side of the dance floor. The music was slightly less loud over here, the speakers pointing in the opposite direction. Claire watched the crowd, and after a short while, she started to sway to the music.

After a few songs she asked, "Are you going to ask me to dance, or am I going to have to ask that blonde over there?" She nodded toward a familiar face on the other side of the room. I didn't know her, and I certainly didn't want Claire to know her either. "She keeps looking over here, so it's either you or me she's interested in. I have a fifty-fifty chance."

Claire would dance with someone she knew was interested in her? I must have asked that question out loud because she answered.

"She might be after my body, but I just want to dance. She won't get anywhere."

Claire looked at me with an expectant expression and said, "Well. Are you going to ask me to dance?"

"That's why we're here." I put my beer on the table. "Let's go."

Claire was a fabulous dancer and kept us on the floor for five or six songs. This was nothing like our dances on New Year's Eve. I loved watching her move. My experience was that how a woman was on the dance floor was how they danced between the sheets. Claire was heart-stopping, her moves sensual and confident. It didn't appear that she had an inhibited bone in her gorgeous body. I was going to die before the night was over.

I was standing at the bar getting us another round when a hand slid down my back and settled on my ass.

"Hey, lover. Haven't seen you here in a while."

I saw the woman's reflection in the mirror behind the bar, and it took me several seconds to remember her name. I shifted so her hand would slide off my ass. Thank God.

"Hey, Donna. How have you been?"

"Missing you," she said, sidling closer to me. Her breath in my ear had once wet my girl parts. Now it smelled like scotch and was disgusting. I once found that attractive? Not now. Not after meeting Claire.

"I've been busy," I said, my excuse noncommittal. The woman beside me at the bar left, and Donna stepped right in.

"You're here now," she said, running her finger down the front of my shirt.

I grabbed her hand before it reached my buckle. The bartender placed my two beers in front of me, and when I handed her a twenty, I saw Claire's reflection in the mirror. What was that expression on her face? Rage? Jealousy? I have got to get my eyes checked.

"I'm here with someone," I said, picking up my change and the two bottles.

Donna leaned in. "I won't tell if you don't."

My stomach turned for more reasons than one. How had I found this woman attractive? Well, I admitted, attractive enough to fuck a few times. Now I just wanted to get away from her.

"Sorry, Donna. I don't do that. Take care." I got out of there as fast as the crowd would let me, feeling like I needed a shower.

"Friend of yours?" Claire asked when I got back to the table.

"No."

"Someone who wants to be your friend?"

"No." God, I wish she wasn't so observant and curious.

"No, I suppose not. It looked like she was interested in something other than being your friend. Unless it comes with benefits."

Trying to disappear in my beer, I didn't say anything.

"Did you have sex with her?"

I'd expected that question in some form, but I choked on my beer, nonetheless.

"I thought so," Claire said ruefully.

Whose idea was it to bring her here? What was I thinking? Oh, yeah. The opportunity to hold her in my arms again. Silly me to imagine this would go smoothly.

"You must've been pretty good because she definitely wants more."

"Can we talk about something else?" I knew I was blushing.

"Why? Don't girlfriends talk about their sex lives together?"

I wasn't sure if she was teasing me or simply asking a question.

This time I did look Claire directly in her eyes. "Yes, I am pretty damn good, but I don't want to think about or talk about another woman when I'm with you."

Claire held my eyes for longer than a typical straight woman does. I wasn't complaining. The lights dimmed, and a slow song started. She took my hand and led me to the dance floor. Again, who was complaining? Certainly not me.

She stepped into my arms again like she did it every day. Her hand in mine was warm and sent tingles up my arm and down to other parts. Her left hand slowly slid up my arm onto my shoulder, sending bolts of heat through me. The two sensations collided, splitting like atoms between my legs.

As I led us around the dance floor, I held her away from me at a respectable straight-woman-dancing-with-a-lesbian distance. It wasn't long before she moved closer. After two times around the floor, she had erased the distance between us, and we were touching. Her breasts were pressed against me, and I couldn't help wondering if she was wearing the black or red lingerie she bought at Victoria's Secret. Her cheek was against mine, her skin soft, her perfume intoxicating. Her hand rested on the back of my neck, and I couldn't have moved even if I wanted to. Somehow, I managed to get us around the dance floor, my muscle memory dictating our two-step dance moves. Three slow songs later she was still in my arms, and I had stopped keeping my thoughts from going to places they shouldn't.

Back at our table, I excused myself to go to the bathroom. I needed to pee, but I also needed a few minutes away from Claire to stop the pounding in my chest and other places. After splashing cold water on my face, I looked at my reflection in the mirror. Somehow, I was alone, so I gave myself a pep talk.

"Just keep it together a little longer. Then you can take her home. Don't do something stupid, no matter how bad you want to. This being a mature, grown woman sucks."

Instead of going back to our table, I detoured to the bar. I gave my order and turned my back so I could ward off another sneak attack from Donna or any of the number of other ex-lovers here tonight.

I looked immediately at Claire, and my heart stopped. A tall, very butch blonde stood at our table, way too close to Claire. I knew hitting on someone when I saw it, and this woman was swinging to score.

Forgetting about our drinks, I started over to Claire's defense. I had taken only a few steps when our eyes met. Claire gave me a small shake of her head. "I got this," it said, loud and clear.

Back at the bar, I watched them for a few minutes. Claire stood her ground, and several minutes later the woman walked away. I couldn't help but smirk as she passed in the opposite direction.

"Everything okay?" I asked after I'd hurried back, looking for any sign Claire was upset. She was, after all, a straight woman in a lesbian bar. I put her beer on the table in front of her.

"Sure. Why wouldn't it be?"

"That woman was hitting on you, and this is your first time in a lesbian bar."

"No, it isn't."

I almost dropped my beer. "It isn't?"

"No, silly. Just relax."

What the hell did that mean? *With who? When? What did she do?*

"I caught my second wind. Dance with me again?" she asked a few minutes later.

My mind was still wrapped around Claire in a lesbian bar.

"Or I'll have to ask Mac."

"Mac?"

"The woman just talking to me."

"It looked to me like she wanted more than to just dance with you," I said, hoping I didn't sound as jealous as I felt.

"Yes. She made that very clear, but I'm not interested in her."

Did she just emphasize the last word? The music was loud, pounding in my ears, and Claire's offhand comment was making my head spin. This time when she took my hand, she could have led me to the ends of the earth for all I cared.

The clock on the dash read twenty after two when we pulled into her driveway. We had danced until they threw us out, then grabbed a bite to eat at a nearby Waffle House. Neither one of us wanted the night to end.

"I'll walk you up," I said, my throat sore from choking back the words I desperately wanted to say. Holding her in my arms, feeling her hands on me had skyrocketed all my feelings to the surface. I had it bad for Claire, and I had to figure out what I was going to do about it—and soon.

"What are you doing for Valentine's Day?" she asked after opening her front door.

"Valentine's Day?"

"Yeah, you know. The day that causes angst among couples and a spike in sales in the flower industry."

"Oh, yeah, Valentine's Day." I paused. "Nothing."

"No date? No special someone?"

Claire and I had talked about my almost nonexistent social life. I'd told her how I had devoted the past few years to my career and was now ready to think about getting serious with someone. Of course, she had no idea she was that someone.

"Not this year. What about you? Are you still seeing Alan?" Claire had told me about a guy she'd met at the deli counter several months ago, but she hadn't said anything about him lately. I hadn't asked, because the last thing I wanted to hear was how good, or bad, he was in bed.

"No. There wasn't anything between us. How about you come over, and we'll barbecue or something?"

I was much more interested in the "or something" than anything to eat.

"Yeah. Sure. What time?"

We settled on a few more specifics before she pulled me into her arms and hugged me.

"I had a great time," she said, her mouth very close to my ear. Her arms were around me, and she was holding me really tight. We were pressed together like we'd been for almost every song we danced. We fit perfectly, and I never wanted to let her go.

Saying something to Claire was a risk, a big risk. I wasn't sure if she was giving me signals, but I also didn't want to go where I wasn't wanted, and I certainly didn't want to lose my friendship with her. It was the most wonderful, yet painful friendship I had ever experienced.

CHAPTER FOURTEEN

I was wearing a new pair of jeans, and my boots were clean and shined. I'd had my favorite shirt pressed at the laundry and was wearing my lucky boxer briefs. They weren't lucky as in "get lucky," but they seemed to bring me luck whenever I had them on. And I certainly needed that tonight. Tonight, I was going to tell Claire that I wanted to be more than friends. To say I was scared shitless would be a significant understatement.

During the two weeks since we went dancing, I'd wavered between asking myself if Claire was giving me signals I desperately wanted or I was reading something into what was not there.

I had practiced what I would say for days. How I would tell her I wanted more than a friendship with her, and not friends with benefits either. My hand was shaking when I pushed the doorbell. No going back now.

Claire greeted me with a kiss on the cheek, and I almost blurted it out right there. That would not be good. I had all my persuasive words ready to go and didn't want to be rushed.

She seemed nervous, and while she cooked and we ate, we seemed to have difficulty finding something to talk about. After dinner we sat on the couch, the tension almost palpable. That never happened. Maybe this wasn't the right time for this conversation. But with so much at stake, would it ever be the right time?

I couldn't wait any longer. It was almost nine, and if I was going to crash and burn, I wanted to do it sooner rather than later. I squared around to face Claire, whose expression was neutral.

"I have something I want to tell you." I started cautiously.

"I do too," Claire said, not quite meeting my eyes.

I felt sick to my stomach. My gut instinct was always right.

"You go first," she said.

I should have made her go first, chivalry and all that, but I just wanted to get this over with and out of here as fast as I could.

"Okay." I straightened my shoulders as I was gathering strength before a storm. "I've met someone."

Claire's expression changed. Disappointment? Heartbreak? No. That couldn't be right.

"Tell me all about her," Claire said.

It sounded like her throat was tight and she could barely get the words out. WTF? Shouldn't she be happy for me? Isn't that what BFFs do? I must have had an odd look on my face because she leaned forward and touched my hands that were clenched in my lap.

"Tell me about her," she repeated. "If she makes you happy, I want to hear all about her."

"Well," I said, my carefully rehearsed words disappearing into the heavy air around us. Panic threatened to overwhelm me, but I took a deep breath and jumped in with both feet, stepped off the cliff, and took the plunge.

"I met her several months ago. The first time I laid eyes on her I somehow knew she was different from any woman I'd ever met. It didn't start out as anything romantic, but it grew into that over time. At least for me it did. I didn't know what was happening. It just crept up on me. We spent more and more time together as friends, just hanging out and doing things, and before I knew it, I realized I'd fallen for her—hard. She's changed my life. She makes me want to be a better person. She makes me see every ray of sunshine and every sliver of hope."

I'd been afraid to look at Claire, but now I couldn't take my eyes off her. I couldn't read her expression, but I plunged ahead anyway.

"I've always been afraid of commitment, but I want to spend every minute with her. I think about her all the time. What it would be like to fall asleep next to her every night and see her face the first thing every morning. I want her waiting for me when I come home, and I want to come home to her every night, knowing I can depend on her and that she'll have my back. I want to support her in everything she does. I want to spend the rest of my life with her. I even want to have a few kids with her." I chuckled at that last one.

"That's wonderful, Hayes. I'm so happy for you," Claire said, but I didn't detect any emotion behind her words. "Does she feel the same way about you?"

"I haven't said anything to her."

She frowned. "Why not?"

"Because I don't want to lose her, lose our friendship."

"And if you tell her, you will?"

"That's my biggest fear. I may lose everything that matters to me if she doesn't feel the same."

Claire interrupted me. "You need to take the chance, Hayes. You need to tell her. Remember when I was talking to you about the doubts I had when I decided to open my own firm? You told me your motto is no risk, no reward."

I nodded, my throat as dry as dirt on a hot summer day.

"Is she worth it?"

"Yes, absolutely." My nerves were a mess, but my conviction was absolute.

"Is the potential of what you could have with her more than what you might lose?"

"Yes."

"Then there's your answer," she said simply. "No risk, no reward."

"What would you do?" I asked.

Claire's entire demeanor changed. She took my hands and looked me right in the eyes.

"I'd tell her. I'd tell her that the stars beam in her eyes and the sun shines in her smile. That the wind blows when she speaks and clouds disappear whenever she's around. I'd make sure she knows that your heart pounds whenever you think of her and that you can't think about anything other than her. That you can't wait to be with her again the minute after you part. That you crave her touch and ache for her kiss. That you want her by your side in this crazy, unpredictable world."

Her voice changed to almost a whisper, her eyes sparkling now.

"That you want to watch the stars come out at night and fall asleep in her arms. That you react like never before when she looks at you. That you want to feel her hands on you. That she makes you laugh and feel like you're the most important person in the world."

"It seems like you read my mind."

"Just tell her, Hayes. You may be surprised to find out she feels the same."

Electricity pulsed around us. This entire scene had shifted, and I wasn't sure if I was on the right side.

"Tell her, Hayes."

She was prompting me. Could I do it?

Claire sounded calm, confident, and encouraging. With her by my side, as friend, or lover, I could do anything. I took a deep breath, confident I was doing the right thing.

"I've met someone, Claire." My mouth was so dry, and my heart was stuck firmly in my throat. "And that someone is you."

Claire didn't say anything, but the growing smile on her face was like shouting from the mountaintops.

"Today seems to be the day for reveals. I've met someone too, Hayes. And my someone is you."

TAKING A RISK

Erin Dutton

Valentine Memories

Is it corny to say that my wife and I are not the kind of couple who needs Valentine's Day to know how we feel about each other? Yes. But it's true. In fact, most years, we barely celebrate it at all. The most romantic moments in our life together seem to happen in small flashes—a day on the beach in P-town, a sweet kiss in the darkness of our RV while we're on a new adventure together, or the inexplicable way I feel when I make her laugh.

But when I think of Valentine's Day, two occasions stand out in my mind.

In 2009, the first year Christina and I celebrated the holiday, we were a new couple, just barely dating for two months. We stayed in, at her house. But she didn't have a kitchen table (long story), so we spread a blanket on the floor instead. We dimmed the lights, lit some candles, and shared two courses of fondue—cheese and chocolate. To this day, those are two of my favorite food groups.

I was already in love with her, but on that day, I couldn't have even conceived of all we had yet to share. I wasn't capable of understanding that I would love her more than I'd ever loved anyone before.

A decade later, we spent Valentine's Day with three of our closest friends. Again, we were eating fondue, this time at the Melting Pot, because as much as I like those guys, eating with them on the floor in our dimly lit kitchen would have felt very strange. This memory also makes me smile because these three guys, two of whom have known Christina since her twenties, have now become a part of my family. I'm thankful she knew them then, and I'm so grateful to have them in *my* life now.

I love a good rom-com and all that it romanticizes. I do write romance, after all. Reading a story that moves me emotionally makes me come back for a reread. And that's what I aspire to write with every book. Having Christina in my life has enhanced my feeling about the idea of happy endings because I now know that it's everything that comes after the happily-ever-after that matters most.

Erin Dutton

CHAPTER ONE

I know we talked about expectations during your interview, but I want to reiterate. We may be a small-town department, but I hold everyone to high standards. It's no longer the era of good-ole-boy policing."

"Yes, sir." Jo Forsythe followed her new boss, chief of police Paul Cade, through the lobby of the Harbor Springs Police Department.

He was the epitome of so many officers she'd worked with before. Tall, with a solid physique, he had a torso that looked even more barrel-shaped because of the ballistic vest under his uniform shirt. But she knew better than to assume anything about him personally or about his leadership. During her research for this job, she'd learned that he was ten years her senior and, two years ago, at the age of forty-five, was the youngest man ever named chief in Harbor Springs.

He swiped an access card and led her into the area restricted from the public. He had conducted her interview by videoconference, so this was the first time she'd been inside the building.

Several desks dotted the open area of the main room. They were modern in style and appeared quite new, as did the ergonomic desk chairs pushed up behind them. A no-frills desktop computer and monitor occupied each one.

"These desks are for paperwork, interviewing witnesses, and such. You can just grab a free one when you need it. They aren't assigned. I encourage my officers to spend their down time patrolling and interacting in the community, not lounging at a desk in the office."

"Makes sense. You've already got nicer equipment than my old department did. They used crappy, uncomfortable furniture to encourage us not to lounge. That and nonstop calls from dispatch."

He nodded. "The idea of the big-city agencies with the cutting-edge design and tech portrayed on television is misleading, isn't it?"

"Sure is. Big city just means big government and complicated budgets too lean to cover all the corners."

"Public money can be as hard to come by around here as well. But last year, we caught the guy who had been vandalizing Mrs. Beacon's flowerbeds. To show her appreciation, she endowed the department directly with a big chunk of her departed husband's money. So, the officers got new ballistic vests and body cams, and the bullpen got a much-needed makeover."

"Flowerbeds, huh? Serious business."

"It was to her and her azaleas." He resumed walking toward the back of the building. In a room to the left, through a large window, she could see a woman seated at a workstation with several monitors. "That's dispatch."

Jo tried not to compare the lone employee with the large communications center at her old department. She'd known this move would be a change, and comparing every component of her new life with her old would wear her out quickly.

"Mrs. Beacon's botanical caper had more intrigue than you'd expect." He glanced over his shoulder with a grin. "Turns out the guy had a grudge against the late Mr. Beacon for a business deal he felt he was screwed out of—one that made the Beacons a ton of money and left his widow quite comfortable."

"And flower vandalism was his chosen form of retaliation?"

Cade shrugged. "I grew up with him—knew him practically all our lives—and he's so low-key I'm surprised he even had that in him. I know it's not the kind of action you're used to—"

"That's okay." She glanced around the room, already happier than she'd been in months in the city. "This is exactly what I was looking for."

She didn't want him to feel he had to apologize for the size or pace of the town, or to think that she was judging his department in some way. She'd come here seeking a quieter life, wanting to feel like she belonged someplace.

"My office is back here. But when I can convince Miss Freda to handle the paperwork part of my job, you're as likely to find me out around town as in here." He smiled warmly at a woman who approached and handed him a cup of coffee. "Miss Freda, this is our newest officer, Jo Forsythe."

"It's nice to meet you, Officer Forsythe." The crinkles at the corners of Freda's kind eyes and the perfectly set style of her silver hair reminded Jo of her grandmother, who'd had a standing weekly appointment at the salon. She was slim and neatly dressed in a knee-length skirt and matching cardigan.

"Please, call me Jo." She'd learned a long time ago, when it came to chiefs, it often mattered more how she treated their administrative assistants. No doubt Miss Freda kept the place running smoothly.

Cade took a sip of his coffee, then waved a hand toward the front of the room. "I'm going to have you riding with Brianna Willis. But she took some personal time today to drive one of her kids to the doctor. So, you'll be with me until tomorrow." He didn't wait for her response before striding off toward the front of the building as if on a mission. "Miss Freda, we're heading over to McCall's Sporting Goods. You can get me on the radio if you need anything."

Jo lengthened her stride to keep up as they passed through the lobby and out the front door. In the parking lot, Cade climbed behind the wheel of a marked SUV.

"Is there a problem at the sporting-goods store?" Jo barely got the passenger door closed before he began backing out of his parking spot.

"No. We've got an ammo order in, and since you're here, I could use an extra pair of hands picking it up." His measured tone contradicted his hurried motions. He spoke as if every word had been carefully considered, even when communicating the simplest phrases. On the other hand, he drove like he was responding to a hot call.

"You order the department's ammo from a sporting-goods store? Wouldn't you get a better deal using a bigger supplier?"

"Maybe. But I like to support our local businesses. And Kayla gives me the best deal she can swing while still making a little bit of money." He glanced at her. "Don't worry. I'm not cheating the taxpayers. It's all listed in the budget. The people of this town want to take care of their neighbors."

Another big difference between her new life and her former one. She didn't even know her neighbors in Atlanta, let alone consider their welfare beyond the basic life necessities.

♥

The only car in the lot of McCall's Sporting Goods, a bright-blue Mini Cooper, was parked several spots from the building, indicating it likely belonged to an employee. As Cade circled and pulled into a place near the front, Jo spotted an equality sticker on the back window of the

Mini Cooper. Interesting. And not at all what she expected to find in rural Georgia.

Ever since she decided to leave Atlanta, she'd been preparing herself for the chance she might not be accepted here. But maybe she'd been too quick to judge, letting her own assumptions about small-town life dictate her emotions. She needed to be as open-minded as she wanted everyone else to be.

Whereas the businesses on the opposite side of the street lined up, sharing walls and competing for shoppers with window displays and colorful signs, McCall's stood alone, a large square, brick structure with little in the way of architectural interest, unless you counted the forest-green awning over the row of front windows.

Inside, the mood changed. A creatively designed display, including a flickering LED campfire and a huge, realistic-looking stuffed bear holding a marshmallow stick, greeted shoppers as they entered the store.

"Good morning, Chief."

Jo turned away from the bear and toward a woman who stood next to the one cash-register counter. She was pretty—in a natural, I-roll-out-of-bed-looking-great way. Soft waves of dark hair curled under just a bit as they touched her jawline. The cut of her jeans and the tailored fit of her red flannel shirt made her appear as if she'd stepped off the cover of an L.L.Bean catalog. The same outfit would make Jo feel more like the Brawny paper-towel man—minus the stubble. She lifted a heavy-looking box, and Jo squelched her urge to step forward and help—somehow feeling certain she wouldn't welcome the implication that she couldn't handle the weight.

"Kayla, how are you?" Cade's deep voice suddenly flowed like warm maple syrup, and a smile born of deep affection transformed his expression.

"I'm doing good, Chief." She placed the box on the counter and faced them both. "You caught me at the perfect time—it's the weekday-morning lull. I'll go get your order from the back."

"Kayla, this is my newest officer, Jo Forsythe. You'll be seeing her around, training on the evening shift with Brianna."

"Nice to meet you, Officer Forsythe." Kayla's tone was polite, but her expression seemed tight, and she barely glanced in Jo's direction, her icy-blue eyes flicking away quickly behind rectangular-framed glasses.

"Please, call me Jo."

She nodded and turned away. "I'll be right back."

"She's super friendly," Jo muttered sarcastically when Kayla had disappeared down an aisle and through a door marked EMPLOYEES ONLY.

"Be careful now. This town is pretty protective of Kayla and her wife. Folks won't abide you saying anything negative about her."

Jo couldn't deny a twinge of disappointment that Kayla had a wife. But she was still happy to discover a lesbian couple about her age in town, potential friends to hang out with. Six months ago, her ex, a fellow police officer, had gotten most of their friends in the split. She'd fed them lies about how Jo ignored and neglected her, when, in fact, she'd been the one who stepped out. Jo was over the loss of the relationship. And the isolation from those she once considered friends had helped make the decision about moving even easier. So, after Christmas, she'd packed up her belongings and resolved to start over someplace new.

♥

"Mint mocha latte, please." Jo gave her order to the young barista behind the counter of her new favorite coffee spot.

"Yes, ma'am." He glanced at Brianna, Jo's training officer, and said, "Black coffee."

Brianna gave a small nod, and he grabbed two to-go cups from a stack next to the register before turning away.

"You weren't kidding about being a regular here." During the week Jo had been shadowing Brianna, they'd visited Beans to Brew nearly every day. So far, all the employees knew Brianna's coffee order without asking.

"Since I refuse to patronize the chain-coffee-which-shall-not-be-named that just opened on the edge of town, yes, I am a loyal customer. Been coming here since I was eleven."

"You were drinking coffee at eleven?" That explained a lot. Brianna seemed to have endless amounts of energy, despite having a full-time job and three kids at home. She gave off a no-nonsense vibe, from her short hair to her minimalist makeup. She worked efficiently but also took time to greet people and ask after their families.

"It was hot chocolate back then. Coffee started at sixteen, I think."

As they waited for their order, a chime indicated another customer entering. Through the window, Jo noticed the distinctive Mini Cooper from the McCall's lot now parked beside the curb. Interesting.

"I'll be right with you." The barista didn't look up from preparing Jo's latte.

"I'm not in a hurry."

Jo recognized the pleasant tone as the one Kayla used with Chief Cade, not the cooler one she leveled at Jo. Kayla didn't seem interested in seeing who else was inside, instead swiped through something on her phone screen. Jo took the opportunity to observe her unnoticed. Today's flannel was blue, shades of light and dark, and appeared so soft that if Jo were closer, she might be tempted to touch it. That would be inappropriate.

Kayla glanced up, caught her, and scowled. Stung, Jo looked away and directly into Brianna's narrowed eyes. Damn.

Brianna shook her head. "Don't even look that way, friend."

"I know. Cade told me she's married."

Brianna's brows drew together. "He said that?"

"Well, he mentioned her wife."

"Oh." Brianna bit her lip.

While the end to their conversation felt awkward, Jo let the subject drop. A minute later, as they picked up their order and headed for the door, she snuck a glance at Kayla and found her staring back at her. She gave Kayla a welcoming smile, hoping to quell whatever animosity Kayla felt. In a town this size, they were sure to run into each other occasionally, and even if they wouldn't be friends, Jo preferred to at least be cordial.

♥

Kayla watched Jo Forsythe follow Brianna out the door, already hating the spread of warmth in her stomach when Jo smiled at her. She'd been rude when they met. She was adult enough to admit that, just not enough to do anything about it. The polite thing would have been to go over just now and apologize, but she hadn't left her place in line.

She didn't want to acknowledge that just the sight of Jo in her uniform when she walked into McCall's with Paul Cade had shaken her. She moved with the too-familiar swagger that a lot of women in uniform had, as if they inherently knew they had something to prove.

Luckily, the coil of tawny hair pinned in a bun just at the nape of her neck didn't feel reminiscent. Nor did the golden color of her tanned forearms or the peek of paler skin on her bicep when her short sleeve rode up slightly.

She wasn't surprised she noticed so much about Jo physically. For over a decade, she'd lived with the most observant woman she'd ever known. Surely she'd taken on some of that attention to detail. But she didn't just take in Jo's physical attributes. She'd also seen how her friendly expression had shut down when Kayla responded so coldly. And just now, she'd felt Jo reaching out, tentatively, from across the room. But that was ridiculous, wasn't it? She couldn't have sensed the emotions of a woman she'd barely met and felt them so acutely, so certainly.

She'd seen a quiet exchange between Brianna and Jo and wondered if it had something to do with her. If Brianna had been alone, Kayla would have gone over to say hello. But Jo's presence had her keeping her distance.

Shaking her head, she retrieved her coffee order and headed for her car, ignoring the blueberry muffins that also called out to her from the display case. Neither those muffins nor Jo Forsythe would be good for her.

Instead, she should be focusing on the to-do list sitting on the desk in her office. Her two part-time employees would return to college for the spring semester soon, and she'd be mostly on her own at the store. She didn't mind working alone though. Her customers kept her company, coming in to browse or buy, and some, it seemed, just came in to chat or check up on her.

She had plenty to keep her busy at work, but lately she'd been thinking she might be ready to make some changes in her personal life.

CHAPTER TWO

"Finish up that report on the incident at the goose pond in the park, and we're through for the day."

"Almost done." Jo clicked through several fields on her tablet. "Did you even know geese could run that fast?"

"I did actually, but that's a long story." Brianna's voice carried a trace of humor that had been missing from their interactions for most of the day.

"Well, now you have to tell me."

"Not today." The chill was back.

Brianna parked their patrol car in one of the designated spots. She would hand off the keys to one of the third-shift officers when they got inside. "Enjoy your days off. I'll see you Tuesday."

"Did I do something wrong?"

"No. Why?"

"You've been standoffish this evening. Since the coffee shop, I guess."

"Nope. I'm good."

Even Brianna's dismissal felt off, and Jo didn't want to wonder for the next two days what she might have done to change their dynamic. She'd been called persistent to a fault, and her worrisome brain turned their interaction in the coffee shop inside-out looking for a clue.

She followed Brianna toward the station, a few paces behind, until it hit her.

"Kayla McCall."

Brianna stopped, her back snapping straight, and she slowly turned around.

"You got weird when you saw me checking her out."

Brianna twitched her lips into a firm line.

"Listen. She's a head-turner, yes. And I couldn't resist looking. But I told you, Cade said she's married. Off-limits. I'm not interested in a woman who's already taken."

"She isn't."

"Taken? Or married?"

"Yes. Both."

"Cade said—" She struggled to remember his exact words. "He said that the town was protective of her and her wife."

She could see the conflict in Brianna's eyes, who, after several seconds of careful consideration, grabbed Jo's arm.

"Come with me." Brianna didn't release her until they stopped in the lobby of the station, in front of a framed photograph of a female police officer. The woman wore a class-A uniform and stood in front of a blue backdrop with an American flag behind her—a standard departmental headshot. Her short, ginger hair fell in unruly ringlets against her forehead. But that was the only part of her appearance out of place. Otherwise, she was well-buttoned up: uniform starched, posture rigid, and a solemn expression.

Under the picture a small shadow box held a silver badge and a plaque with the name Macy Tadd on it, followed by the letters EOW and a date from four years ago.

"Only officer this department has lost in thirty years." Brianna paused long enough to give Jo a hard look. "Also, Kayla's wife."

Brianna's eyes welled, and Jo could feel that her pain was about more than just Kayla's loss or that of the department. Brianna sniffed and looked away, back at Macy's photo.

"She was your friend."

Brianna nodded. "My best friend. We'd known each other since kindergarten."

"Did you both grow up here?"

"Yes. After high school, we got Criminal Justice degrees at Georgia State, then came back."

"I'm sorry for your loss." She glanced again at Macy's photo.

"It was a loss for the whole town. Macy was homecoming queen, the most popular girl, but also the nicest. When she and Kayla got together, Harbor Springs embraced them as a couple. In such a small Southern town, that could have gone another way."

Jo nodded. Atlanta was considered progressive within the state of Georgia. In fact, in a lot of Southern states, once you ventured outside of the metropolitan areas, values got conservative very quickly.

"What happened?"

"Traffic accident. We had one of those freak ice storms that happen every few years. She was helping a stranded motorist, when another car skidded into them."

Jo bowed her head solemnly, knowing Brianna didn't need her to respond. Every officer she knew was aware of the inherent danger of their profession. She'd learned years ago to balance self-protective vigilance without letting it topple into a paranoia that could cause her to make a mistake when lives were on the line. Fear had no place in police work. Jo had found that respect served her much better.

♥

Jo shoved open the door of her rental house and dropped her keys into a bowl on the console table just inside. She headed directly for the bedroom, unsnapping the keepers on her duty belt along the way. After she'd secured all her gear and tossed her uniform into a hamper in the closet, she pulled on her comfiest sweats and an old T-shirt.

This week, but especially this day, had beaten her up a bit. She'd expected a slower pace from the city, but she'd worked just as hard. Things would calm down once she was fully trained in the local policies and procedures. Brianna had them grabbing every call so she could get the experience she needed. The other officers on their shift had probably really enjoyed the break they'd gotten this week.

She settled on the sofa with a cup of hot cocoa, needing a bit of relaxation before she could go to bed. She'd been lucky to find this furnished house in the center of town, one block off the main street. The living room had been set up exactly like she would have done herself, the sofa near the set of three windows that overlooked the front yard. It was dark now, but in the morning, she sat here and watched the town waking up around her.

One of her neighbors had walked his basset hound by every day this week. Small packs of kids walked or rode bikes to the school three blocks away. She'd always been an early riser, and working the evening shift hadn't changed her routine.

Overall, she was settling into Harbor Springs quite well. She'd discovered, during a midmorning walk one day, that the deli on the corner started their lunch service at ten a.m. and that their bacon, blue cheese, and shaved-steak wrap tasted incredible. She'd stopped in the consignment shop to check out their wares, made a mental note to visit the hair salon when it was time for a trim, and waved at a pharmacy employee that was setting up a new window display of Epsom salts and bubble bath.

Imagining the quaint downtown area only a few minutes' walk away brought McCall's Sporting Goods to mind. Kayla McCall was a widow. Jo's old department had lost officers, and though she wasn't close to any of them, she felt the loss of a member of the team. But that was nothing like what Kayla and Brianna had gone through when Macy died. She couldn't imagine the depth of that pain, to say nothing of the hole left in the community.

She was struck with a ridiculous desire to comfort Kayla. Where did that come from? She wasn't a casually physical person. She didn't hug her friends when she said good-bye, and she didn't touch someone's arm or shoulder while talking, even during a serious conversation. Why, now, did she find it so easy to imagine taking Kayla in her arms and tenderly cupping the back of her head? If she were going to take this fantasy to its probable conclusion, she had to also picture Kayla pushing her away and glaring at her. Of course, Kayla wouldn't welcome the sentiment from a woman she didn't even know, and seemingly didn't want to.

Feelings inexplicably hurt by a rejection that hadn't actually happened, Jo stood and strode to the kitchen, where she rinsed her mug and placed it in the sink. She'd spent enough time thinking about Kayla McCall.

♥

Kayla picked up her order from the deli counter, then headed to the park next door. Mondays were her favorite time for a solo picnic. The families that filled the space over the weekend were off to school and work, so she often had the park to herself. When the weatherman forecasted an unseasonably warm, sixty-five-degree January day, she decided to take advantage.

Reaching her favorite oak tree, she spread out a blanket in the grass. Her plan for the afternoon involved lunch and an hour or so with the newest book by her favorite romance author. Usually, she tried to keep herself to her schedule, but she already had a feeling this story would suck her in for at least a couple of hours. She couldn't resist a good ice queen.

She'd just opened her novel when she saw Jo cross the street and enter the park. She bent her head even farther, hoping if she appeared engrossed, Jo would leave her alone. She peeked over the top of her glasses and caught the moment Jo noticed her. She took a few more hesitant steps, and Kayla hated how endearing her indecision was. When it became clear Jo had detoured toward her, she set her book aside.

Seeing Jo out of uniform for the first time did strange things to her. She felt angry at Paul Cade, because making Jo cover up those legs with navy polyester was a sin. Her thighs flexed as she walked, and her calves curved gracefully in at her ankles, which Kayla spent far too long studying. But what did Jo expect when she wore those no-show socks inside her running shoes? Kayla had to look.

In loose-fitting athletic shorts and a ringer-tee, Jo appeared younger. Somehow, her uniform hardened the roundness in her cheeks and the slight fullness under her chin. Her steps seemed lighter, less like she was taking on the world.

She stopped just a few feet away, at the edge of the dappled shade in the grass from Kayla's tree.

"Great minds think alike, I guess." She held up a bag from the deli, then glanced around. "I was headed for that picnic table over there. And—well, it's a small town, and we're bound to keep running into each other, so I thought I'd be cordial and say hello." She seemed uncomfortable—nervous maybe. Kayla couldn't blame her. She hadn't exactly been welcoming to Jo so far.

"Okay, then. Hello back." Her face flushed at how awkward she sounded as well.

Jo gave a curt nod, then turned to go. Kayla held back a sigh. Jo was right. They couldn't avoid seeing each other around town. She could be friendly—she should be. She didn't even know Jo, so what reason did she have—other than the uniform she wore—not to like her?

"Wait," she said before she could stop herself. Jo angled back toward her. "Do you want to join me?"

Jo tilted her head to the side, then smiled. "You *have* staked out the best spot in the park, so if you're willing to share, I should take you up on it."

She scooted over a bit, making room on the blanket and pretending that smile hadn't made her insides flutter. Jo sat as close to the edge of the blanket as possible, leaving plenty of space between them. That was fine with her, because she didn't want to take a chance that Jo's bare leg might accidentally rub against her thigh.

"How about this amazing weather, huh?" Jo asked as she unpacked the contents of her paper bag. Her lunch consisted of a bottle of flavored water and a wrap, just like Kayla's. She set the bottle in the grass to her right and peeled back the paper around one end of the wrap. Kayla picked up her own.

"I got the buffalo chicken." Kayla kicked herself for still sounding like she couldn't have productive conversation. But was lunch-food talk any worse than Jo's comment on the weather?

"I haven't tried that one yet. I got stuck on the steak-and-blue-cheese, and I keep getting it."

"How do you know another one isn't better?"

Jo shrugged. "When I find something I like, I stay with it."

Kayla took a bite so she wouldn't ask if that was true in all aspects of Jo's life. Such an inquiry could only come off as flirty, when actually she was just curious. Both Macy and Brianna were adventurous with a menu, and, for some reason, she'd equated the willingness to take a risk as a characteristic of their career choice.

"So, McCall's Sporting Goods, huh? Let me guess. Your dad started the place and—"

"And since he didn't have any sons, he passed it on to me?" Kayla shook her head. "Not much of a feminist, are you? Actually, my grandmother founded McCall's."

"Really?"

"Yep. She and my grandfather were outdoorsy types—hiking, fishing, camping—and when my grandfather died in his late forties, she had an awakening about the fragility of life. She used his life insurance to open the store that had always been a pipe dream for them."

"Wow. That's brave."

Kayla shrugged. "I guess, without him, she had nothing left to lose. My mom was grown and married by then."

"Did either of your parents work there?"

"Neither was interested. They were Realtors, and to stay in the game, they had to cover basically the whole county. So, growing up, while they showed houses in neighboring towns, I hung out at the store with Gran. I didn't actually start getting paid to work there until I was in high school, but by then I knew everything about the business. After graduation, I never left."

"Never thought about doing anything else?"

"I guess I also stick with what I like."

♥

Jo lay flat on the blanket and stared up through the leaves above her. She peeked at Kayla out of the corner of her eye to see if Kayla's expression indicated she was getting too comfortable. She'd decided to take Kayla's invitation to join her to heart and not believe that she'd just been polite and couldn't wait for her to leave. Normally a well-mannered person, she was apparently perfectly willing to overstay her welcome when it came to Kayla.

Kayla gathered the trash from their lunches and shoved it all into one of the paper bags, then set it off the blanket in the grass. She pulled her knees up toward her chest and wrapped her arms around her legs.

"What a great spot. You're probably going to find me squatting here all the time now."

"I'll call Brianna and take out a restraining order."

"On behalf of the tree?" Jo grinned.

"Yes. I'm its proxy."

"Joint custody?"

Kayla shook her head. "You'll have to wait until you're invited again."

Jo folded her arms and rested her hands behind her head. "I'm looking forward to it." Against her better judgment, she liked the idea of Kayla wanting to share her space with her.

She should have stuck with the plan, shared a pleasant greeting, then gone on to the picnic table and left Kayla alone. Brianna was right. Entertaining the idea of anything developing with her was an invitation for heartache. And even if she could get through Kayla's icy demeanor and they became involved, when it ended, as things inevitably do, she would not only lose Kayla and Brianna, but risk alienating the whole town. Establishing herself as the town pariah didn't fit with her plan to put down roots and become a part of someplace.

"Is Jo short for something. Joanna? Josephine?"

She rolled her head to the side and met Kayla's curious gaze.

"You can tell me."

"You can't laugh." She sat up and stretched out her legs in front of her.

Kayla nodded solemnly, as if determined to try to keep that promise.

"Journey."

Kayla pressed her lips together hard, clearly smothering a smile. "That's unique."

"My mom was sixteen when she had me. Her parents wanted her to give me up, but she refused. She had this grand idea that I was going to be her journey to happiness."

"Were you?"

Jo shrugged. "She'd have said yes. But what else is a mother supposed to say? *I gave up everything to raise you, and you turned out a disappointment.*"

"Surely she can't say that. You seem to be a nice person. You have a respectable job."

"I got the impression you weren't so fond of my profession."

"That's complicated." Kayla's tone indicated they would have no further discussion on the matter. She'd opened the door with her comment about Jo's career choice, but Jo decided not to push the issue.

"So was our relationship. We didn't always get along. We grew up together, so she wasn't much of an authority figure at times. But my grandparents basically shunned her, so it was us against the world."

"No other family?"

She shook her head.

"Is she still in—Atlanta, was it?"

"She passed away. Five years ago." The pain had dulled over time, but an ache still accompanied thoughts of her mom.

"I sometimes felt I had too much family around. Between my own relatives and Brianna and Macy's, too, someone was always watching what we were doing. We couldn't get away with anything."

"I imagine that's part of living in a place so small everyone knows each other."

Kayla laughed. "You say that like it's one of the good things about Harbor Springs."

"Isn't it? Even if you're otherwise alone, there are people who see you and would probably look for you if you went missing."

"Is that why you moved here? So someone will look for you when you go missing?"

"Yeah, maybe." She could leave it at that, a casual answer to what might be a joking inquiry anyway. "I didn't specifically choose

Harbor Springs. After a breakup a while back, I wanted to get away from the city. But that wasn't the only reason. I wasn't running from a great tragedy, just a life that felt isolated and impersonal. Over time, it stopped feeling like I was making a difference professionally, or that the people I served cared or even wanted me there. That probably doesn't make sense, does it? I sound crazy, huh?"

"Not crazy. Brave. But how did you know moving someplace smaller was the answer?"

Jo shrugged. "I didn't. I knew I wasn't happy in Atlanta. I started looking at openings in law enforcement elsewhere and came upon Chief Cade's posting. It didn't hurt that I left my old department in good standing and can go back there within six months without penalty if this doesn't work out."

"A safety net."

"Of sorts. I hope I won't need it. It may sound cheesy, but I want to be part of this community. I want people to know me." She toyed with a tuft of grass beside the blanket, purposely not meeting Kayla's eyes. She didn't want Kayla seeing how badly she wanted her to be someone who knew her.

"Fair enough. But, so you know, you haven't been here long enough to warrant a search party if you go missing, yet."

Jo smiled, taking Kayla's teasing as a good sign. "You let me know when I have."

CHAPTER THREE

It's up here on the right." Brianna pointed to a building midway down Main Street. "The Tadds have owned the pharmacy for as long as I can remember."

"The Tadds?" Jo pulled the cruiser into a spot next to the curb in front of the pharmacy.

Brianna nodded as she shoved open her car door. "Macy's folks. They moved to town right before Macy was born."

Inside, the pharmacy looked just as Jo imagined it had when the Tadds bought it four decades ago. The shelves and fixtures weren't modern but were clean and organized. A counter just inside the door held a cash register, probably newer than the original, but not a computer point-of-sale system like she expected to see in a retail store these days.

"Brianna, so good to see you."

"It's always good to see you, too. Mrs. Tadd, this is Jo Forsythe. She's new to the department and the area. Jo, this is Macy's mom and my second mother." Brianna smiled at Mrs. Tadd with clear affection.

Jo shook her hand and exchanged greetings. She guessed Mrs. Tadd was in her sixties, and her perfectly coiffed silver hair no doubt had been set at the salon a few shops away. She imagined Mrs. Tadd sitting in the chair next to Freda from the office, catching up on the latest goings-on around town.

"It's wonderful that Chief Cade has finally hired another female officer. He'd never admit it because that would make him sexist, but I believe he hesitated to do so after Macy. You girls were like daughters to him." Sadness and pride commingled in her expression.

Brianna cleared her throat. "Mr. Tadd called the station and said you had a shoplifter."

"Just some high school kids trying to prove themselves. I don't want to get anyone in trouble."

"If you let them get away with it, you won't be able to keep them out of here." She glanced at Jo. "We're already here. Let us at least take a report. Then you have the option to prosecute if you want to."

Mrs. Tadd still seemed reluctant, but Brianna's reasoning won her over. "Okay."

Jo retrieved the tablet from the car, and by the time she returned, Mr. Tadd, the pharmacist, had come out from the back room. After a brief introduction, Jo began gathering information for the report. Brianna stayed close and chatted with them both between questions.

The Tadds seemed like great people, and their affection for Brianna was clear. They spoke lovingly of Kayla, who apparently still kept in close touch with them. She helped Mrs. Tadd in her garden, and last summer she and Mr. Tadd had put an addition on their deck.

"Every year, Mr. and Mrs. Tadd host a February open house for the department. We all stop by when we can and raise a glass with them," Brianna said.

"It's just our way of showing appreciation. After the excitement of the holidays has faded, I think of it as a midwinter lift. Last year, we turned it into a fund-raiser for Climb Together, an organization that helps out the homeless all around the county. It was such a success that we'll do it again this year." Mrs. Tadd smiled. "You can expect to be included as well."

"I look forward to it. I love that you made it a celebration and something good for the community as well."

She finished the report and advised the Tadds how to get a copy of it and their next steps if they decided to press charges, though she doubted they would. Jo hoped word would get around that a police cruiser had been parked in front of the pharmacy after the shoplifting. Maybe that would be enough to deter future thefts. She made a mental note to speak with Brianna about driving by a few extra times during their shifts as well.

As she and Brianna pulled away from the curb in the cruiser, she said, "Sounds like Kayla still has a great relationship with the Tadds."

"I told you to forget about Kayla."

"It's a small town. I've already run into her a handful of times. Besides, that was more a commentary on how nice it is of them to keep her in their lives—to remain family to her. Not all parents would do that."

"Of course they did. We were childhood friends. They were treating us like daughters before Macy and Kayla got together."

"How was that for you? Was it strange when they became a couple?"

"It definitely changed the dynamic of our friendship. Things shifted from the three of us to the two of them and me. But everything changed again when I got married and started having babies. That's life, right?"

"Yeah. The admirable thing is that you guys seem to have adapted and kept your friendship strong. I grew apart from all my school friends."

"I suppose it's easier to stay in touch here than it would be in Atlanta. You don't have a lot of other people to hang out with."

Jo laughed. "I guess so. I'm too much of a homebody."

"So's Kayla. I used to have to drag them out with me on the weekends. They just wanted to stay in together. Now that I have a family of my own—"

"You appreciate the value of being at home with them."

"Hell, no. I appreciate escaping for a night out on my own." Brianna's grin let Jo know she was mostly kidding.

♥

Jo woke up every morning thankful that she'd moved to Harbor Springs. She already loved the pace of the life she'd been building. She'd never minded working second shift. Waking up without an alarm felt far more refreshing than being jerked from sleep before she was ready. Her body told her when to start the day.

She spent her mornings doing laundry or chores around the house, or walking through town. As she'd told Brianna, in Atlanta she'd been a homebody. When she wasn't on shift, she rarely went out unless a colleague coerced her. But here, she wanted to stay present in the community.

Sometimes, she saw Kayla through one of the large front windows of McCall's. Most days, she limited herself to a friendly wave while she walked on. But once in a while, she went inside and browsed the store. She kept their conversations to small talk, even though she wanted to know more about Kayla. They chatted about community events, and Kayla told her engaging stories about the town's most eccentric residents.

Since the day at the park, Kayla had been much more pleasant toward her. Sometimes she might even say *warm*. She still felt Kayla keeping a buffer between them, but she didn't cut their conversations short, and she rarely scowled at her anymore. Jo marked that as progress.

She'd finished her rotation riding with Brianna after four weeks. Following another meeting with Chief Cade, he had released her to patrol on her own. Since she and Brianna were two of the six officers assigned to second shift, they often still worked together. Having seniority, Brianna continued to tell her what to do, though Jo got to drive her own cruiser. In fact, she'd been assigned to Brianna's old one, and Brianna had received a shiny new SUV. She'd joked it was a bribe from Cade for putting up with Jo for those weeks.

She spent her evenings patrolling, timing her routes so she could be in town around the time most of the businesses closed. Then she headed out of town to familiarize herself with the rural areas outside of town, but still within her jurisdiction. As a city girl, she'd been surprised by how relaxed she was cruising the unlined, narrow roads, though she did sometimes have to turn on the radio because the quiet out there was unnerving.

She took the occasional report on a vehicle accident or theft. Toward the end of her shift, especially on weekends, she could expect to be called to the one bar in town for a disorderly, intoxicated patron.

Brianna often went home for her dinner break, to check in with her family, make sure her kids did their homework, that sort of thing. Jo would cover any incidents during that time, knowing that if she called for backup, Brianna remained only minutes away.

Jo took her dinner breaks in town, parked on the street eating a deli wrap or a salad in her car. She'd gone to the diner once, but sitting on a stool at the counter made her feel a part of that damn Norman Rockwell painting.

♥

"Have a good night," Kayla called as the customer she'd just helped left the store, trailed by her three kids.

She grabbed her phone and opened the app that synced with her point-of-sale system. Gran had taught her early on to never skimp when it came to the sales/inventory software. She'd always had the best system she could afford. Her last upgrade had made tracking sales trends incredibly easy.

She worked through the sales floor methodically, scanning barcodes with her phone's camera and inputting item quantities. The app saved her totals so she could review them one last time before placing orders with the appropriate distributors.

The front-door chime sounded just as she rounded the archery aisle.

"I'll be right with you." She scanned two more labels, finding a good spot to pick back up later.

"No hurry."

Kayla's heartbeat accelerated at the sound of Jo's voice. It had started doing that in the past couple of weeks, and she found it extremely annoying. She was determined to ignore the sensation of anticipation, hoping it would die a natural death and she could feel normal again. Yes, they'd crafted a truce of sorts that day in the park and carried it forward each time they casually ran into each other since. But any giddiness or floaty feelings on her part would only threaten the balance of their acquaintance.

At the front of the store, Jo peered at the bear display. The night before, Kayla had swapped out his waders for a backpack and a hiking pole.

"Hiking gear this week, huh?"

Kayla nodded.

"Where did that guy come from anyway?" Jo shoved her hands into the front pocket of her hoodie.

"I don't know exactly. All Gran would ever tell me is that she won a bet."

Jo flicked her eyebrows up and smiled. "Something so risqué she couldn't tell her granddaughter. Was your Gran a bad girl?"

"Stop it."

"Come on. She had to be, right?" Jo scoffed. "Won a bet? In a town this small, somebody knows what that bet was about. We should ask around."

"No."

"You don't want to know what kind of daredevil genes you have swimming around in there?" Jo waved her fingers the length of Kayla's body. When Jo met her eyes the teasing humor there kicked her in the chest. She missed banter. Yes, she had Brianna, and they had a similar sense of humor. But she craved the intimacy of this kind of flirty back-and-forth.

She'd been seeing Jo around town, sometimes on duty and sometimes not. Usually, she would just wave and continue on her way. Then just when Kayla convinced herself that Jo purposely kept her distance, she would stop to chat or come inside and browse. Against her better judgment, she began looking forward to these visits.

"Can I help you find something?" Treating Jo like any other customer didn't erase the electricity in the air between them.

"Time for new running shoes." Jo glanced down at her feet and a beat-up pair of sneakers. She seemed to be trying just as hard to keep their exchanges casual.

"You're a runner?"

"More of a jogger, really. I'm not breaking any speed records, but it keeps me in decent shape."

"Is this where I'm supposed to say that your shape looks just fine to me?" Oh, God, why did she say that?

"If it's true, I'll take it."

She turned away, but not before a heated blush spread up her neck. "Shoes are over here."

She led Jo to the far side of the store, where a variety of athletic shoes lined the wall. She wasn't as well-stocked on running gear this time of year as usual, but she had several pairs similar to what Jo already wore. "Is there a particular brand you prefer?"

"I'm all about comfort. I can browse a bit and try a few things on. Don't let me keep you from your work."

Kayla nodded, but when she moved away, it was only to the next aisle. She told herself she wanted to stay close in case Jo needed assistance—good customer service and all. But really, she just couldn't push herself outside of the radius of Jo's draw, as if a force acted on her that she couldn't control. So, she busied herself with straightening an end cap of youth football gear.

She heard Jo slide several boxes off the shelf, then the shuffling and crinkling of paper that went along with opening boxes. After donning a pair of shoes, Jo strode quickly up the aisle and back a couple of times.

"These feel great," she said after what Kayla counted as the third pair of shoes.

She took that as her cue and circled into the aisle. Jo bounced on her toes, wearing a pair of navy-blue Saucony sneakers with lime-green trim.

"They look good." They looked amazing, but that had more to do with her fitted, black yoga pants and the swell of her calves sweeping into the lines of her ankles than the actual shoes themselves. Damn, she'd somehow still landed on a commentary on Jo's shape, but at least she managed to keep it silent.

Chapter Four

Kayla sat across from Brianna at a table on the patio of Beans to Brew. No one shopped for sporting goods before church, so on Sundays she didn't open until noon. With Brianna working evenings and Kayla at the store most mornings, Sunday was the perfect day for them to get together. The Beans to Brew staff alleviated the chill in the air with several tall patio heaters spaced evenly among the tables.

As if they needed another reason, on Sundays, the coffee shop expanded their usual coffee and light breakfast offerings to include more decadent dishes. Today, Kayla and Brianna were all-in on the bananas-foster French toast with caramel sauce and spiced pecans.

"This is amazing." Brianna speared a banana slice and held it in the air. "So worth the egg whites and turkey bacon I've been eating all week just to have this."

Kayla rarely ate breakfast, unless her morning coffee counted—it sure felt like sustenance to her. Lunch typically consisted of a quick sandwich during the late-morning lull, while she trolled the internet for the latest and greatest new gear for the store. Her browsing was largely wishful thinking since most of the Harbor Springs residents didn't require more than basic sports equipment and fishing and camping gear. But she liked to stay on top of the trends, so she could make suggestions for the group of local mountain-biking enthusiasts or speak knowledgeably about the latest tech trends in hunting. Her favorite find had been a line of eco-friendly, water-soluble golf balls. She'd ordered some and featured them on a display. They sold surprisingly well.

She glanced up and, over Brianna's shoulder, caught sight of Jo jogging in their direction. Before she could figure out if she hoped Jo didn't see them, or that she did and stopped to chat, Jo looked right at her. She felt in Jo's gaze that the decision was hers. If she looked away, Jo would run right by. She held eye contact as if guiding Jo to them.

"Good morning, ladies." Jo slowed to a stop beside their table. Her cheeks were flushed, and her skin shone with sweat. She touched her watch screen, stopping the timer displayed there. She'd layered for the weather with a short-sleeved shirt over a long-sleeved one. She shoved up the side of her knit cap and removed one wireless earbud.

"Thanks for the advice on the shoes." She glanced down at her feet. "They feel great."

In her peripheral vision, Kayla saw Brianna's posture straighten, but she didn't look at her. "Just doing my job."

"What is that?" Jo nodded toward Kayla's plate. "Another local secret you all are keeping from me?"

"Exactly." Brianna shoved a bite into her mouth.

"Sunday brunch at Beans to Brew—noted." Jo tapped a finger to her temple.

"If I were a better person, I would feel guilty eating this while you're out jogging," Kayla said.

Jo smiled. "Please. I'm all about self-indulgence. Enjoy it." She glanced once more at Brianna before trotting off.

Kayla tried not to watch her go, but—when did she become obsessed with calves, specifically watching Jo's flex as she ran away? And why was Jo wearing those sexy running shorts in February? When she returned her attention to their table, she couldn't be sure if Brianna had seen her looking. She grimaced at the thought of having to explain something she didn't completely understand herself.

"Don't worry. I told her to leave you alone." Brianna must have mistaken the reason for her expression.

"You did?" Why was it Brianna's business to mediate her social interactions?

"Sure. Macy would want me to look out for you."

Kayla's irritation softened. Of course Brianna had the best of intentions.

"I can't keep her from coming to the store and acting like she needs new shoes." Brianna put air quotes around *new shoes.* "But at least she knows where you stand."

Where did she stand? Brianna assumed she didn't want to interact with Jo. But that didn't feel like the truth. She for sure didn't want to get romantically involved with Jo. Right?

"How's that going? Working with her?"

Brianna shrugged. "I like her. She's a good cop and is really eager to fit in here."

"Do you think she will? I thought the pace here compared to Atlanta would drive her nuts within the first month."

"Yeah. I did, too. But she spends time genuinely talking to people, and I get the feeling she enjoys that as much as any other part of the job."

♥

Jo stepped outside and immediately wanted to go back in. She could skip this morning's run, sack out on the couch, and watch a movie. She'd often joked that her motivation seemed tied directly to the barometric pressure. Dreary weather was often the downfall of her fitness routine. She forced herself off the porch and down the walkway. She'd gotten this far, so maybe she'd abbreviate her route a bit—shorten the punishment.

She jogged two blocks north, picking up speed a bit as her muscles warmed and stretched. She hadn't charged her earbuds, so she was without her usual soundtrack of songs specially selected to pace her run. Yet another reason she felt sluggish today.

When she reached downtown, she crossed to the other side of the street—in front of McCall's Sporting Goods. The curbside parking on the south side meant more obstacles while running. She always pictured, in her head, someone throwing their driver's door open and her smacking into it and falling down.

She was engaged in that mental scenario when her right foot hit an uneven crack in the pavement. She stumbled so quickly she never had a chance to regain her balance. And it wasn't a graceful fall—basically Superman-ing across the asphalt, her outstretched hands protecting her from face-planting at the last minute. She rolled to her back with a groan, her scraped palms already burning. She closed her eyes, partly to assess what hurt and partly because she didn't want to look around to see if anyone had witnessed her humiliation.

"Are you okay?"

She flopped the back of one hand against her forehead, covering her eyes. Her disgrace was complete. "Is there any chance you didn't see my big dive?"

"Can I help you up?" The apology in Kayla's tone answered Jo's question.

She moved her hand, startled to find Kayla closer than she thought. Kayla had knelt beside her, her thigh almost touching Jo's, her hand frozen in the air halfway to Jo's shoulder.

"I'm good. I'll probably be able to get up once my pride stops throbbing."

"This is why I don't jog."

Jo winced as she pushed into a sitting position, the concrete rough against her sensitive hands. She rose carefully, pausing when her left ankle felt tender as she put her weight on it. She sat back down.

"Does something hurt?"

"My ankle." She pulled her shoe off, already feeling a bit of swelling in the joint.

"Let me see." Before Jo could react, Kayla slipped her fingers under the edge of Jo's sock and eased it off. Kayla's fingers were cool against her heated skin.

"It's probably okay. I just need to get home and elevate it." Were her feet sweaty? Worse, did they smell?

Kayla cradled Jo's heel, gently pressing along the side of her ankle. Jo managed to avoid sucking in a breath, but Kayla almost certainly felt her tense at the twinge of pain.

"I don't think you can walk even a few blocks on that. Are you certain you don't need to go to the urgent care?"

Jo shook her head. "It's not broken. I don't need a doctor to tell me to take an anti-inflammatory and stay off it."

"Okay. Let's get you inside." Kayla grasped Jo's arm under her elbow.

"What?"

"You can sit on the couch in my office and elevate it. Then when I close in thirty minutes, I'll drive you home."

"I don't think—"

"What are your other options?"

"I could call Brianna to come get me."

Kayla furrowed her brow for just a second, then abruptly released Jo's arm. "Okay, then." She straightened, looking oddly like Jo had hurt her feelings by refusing her help.

"Wait—" She let Kayla get almost to the front door of McCall's before she spoke. She hated asking for assistance, especially from

Kayla. But she didn't want to sit on the sidewalk waiting for Brianna. And spending a little time with Kayla could be an added bonus. "Okay. Let's just do this before too many other people see me sprawled out."

With Kayla's help, she got up, not gracefully, but they managed. She limped into the store and to the back room, putting as little weight as she could manage on her foot. After a quick stop at the restroom to wash her still-stinging hands, they continued into Kayla's office. It was small, barely room for the desk, filing cabinet, and loveseat, but orderly and tastefully decorated in neutral shades.

Jo sat on the couch with her back against the arm and stretched her legs out. While Kayla carefully lifted her foot and situated a pillow underneath, she looked up at the collection of photographs on top of the filing cabinet to distract herself from the intimacy of the moment.

That was a mistake. The first frame she saw contained a picture of Kayla and Macy. They stood atop a peak, a scenic valley sprawling out behind them. Their cheeks were pink, and both smiled broadly. Macy's hair was windblown and swept across her forehead, while Kayla's was secured under a baseball cap.

When she glanced back at Kayla, she found her staring at the photo as well, her brows drawn together in sadness, but a small smile graced her lips.

"That was a good day."

"I've seen only the one picture of her—the one at the station. She looks so different here." Judging by the lines at the corners of Macy's eyes, she was actually older in this shot than the department one, but the joy on her face made the years insignificant.

"You all look so serious in those photos."

"Because that's the one that goes out to the media. If an officer is involved in anything newsworthy, the department shares that photo. You don't want them reporting that you shot someone while on duty, and then they flash up this image of you just grinning away. Bad optics."

"Yeah. I'm pretty familiar with seeing her picture in the news."

Jo grimaced. "I'm sorry. That was thoughtless."

Kayla shook her head dismissively. "It's okay. At first, it was almost every day, which was tough. Then just on the anniversary, which might have been even harder, counting away the months and years without her."

"I really am so sorry."

Kayla cleared her throat. "Are you all set here? I need to get back on the sales floor and prepare to close." Her chilly demeanor had returned.

"Sure. Go ahead. I'm good." The distance Kayla seemed to want between them was for the best. It would help her stick to her decision that getting involved with Kayla as anything more than an acquaintance was a bad idea. The shift in Kayla's mood didn't bother her at all. Right?

♥

"I need to buy a tennis racket." One of the high-school-age boys spun around as soon as she appeared from the back room. His voice rose, both in volume and pitch, until the last part of the word racket came out as a squeak. He held up a smashed one, little more than broken graphite and a nest of strings.

"Right over here." She led him to an aisle across the store, happy for the distraction from her thoughts for a moment. She'd have to examine her exchange with Jo eventually, but procrastinating this particular task didn't seem like a bad idea. "We'll get you back on the court in no time. Are you looking for a similar racket to the one you had?"

"Yeah. The exact same one."

"Hm. Well, I don't think I have that one. It's an older model. But I'm sure I have something along the same line of quality and price that will work for you."

"Ugh." The huge sigh of frustration seemed a bit dramatic for a broken racket. "Can you order this one?"

"Let me check." She held out a hand, and he gave her the mangled mess. She returned to the front desk and unlocked her computer. While she searched, he paced nervously in front of the counter.

"My dad is going to kill me if he finds out I broke his lucky racket." He shoved a hand through his hair, leaving it sticking up haphazardly.

She clicked through several screens, already certain she would have bad news for him. After some quick research she found the model had been discontinued five years ago. It was too late to point out the risk involved in "borrowing" his dad's lucky racket.

She hated to destroy his hopeful expression when she turned away from the computer.

"Well?"

"I'm sorry. I can't get one. You could try some of the online shops for used goods, but even then it's a slim chance."

"Shit." He pressed his fingers against both temples. "What am I going to do?"

"Unless you think you can keep this from him until you find another one, it might be best to just come clean."

He shook his head vigorously. "He plays three times a week. Maybe I should tell him."

"He might respect you taking responsibility."

"Yes, ma'am."

"Maybe we can soften the blow." She selected a racket from a hook in front of them. "This is a great one. It's not the exact model but should have a similar feel. He might find he has a new favorite." In truth, the racket was actually higher-end than the one he'd broken.

"It is nice." He turned it in his hand, testing the weight, then glanced at the price tag. "I don't have—"

"It's on the house."

"I can't accept it. He wouldn't like that." He hung his head for a moment, then met her eyes, his expression full of hope. "I can come by after school. Sweep up or help you out or whatever. I can start tomorrow."

She smiled. "That sounds great. Take the racket home. We'll work out the rest tomorrow."

"Thank you so much. Are you closing now? Can I do anything to help?"

"I got it. Go on. Get out of here. Talk to your dad. And also clear with him about you helping out here."

"Will do. Thanks." He held up the racket in salute on his way out.

She locked the door behind him. While she spent the next fifteen minutes going through her closing routine, her mind wandered to Jo, waiting in her office.

She'd spent the last four years learning how to survive on her own again. She had the store, her quiet house on the edge of town, and her community. But Jo had been spinning her up since she arrived, inspiring new feelings, new desires. What should have made her apprehensive, instead left her feeling oddly keyed up. Jittery. Excited. For the first time in years, she didn't feel like she was watching her life from the outside—she was living in it. And the glimmer of promise both exhilarated and scared her.

CHAPTER FIVE

Jo stepped gingerly out of her car, slung a backpack over her shoulder, and limped across the parking lot toward the station. When she woke up two days ago to a throbbing ankle, she knew she'd never make it through a full day on patrol. Reluctantly, she called Chief Cade to inform him of her situation. He instructed her to go to the urgent care and get checked out, stating she couldn't come back to work until she did.

She should have toughed it out and gone in, because the physician assistant put her off work for two days. And she wouldn't sign off on her working unless she could do light duty, restricting her time on her feet for several more days. And, she told Jo, she went to church with the Cades so she would find out if Jo defied her order. Jo argued that was a baseless accusation, since the PA didn't even know her, but when given a clear directive, Jo was a strict rule follower.

She also had to wear a walking boot on her left foot, making her already limping gait even more awkward. As soon as she pushed through the door, Freda hurried up from the back of the room.

"Did you get X-rays?" She lifted Jo's backpack off her shoulder.

Jo slumped into a chair at one of the desks in the middle of the station. "I told you it wasn't broken."

"Chief said if you want to work light duty, you had to go to the doctor."

"I know what he said," she grumped. Riding a desk wasn't her idea of a good time, but it beat the past two days of sitting around the house with her foot up. Yet her frustration wasn't Freda's fault, so she assumed a more pleasant tone when she said, "It's a bad sprain. I'm all clear to keep you company for the rest of the week."

"Wonderful. I've thought of plenty of things you can help me with that you can do sitting down." She placed Jo's backpack in a chair beside the desk.

"Why do I have a feeling I'm not going to like any of those things?"

Freda crossed to a stack of boxes near the wall, grabbed the top one, and placed it on the desk in front of Jo. "We've been trying forever to find time to digitize these old reports. How are you with data entry?"

"Aren't there companies that do that kind of thing?"

"In Harbor Springs? Not likely. We just work on this project when we have time. And lucky us, you'll be able to put a dent in the stack this week."

"I'll do my best." She tapped the space bar on the computer in front of her to wake it up, then logged in. Even though she wouldn't enjoy the task, she might as well maintain a positive attitude. Getting these records computerized benefited the department, and she'd get to know Freda better.

She spent the morning inputting handwritten reports from two decades ago, which brought up questions for her about the department's records-retention policy. For high-profile or unsolved cases, she understood the need to obtain records. But three vandalism reports in a row had her thinking that these crimes would probably go unpunished. At her previous department, files this old would have been destroyed years ago. But then again, the sheer volume of incidents there meant limiting retained records because of storage space on servers. Harbor Springs probably didn't have the same problem.

At lunchtime, Chief Cade stopped by with burgers and fries from the diner down the street, so she took a break and ate with him and Freda. He'd used her injury as an excuse to patrol around town in her place. But from what he said, she hadn't missed anything. He did seem to enjoy his time away from the office, until Freda reminded him that he had a meeting with the mayor that afternoon and would need to return to his "chiefly duties."

He glanced at Jo. "Any chance I could convince you to meet with the mayor in my place?"

"No way. You don't pay me enough for that."

He laughed. "Someday, maybe. When I'm long retired and you're running the place."

She shook her head. "Didn't I tell you, I moved here to lessen my stress? I might be perfectly happy riding in a cruiser for the rest of my career."

"We'll see," he said on his way out.

What did he think he knew that she didn't? She was the least senior officer in the department. All the others had ties to the community—family here. She was a transplant who had barely proved herself yet.

♥

Kayla unpacked the last case of baseball gloves and slid them onto long, metal pegboard hooks. She broke down her boxes and carried them to the back room for recycling. She'd stocked up on gloves in the fall because, just before the holidays, she always sold a bunch of them. One dad had told her that he bought the glove months ahead of baseball season so his son had time to break it in. She usually saw another run on them in early spring from the buyers who waited until the school-team tryouts were announced.

She'd spent most of the day restocking the shelves and reorganizing the stock room, but the physical labor failed to distract her from thinking about Jo Forsythe. After closing the store the other night, she'd driven Jo home. The conversation between them had stayed light, but the cabin of her Mini Cooper still felt smaller than usual.

Only a few minutes later, they'd arrived at Jo's rental house, and she helped Jo inside. When she'd offered to stay until Jo got settled in bed, she immediately wished for the words back. They felt awkward, and she didn't want to think about peeling back the covers while Jo slid between them. She had conveniently forgotten about Jo's injured ankle. Luckily, Jo plopped down on the sofa and insisted she could manage on her own from there. Kayla made her a towel-wrapped ice pack from the freezer and helped her prop her leg up on a stack of pillows.

Now, two days later, she was still thinking about Jo's earthy smell as she leaned over to straighten the pillow behind her back. In that moment, she'd remembered that Jo had been running, and sweating, and would probably want to take a shower before going to bed. Some miraculous filter between Kayla's brain and her mouth stopped her from offering to help Jo with that task before she left.

She hadn't stopped thinking about Jo during the drive back to her house. She'd happened to have been looking out the store window when she saw Jo jogging her way. And, though she knew she should turn away—get back to work—she didn't. So, when Jo tripped, Kayla saw her fall. She rushed outside just as Jo rolled over and noticed her. Jo's embarrassment had been obvious and expected, as had her pride, when Kayla tried to help her. What caught Kayla by surprise was the depth of sympathy in her eyes when she looked at the photo of Kayla and Macy. The openness in her gaze when she turned to Kayla had been almost too much to bear. She'd expected the same reservation that Brianna and Macy defaulted to in emotional situations. Without realizing it, she'd attributed that characteristic to the fact that they were both police officers. But here was Jo, unguarded and tugging at her in ways that no one else had.

It had felt wrong to just drop Jo off to fend for herself. She could convince herself her feelings were inspired by Jo's injury. But did she want to? Why shouldn't she just admit that she was interested in knowing more about her?

Ideally, she'd have sat down on the other end of the sofa and talked to Jo until they both fell asleep. The next morning, they would wake up and act like they hadn't meant to spend an innocent night together. But over breakfast, she'd admit that she'd had a really good time and would like to do it again. And Jo would shyly agree. That could have been the slow, easy start to finding out if they worked as a couple. Instead, things felt so complicated, and her mind was clouded with loyalties and promises that she already knew Macy would release her from if it meant being happy again.

She stopped abruptly, realizing she still stood in the middle of the baseball aisle, which wasn't an ideal place for an aha moment. But there it was—Macy would want her to move on—to make a new life. That didn't diminish the value of what they'd had.

The chime at the front door dinged, indicating a customer had entered. She rushed to the front to greet them and seek distraction from figuring out her next step.

♥

Her next step, it turned out, involved talking to Brianna. That she wanted to talk to her was also what made her nervous about the conversation—she knew all the players. She could have waited for their next brunch date—she should—this wasn't an urgent topic. So, when she closed the store, she steered her car toward her house. But when she saw Brianna's SUV backed into a spot in front of Beans to Brew, she pulled into the empty space next to it, her driver's window lined up with Brianna's. Brianna sat inside the SUV sipping a coffee and watching the street in front of her. They both rolled down their windows.

"Hi." Kayla rested her arm on the door sill.

"Hey." Brianna looked over her shoulder toward the coffee shop. "Are you going in to get something?"

"No." Kayla shook her head, then realized she didn't have any other logical reason for parking here. "I—uh—just saw you sitting here and thought we could chat for a few."

"Okay." Brianna paused, but Kayla didn't go on. "About anything in particular?"

"Yes—well, not really. I just closed up and was driving and you— had coffee." *What?* Now she sounded like an idiot. The confidence she'd found in the store earlier had fled, and she didn't know how to start this conversation.

Brianna nodded toward the park across the street. "Do you want to take a walk?"

"Yes." Maybe some motion would propel her thoughts as it did her body. She waited until Brianna got out and moved aside before opening her own door.

As they strolled across the street side by side, she zipped her coat. The day had been overcast, never warming above fifty, and evening had dropped it into the forties, so they had the park to themselves.

"What's going on? You're acting weird." Brianna paused and turned toward her, but Kayla waved her on, indicating they should keep walking. She didn't want to have this conversation face-to-face.

"I've been thinking about dating again." Her words sped up as she reached the end of her sentence, in a hurry to get them out. When Brianna didn't respond right away, she fought the urge to fill the silence. She wouldn't be able to come up with anything productive to follow that comment until Brianna engaged with her.

"Why didn't you want to tell me that?" This time when Brianna stopped, Kayla turned to face her.

"Macy was your best friend. I can see how you might not be comfortable with me seeing someone else. Hell, I'm only just realizing that I'm good with it."

"You think it might be time?" Brianna didn't seem on board with the plan.

She nodded. "After Macy died, I was so lonely—for her. I missed everything about our time together. Truthfully, I still miss plenty and always will. But lately my loneliness is also about wanting someone there—to have a partner in life."

"That makes sense." Brianna's expression had softened only a little, but the idea did clearly still bother her. "Macy would want you to be happy."

"I know it's hard to think about—and I'm sure it will feel strange at first. But it's been four years. I have to at least give it a shot."

"Or you could forever be known as the town widow." Brianna smiled. "Are you considering anyone in particular, or is this a general conversation about your readiness?"

Kayla's face grew hot. Telling Macy's best friend that she might want to date again was one thing, but letting on that she was interested in the new woman on the force was another entirely. "I'm not sure."

"This revelation does seem to coincide with the arrival of another out, available lesbian in a town with not too many of those."

"Judy Finster is bi." She threw the possibility out as a defense but knew it was limp, at best. Brianna wasn't bi-phobic, and even the implication was rude.

"You are correct. I didn't mean to limit you to only lesbians. But, unless you know something I don't, Judy Finster is also happily married. Hence she doesn't meet the *available* part of the criteria."

Kayla nodded. "This is hard for me to talk to you about."

"It's not a picnic for me either, friend." Somehow, her sarcasm softened the words. She turned away and sat on a park bench. Tilting her head back, she met Kayla's eyes. "I told you the other day, Jo's a good person. If you're into her, you should give it a shot."

"You warned her away from me."

"That's when I thought you wouldn't be interested—especially not in dating another police officer."

She fisted a hand and wrapped the other around it, popping her knuckles—a nervous habit Macy used to chastise her for. "I admit I'm not thrilled about that part. Logically, I know what the odds are of something bad happening. But my heart is hesitant. Macy faced those same odds, and look what I went through."

"Then why her?"

She shrugged. "I like her." Such a simplified response, but she didn't feel obligated for anything more complex.

"That's where you start." Brianna stood and rested a hand on Kayla's shoulder. "Maybe you'll find she has some annoying habit you can't stand, and you'll have stressed over this for nothing."

Kayla smiled. "I'm concerned that you really do want me to be the town widow."

CHAPTER SIX

"I'm out of here, Freda. Have a good night." Jo slung her backpack over her shoulder and shoved her cell phone into her pocket.

She stepped out the front door, pausing to let her eyes adjust to the sunlight. The streets were busy with Harbor Springs' equivalent to rush hour as the high school dismissed and those working some earlier shifts began heading home. But no number of cars and school buses could have made her miss seeing Kayla's Mini Cooper.

Kayla waved, then slowed to pull into the station parking lot. Jo walked that way, pausing beside Kayla's car.

"Hi. How's your ankle?" Kayla removed the tinted lenses that clipped onto the frame of her glasses, giving Jo an opportunity to see that her wide smile made faint crinkles at the corners of her eyes.

"Getting stronger every day. Hopefully, I'll be back in my cruiser soon. I like Freda and all, but I'm counting the days until I'm not her lackey." She glanced behind her as if making sure Freda wasn't sneaking up on her. "That woman is drunk on power."

Kayla laughed. "She does run a tight ship. But with Paul, she kind of has to."

"True."

"It's weird seeing you leaving the station this time of day."

"Yeah. You, too." Jo glanced at her watch. Usually, around now, she was searching for a reason to drop by McCall's while out patrolling. "It's not closing time."

"One of my part-timers is minding the store while I run to the bank." She propped her arm across the top of the door, through the open window, and rested her chin against her forearm.

As the sun moved out from behind a cloud, Jo felt at a disadvantage. She had to squint to see Kayla, but she felt like Kayla could see right through her.

"Would you like to have dinner sometime?" Kayla asked, as if proving that she could, indeed, see that Jo's deepest wish was to spend time with her.

Jo was surprised at her ability to radiate calm when under the surface she was anything but. Had Kayla McCall just asked her out? Before her emotions could get out of control, her logical side put the brakes on. "As friends?"

"I'm thinking more like as a date."

"Oh." She wanted to—good Lord, how she wanted to. But Kayla had been hurt beyond Jo's comprehension when she lost her wife. And the entire town loved Macy Tadd. If it didn't work out—or worse, if something happened to her—she didn't want to cause Kayla another ounce of pain. "No, thank you."

"Coffee then? Less of a time commitment if you find me completely uninteresting."

"What if I already find you uninteresting?" Perhaps a bit of teasing would make the situation more bearable for them.

Kayla leaned back against the car seat and placed a hand on her chest. "Ouch." The corners of Kayla's mouth twitched, then tightened so quickly that Jo thought she imagined the beginning of a smile.

"Word around town is that you don't date police officers." Struggling to hold on to the composure that threatened to abandon her at any moment, she tried recalling their first meeting. Kayla had been immediately cool and distant. She'd known from the jump she wanted nothing to do with Jo and had made it clear. How, then, did they get here?

"Maybe I could make an exception for you."

Jo was dying—she was sure of it—no heart could handle being given this much hope and turning away from it. What Kayla was offering was potentially everything she'd wanted—the reason she moved to Harbor Springs. A chance at a community, a partner, maybe even a family. Or it could crash and burn. "We can be friends."

Kayla hesitated, her eyes flickering away from Jo's in what might be embarrassment. "Sure. Yeah. That sounds great." She gave a short nod as if affirming something to herself. "I should go to the bank and get back. See you around."

She pulled away, rolling up her window as she left the parking lot.

Jo didn't have anything else to say anyway. She felt sick, which was ridiculous given that she barely knew Kayla.

Jo remembered when she first arrived and believed that Kayla was married. She'd have been happy then to have Kayla (and her wife) as friends. Now, the idea of living in Harbor Springs, being friends with Kayla, and potentially, someday, watching her fall for someone else made her feel queasy.

♥

"I asked her out." Kayla barely waited until Brianna sat down. She'd already ordered for both of them, but she wasn't sure even bananas-foster French toast could soothe the burn of rejection. Between surprising Brianna to break the news about her readiness to date and catching Jo outside the station two days ago, she'd apparently taken up stalking people in her car.

"That's great."

"She turned me down."

Brianna frowned. "Wow. She's dumber than I thought."

"You don't think she's dumb."

"I didn't. But I might now. Did she say why?"

The waitress brought their food. Kayla waited until she'd left before she replied. "Not really. Just that she wants to be friends."

Brianna laughed. "No, she doesn't. I've seen the way she looks at you."

"Yeah?" Kayla dug in, and the rush of sugar helped a little.

"She's been checking you out since day one. Why do you think I warned her away?"

"It's just my luck that when I decide I'm ready to start dating, I get rejected."

"That's it? You're all out of moves?"

"What can I do? She said she just wants to be friends."

Brianna laughed again.

"I really wish you would stop doing that."

Brianna flagged down the server and ordered two mimosas, despite Kayla's protest.

"Look, I am all about respect and consent, but don't you think you might be giving up a little too easy?"

"Why would she say that if she didn't mean it?"

"Think about this from her perspective. She likes you. But Macy is basically a legend in this town. Everyone loved her—you loved her, enough to marry her. Those are big shoes to fill."

"You think she's worried about what people will think." She put down her fork, giving the idea serious consideration. Jo wasn't used to being part of a community where everyone knew way too much about their neighbors. Kayla had long ago learned how to disregard any perceived judgment. She never would have survived coming out during her late teens in Harbor Springs otherwise.

"Maybe. And I don't know if you realize it or not, but you might be a little spoiled."

"What do you mean?"

"You've been with one woman your whole life. And from what I remember, she made the first move. You've never had to chase a woman."

"You're right. I don't even know how. What do I do?"

"How should I know? I've never romanced a woman, either."

♥

Jo had just poured her third cup of coffee when Brianna entered the station, followed by the kid that worked the counter at the bakery.

"Look who I found loitering outside." She hitched a thumb over her shoulder.

"I have a delivery for Jo Forsythe," he announced as if she were a stranger, even though she'd chatted with him several times at the bakery.

"Right here." She raised her hand, and he set the white bakery box on the desk in front of her. "Thanks." She slipped a tip into his hand. If she were a stranger, would she know that he'd just graduated high school and worked at the family bakery to make money for his first semester at college?

"Enjoy." He handed her a small white envelope and grinned before heading out the door.

Freda and Brianna had gathered around during the exchange and waited with obvious anticipation for her to open the box. The only one missing was Chief Cade, who, thankfully, was tied up on a conference call in his office.

"Did you order something for us?" Freda asked.

She shook her head and lifted the lid. A dozen cupcakes arranged together and decorated to resemble a bouquet of daisies with lush green leaves filled the box. She slipped out the card, keeping it angled so only she could read it.

> *YOU DON'T SEEM LIKE A FLOWERS KIND OF GIRL.*
> *HERE'S HOPING THESE SWEETEN YOUR VALENTINE'S*
> *DAY ANYWAY.*

"Who are they from?"

"There's no signature."

"Looks like you've got a secret admirer," Freda said. "What a romantic Valentine's Day surprise."

"I don't know how much of a secret it is. One phone call to the bakery will solve that mystery." Brianna picked up her cell phone and looked to Jo for approval.

"Let's not."

"You don't want to know."

Jo shrugged. "Not yet." She knew who she hoped the gift was from, and if Kayla hadn't sent it, she didn't want to burst that bubble right away. She'd always said Valentine's Day wasn't a big deal to her, but hoping that Kayla had been thinking about her, even after she turned down her date invite, made her feel good.

"I'll get plates." Freda rushed toward the small kitchen.

"You really don't want to know?" Brianna dropped into a chair next to Jo's desk. When Jo didn't answer, Brianna threw out a few names—the crotchety old man they'd taken a report from the day before, the cougar who owned the hair salon and flirted with everyone, man or woman, and the delivery boy himself, just turned eighteen and looking for a fling.

Jo laughed. "Are those your best guesses?"

"Maybe the librarian. I don't know her very well, but she is an eligible lesbian bachelorette."

"I've never been to the library."

♥

"Sir, put the knife down, and let's talk about this." Jo stood on the lawn of a farmhouse on the outskirts of town.

She could see the lights of the nearest neighbor's house through the trees, but otherwise she was out here all alone. Just her and the homeowner currently wielding a large chef's knife twenty feet away from her. She'd drawn her Taser when he stumbled out of the house, but then she'd seen the knife. If he rushed her, that Taser might not be enough to stop him.

"Get off my property," he shouted, his face glistening with sweat in the glow of the porch light. From the slight slur in his words, she suspected alcohol played some part in all of this. She hoped that was the only substance involved.

"I can't do that until I talk to your wife."

He blocked her path into the house to check on the woman who had called 9-1-1. She'd said he'd been threatening her and that she intended to leave him this time. Then the dispatcher heard shouting in the background, and the phone went dead. Jo didn't know what her current status was.

"You don't need to talk to that bitch."

"I have to know she's okay before I leave." She wasn't going anywhere without this guy in cuffs, but he didn't need to know that yet.

He squinted at her. "You a new cop? I ain't never seen you before."

The dispatcher had indicated they'd had previous calls to the location, but his statement was even more telling. He knew the local law enforcement by sight, and not in a good way.

Blue strobes flashed across his face, deepening the angry shadows in his features. He looked over her shoulder, but Jo never took her eyes off him. Blue lights meant backup, probably Brianna, but it didn't matter specifically who it was. All she cared about was not facing this guy alone in the impossible darkness cast by the lack of streetlights.

Tires crunched on the gravel, then came to a stop. A car door opened, then closed. She felt the presence of another person behind her left shoulder and breathed a little easier.

"What's going on, Nate?" Brianna didn't raise her voice, but her tone was firm.

He blinked, canted a bit to the side, then recovered with several stumbling steps. "Same shit, *Officer Willis*." He put a sarcastic twist on Brianna's name and title. He jerked his chin toward the house. "She's not coming out."

"You know how this goes, Nate. She called us. We need to talk to her."

"I'm not going to jail." He threw his shoulders back and puffed out his chest.

"Sir, if you'll put down the knife and let us talk to your wife, this will go a lot more smoothly," Jo said.

His face pinched as he formulated a response, but before he could say anything a woman appeared in the doorway. Her face was a mess—a crusted line of blood ran from an open wound on her temple down to her jaw. Her other eye was swollen half shut. She leaned against the doorjamb as if she needed its support to stay upright.

Jo took a couple of steps forward in response to her appearance before she even realized what she was doing. Dispatch had said she reported he'd threatened her. This was a hell of a lot more than threats. Brianna keyed up her shoulder mic and spoke quietly into it, telling dispatch to notify the volunteer ambulance service and have them stay clear of the scene until further notice. She wanted them close but not in danger. Jo also suspected seeing an ambulance could escalate Nate's agitation, knowing his wife wouldn't be staying in the house tonight.

"Brianna, I'm fine." The defeat in the woman's voice made Jo angry.

"Claire—"

"It'll be better if you leave."

How could it be better to be left here with this guy? Jo wanted to ask, but she knew better. The question would only rile Nate more, and Claire's answer wouldn't make sense to her. But she'd seen it so many times. Claire already knew how much worse things would get if Nate was arrested. She'd told dispatch that this time she was leaving him, but apparently she'd already decided to walk that decision back.

"Please. I shouldn't have called." She was afraid. That much was clear in the apprehensive glances she directed toward Nate.

"You heard her. Leave us alone." Nate surged forward, knife swinging in an arc in front of him. Just as Jo's finger twitched against the trigger of her Taser, he tripped and fell forward, landing facedown. The knife dropped into the dirt close to Brianna's feet.

He flailed his arms, hands searching for his weapon, but Jo stepped closer. "Stay down."

Brianna kicked the knife aside, and while Jo covered her with her Taser, she knelt and secured his hands behind his back in handcuffs. Jo holstered her Taser and helped Brianna get him to his feet. After patting him down, they secured him in the back of Jo's cruiser. Brianna radioed that the paramedics could enter.

"Wait. Let him out." When Claire tried to approach the car, Brianna stepped in front of her and stopped her.

"He's going to jail tonight."

"No." She jerked free. "I won't press charges." She skirted Brianna and pressed her palm to the window of the cruiser. "I'm not pressing charges." This time her words, directed at Nate instead of them, sounded more desperate.

H ell of a first shift back out here, huh?" Brianna joined Jo at the officers' work desk inside the county booking facility.

"It still beats data entry at the station." Jo clicked the mouse button to submit her affidavit. "Do you think there's any chance she'll assist the prosecutors on the domestic-assault charge?"

"Probably not." Brianna sat in the chair next to her. "We all went to high school together. Nathan and Claire were that couple who started dating in like ninth grade and never split up. Back then, I'd have told you they were meant to be. The first time I responded to their place, as a rookie, was a shock. Now, all these years later—well, he'll stay in jail for twenty-four hours. She gets a night without him, and a social worker will visit her in the morning to offer options."

"We've got the pictures of her injuries, my body-cam footage, and our account of what he said to us. The DA will still prosecute even without her cooperation." Jo spun toward Brianna in her chair.

Brianna nodded. "He will. The case would be stronger if she would testify. If nothing else, he might catch some time for pulling a knife on you."

Jo swiveled back to the computer screen and logged out. Most of the time, she loved her job, but today, she was glad her shift was ending.

"You look like you could use a drink. I'm meeting Kayla after we get off. Why don't you join us?"

"Yeah?"

"Sure. You said you wanted to make friends here." She seemed to put extra emphasis on the word *friends*.

"You aren't worried I'll hit on Kayla?"

"From what I heard, you've already turned her down. So, I don't have anything to worry about, right?"

"Right." Brianna seemed to be waiting for more reassurance. Jo didn't have the energy to throw out a spiel on how, being new in town, she didn't want to burn bridges by getting involved with Kayla and risking it ending badly. A drink with *friends* would be nice, but what she really wanted was someone to draw a bath, pour two glasses of wine, then slip into the tub behind her and hold her before tucking her into bed. That wasn't too clichéd, was it?

She went home first, to change and leave her car. Grabbing a heavy coat, she decided to walk to the bar. The streets were quiet, the businesses having closed hours ago. Except for a few places on the edge of town, near the interstate, Harbor Springs shuttered by ten p.m. As she neared the bar, the only one in town, the still night gave way to the faint sounds of music. The place was a typical roadhouse, slightly run-down and boxy, a gravel parking lot surrounding the building on three sides. Kayla's Mini Cooper was one of a dozen vehicles parked there.

She hadn't seen Kayla since she received the cupcake delivery. Should she ask her about it? Would Kayla bring it up? And even if she had sent them, what did they actually mean? Could be that Kayla intended them as a friendly gesture to smooth over the awkwardness of her asking Jo out. The note had been benign enough to keep her guessing and just flirty enough to make her wonder.

The inside of the bar had been kept up much better than the outside, but still no surprises here. Booths abutted the outside walls, tables dotted the center area, and crowds gathered around two pool tables in the back. A stage, no more than a platform raised the height of one step, took up a corner opposite the pool tables.

♥

Brianna and Kayla had already claimed a round table, far enough from the band that they had a chance at actual conversation. She wouldn't be bringing up the cupcakes in front of Brianna, though. She'd already made her feelings clear.

"Hi, Jo." Kayla smiled as Jo slid into one of the two available chairs—the one closer to Brianna.

"I ordered you a beer," Brianna said.

"Thanks."

As if she had timed it perfectly, a waitress set a glass down in front of her at that moment. Jo took a long drink from it.

"You two had a tough call, huh?" Kayla lifted her own glass, some kind of mixed drink that she sipped through a dainty straw.

Jo glanced at Brianna.

"She didn't say anything. I heard from the bartender before either of you got here that Nate and Claire were at it again."

"How?"

Brianna shrugged. "Only a few houses on that road. When folks see blue lights headed that way, they know what's going on. But thanks for automatically assuming I'm unprofessional enough to gossip about what we do."

"I'm sorry. I didn't think there was any other way—"

"We have plenty of busybodies in Harbor Springs, but I'm not one of them."

Kayla rested a hand on Brianna's shoulder. "I concur. There's no one I trust more with my secrets."

"Or your drinks." Brianna visibly shook off the serious moment. "Refills, anyone?"

Kayla shook her head, and Jo held up a finger, indicating she'd have one more. That would cap her night and keep her warm for the walk home, yet not be enough to push her into melancholy. Brianna gave her a thumbs-up and headed for the bar.

"You okay?" Kayla leaned forward to compensate for the noisy crowd around them.

"Yeah. Just letting go of the day."

"Today got to you?"

"I've had knives pulled on me before—even been sucker punched in the face by a woman while arresting her abusive son." When Kayla grimaced, Jo said, "I'm sorry. I shouldn't talk about the dangerous parts of the job."

Kayla waved a hand. "It's okay."

"Does it bother you? Being friends with Brianna, you must still hear about this stuff." She could imagine that being reminded of the dangers they faced, even in small-town policing, would be hard for Kayla.

"At first, it did. Now—well, it still does." She chuckled. "But maybe just the normal amount. Nobody wants to hear about someone they care about getting punched in the face, right?"

Jo couldn't tell in the dim lighting, but she thought she saw a flush creeping up Kayla's neck as she averted her eyes. She decided not to tease her about whether Kayla had just admitted to caring about her. Instead, she folded her heart around the warm kernel the words had created in her chest. Outwardly, she opted for a more clinical response.

"Domestic calls are unpredictable. The hardest part is when someone who has just had the crap kicked out of them pretty much begs you not to arrest their partner or family member." She shook her head. "I know the psychology behind it. But a part of me will never understand that kind of unhealthy dedication."

"Spoken like someone who's never been married."

"True." She looked at Kayla for a moment longer than was comfortable. "You have."

"I have." Kayla pressed her lips tighter and nodded.

She clearly didn't want to talk about Macy, and Jo almost gave her an out. But her curiosity won out, and she remained silent.

"I hope we didn't have an unhealthy amount of dedication. But I can certainly understand finding yourself doing things you didn't think you would for another person."

It didn't feel like she was talking about Macy. So, then what? Surely not asking Jo out, though she probably never thought after their first meeting that she'd be doing that. Kayla had so clearly shut her out that day, presumably just because she was a police officer. She remembered Kayla's voice softening as she admitted she might make an exception to go out with her. What had changed?

"Jo, I—"

"Okay. Here we go. Round two." Brianna set two glasses on the table and sat down. "What are we talking about? I need some adult conversation to hold me over before I spend my two days off with the kids."

Jo held Kayla's eyes for a moment longer, but she couldn't read anything in them. What had she been about to say? Brianna didn't leave the table again, so she wouldn't get a chance to find out. Instead, she let herself get lost in casual conversation about the insane schedule Brianna juggled to keep up with extracurriculars for three kids.

♥

"Has she even mentioned the cupcakes?" Brianna opened a camp chair and set it next to Kayla's blanket. She'd been invited to a few of Kayla's Monday picnics in the park, and after the first, she always brought a chair, stating she was "too grown" to sit on the ground.

Kayla shook her head. She handed a wrapped sandwich to Brianna and opened her own.

"To me either. She said, that day, that she didn't want to try to find out who sent them. I tossed out a casual inquiry the next day, but she brushed it off, too."

"Do you think she knows it was me?"

"I think she hopes it was. What's your next move? Another secret gift?"

"I didn't think that far ahead."

Brianna laughed. "You expected your gesture to impress her so much she'd come running into your arms?"

Kayla's face heated. "Stop it."

"Okay. I'm playing. If it helps, I think you nailed it. The cupcakes were original and sweet, no pun intended."

"It took so much nerve to place the order, I didn't know I was even going to go through with it until I was swiping my card at the bakery."

"Regrets?"

She took a beat to consider her answer, but she didn't really need it. "Not one."

"Well, are you going to keep playing secret admirer?"

"I don't know. But if you're not going to help me, you're no longer welcome at my picnic."

♥

"Good morning." Kayla picked up a shopping basket as she entered the pharmacy.

Mrs. Tadd called back a greeting, and Mr. Tadd waved from behind the counter. Kayla chose a few essentials. She didn't have to search for anything. The Tadds hadn't changed the layout of the store in all the time she'd known them. She could get most of what she needed at the grocery store and save herself a trip, but she'd always made it a point to patronize the pharmacy.

"Kayla, do you have a moment to chat?" Mrs. Tadd asked.

"Sure."

"Come on, sit down." She pointed to a couple of padded chairs where customers would wait while their prescriptions were filled.

"Word around town is that Jo Forsythe got a sweet gift from an admirer."

Kayla could kick herself for not going to the next town over to place that order. She'd forgotten that the Tadds had a standing poker game that also involved the bakery owner. And that Mrs. Tadd could be the most direct woman she'd ever met.

"This town has too many gossips."

"Maybe so." Mrs. Tadd sighed, then, more softly, said, "Macy would want you to be happy."

Kayla didn't know how to respond. Even a year ago, she would have petulantly blurted that Macy was supposed to stick around to make her happy. But she'd reached a place of peace and understanding that, if the roles were reversed, she wouldn't have wanted Macy to be alone for the rest of her life. And Mrs. Tadd was right: Macy would desire the same for her. But believing that, and discussing it with Macy's mother, were two very different things.

Mrs. Tadd patted her knee. "It's okay, dear."

"I haven't even looked at anyone else since Macy."

"I know. But maybe it's time."

Kayla nodded, hoping the lump in her throat wouldn't propel her into tears.

"It feels awkward to talk about this." It wasn't a question for Kayla. It was a statement of truth between them, on both sides of the conversation. "Tell me what about Jo has you looking for the first time in four years."

"I'm not sure I know exactly. I'm drawn to her." She scoffed at her own words. "That sounds silly and far too vague." She pictured Jo, her quick smile and the tender way she gazed at her when she thought she wasn't looking. The depth in those eyes brought a swell of emotion that caught Kayla off guard every time. But when she tried again to answer Mrs. Tadd's question, what came out was a superficial response in comparison. "Obviously, she's attractive. But she's also very sweet and surprisingly genuine."

"I noticed that, too. I expected a bit more of the tough, big-city, officer type. Perhaps that's why she came to Harbor Springs. She fits better here."

"I'm not completely sure I can give my heart again, let alone to another police officer."

"I never got the impression you minded Macy being an officer all those years."

"I didn't. Until I did, right?"

"Kayla, the odds of—"

"I know. First loss for the department in thirty years." Kayla heard the edge in her voice but couldn't soothe it. It didn't help to know how rare an officer death was, when her wife had been that one in fifty thousand. She still didn't understand how people thought telling her that fact would comfort her after Macy's death.

"If, for whatever reason, you don't think you can love again, why the gift?"

"Because I *want* to feel something again."

"And that's okay. It doesn't take anything from what you and Macy had."

"Gran used to tell me that time isn't guaranteed, so go after what you want."

"That does sound like your gran."

She cocked her head to the side. "I'm not sure when I stopped doing that." If she was being honest, she'd stopped long before losing Macy. They'd settled into their life together, and she hadn't wanted or needed anything but Macy and the store. Without Macy, she'd shifted her focus to her business and told herself she could be happy with just that.

"If the cupcakes are any indication, I'd say you've started again. I feel I should mention that a certain someone has RSVP'd for the annual gathering Sunday afternoon." Mrs. Tadd smiled. "Not that you need it, dear, but you have our blessing."

She hadn't realized how much hearing that would mean to her. The Tadds had made it clear four years ago that they would always consider her family, and she'd vowed the same. Now, more than ever, she knew that fact wouldn't change.

CHAPTER EIGHT

Jo awoke Sunday morning to the sound of her doorbell. Grumbling, she climbed out of bed and trudged through the house. She glanced at the clock in the living room as she passed. She would normally be awake by nine a.m., but she'd stayed up until the early morning hours bingeing a documentary series about serial killers.

By the time she swung open the front door, she spotted a kid—she guessed about ten or eleven—jump on a bicycle at the end of her driveway and pedal away. She didn't see a face, just the back of a head of curly, dark hair and a striped T-shirt on a lime-green BMX-style bike.

At her feet, a cardboard box with a folded top, the kind restaurants used for leftovers, sat on the top step. She picked it—and the card underneath—up and carried them inside the house. She hadn't seen that bike before, so she didn't think the kid lived on her street. The outside of the box felt warm.

She set her gifts on the kitchen island and opened the card first.

IS THIS THE WAY TO YOUR HEART?

She lifted open the flaps on the top of the box, and immediately a sweet, fresh-baked aroma drifted up. She leaned down to draw it in more fully.

"Oh my God. If this tastes anywhere near as good as it smells, this is absolutely the way to my heart."

She recognized the French toast, bananas, and caramel as the dish she'd seen Brianna and Kayla enjoying outside Beans to Brew. When she took a bite, she couldn't stop a moan. Now she understood Kayla's comment about feeling bad if she were a better person. She would take eating this amazing dish over jogging every single day.

She picked the card back up. If she'd had any doubts, this had to be Kayla, right? Who was the kid? One of Brianna's? So Kayla had enlisted Brianna's help. She tapped the edge of the card against her chin.

Kayla had sent a pretty clear message without directly saying she was behind the gifts. Jo felt certain there wouldn't be any more surprises. The next move was hers. She still had all the same reasons for avoiding getting involved with Kayla, and a couple of thoughtful gifts shouldn't negate them.

But they did. Kayla had plenty of reason not to want to get involved with a police officer again. In fact, when they first met, Jo had been certain she'd never have a chance with Kayla because of that fact. If Kayla could get past her reservations and be willing to give them a shot, shouldn't she as well?

She'd committed to the Tadds' gathering that afternoon and would probably see Kayla there. First, though, she'd finish her breakfast while considering how to respond. She slid onto a stool at the island counter and dug in.

♥

Jo walked around a large circular driveway toward the Tadds' brick colonial home. She'd parked strategically toward the end of the arc, in a manner that allowed for a quick escape should she need it. She carried a bottle of red wine bearing a label from a winery in Tennessee that she'd grabbed at the liquor store in town. Mother Nature had given winter one more shot for the year, and as Jo pulled her coat tighter around her, she hoped it was the last round of icy temps for the season.

When she reached the front and was about to knock on one of the heavy-looking oak double doors, it swung open. Before she could react, Mrs. Tadd had an arm around her and guided her inside.

"Officer Forsythe. It's so good to see you."

"Thank you. You have a lovely home." She handed over the bottle of wine. Mrs. Tadd made the appropriate remark of appreciation, but Jo could tell she wasn't a wine drinker. Maybe she could serve it at the party.

Mrs. Tadd took her coat, then led her from the foyer into a formal living room. Warm wood tones of heavy furniture complemented the traditional styling of the house. Light-colored rugs and artwork kept the decor from being too heavy. While various paint colors, wallpapers, and woodwork seemed to have been kept fresh and clean, the house hadn't been remodeled to alter the style. Where designers touted removing walls to "open up" living spaces, the rooms here had been kept clearly divided and separated by archways and doorways with ornate moldings.

Mrs. Tadd pointed out the direction of the kitchen, dining room, and a powder room.

"Drinks and food are in the kitchen. Usually, the party spills onto the back deck and lawn, but this year it's much too cold. So, we'll have to stay cozy inside for this evening. You'll find some familiar faces, members of your department scattered throughout. And there will likely be some folks from town that you haven't met yet."

When the doorbell rang, Mrs. Tadd turned her loose into the party. She wandered through the formal living room, stopping to greet several people she recognized. Some of the day-shift officers waylaid her in the dining room to introduce her to their wives.

One of the wives mentioned a female cousin who was single. Jo politely brushed off the offer of a fix-up. Sometimes, when a male officer's wife found out another female was on the force, that officer felt compelled to out her to them. The knowledge that she was a lesbian made her much less threatening. She'd never quite understood that concern. They rode around in separate cars all day, so what did the women think they had to worry about?

♥

Kayla stepped away from the group of couples she'd been talking to, under the guise of needing to refresh her drink. Mrs. Tadd's favorite settee near the window provided a quiet place away from any clusters of guests. She'd been sitting there for only a few minutes when she saw Mrs. Tadd draw Jo into the living room. Given her gestures, she was giving Jo her spiel about the layout of the house and the "make yourself at home" sentiments.

She watched Jo move about the room, making sure to glance away and scan the room once in a while, so no one looking at her could tell where she really directed her attention. Jo smiled and chatted with several small groups. She appeared to be navigating toward the kitchen, when she stopped, turned, and looked right at Kayla. This time she didn't glance away, holding Jo's gaze as electricity sizzled through her.

When Jo headed her way, nervousness weakened her arms and legs. She knew Jo had received her offering of breakfast this morning and the note. Her accomplice had told her so. Would Jo bring it up? Should *she*?

"Hi." When Jo sat on the settee, she angled toward Kayla, and their knees touched.

"I was hoping to see you here." Kayla didn't shift away. Instead, she focused on whether she could feel the heat of Jo's skin through the layers of their pants.

"You were?"

"Of course." She wanted to say she'd been counting the hours ever since Mrs. Tadd told her Jo had accepted the invite. But she chickened out. "The Tadds do this every year for the department. You're a part of that family now."

"Right." Jo looked disappointed. "Well, I'll say this. The party has lived up to the hype. The Tadds are very trusting, just setting a donation box next to the front door like that. Anyone could walk off with it."

Kayla shook her head. "Who would do that? Chief Cade would have you all working overtime to see who would steal money intended to help the homeless. Besides, I helped Mr. Tadd install the security camera on their front porch and the one on the garage myself."

"You're pretty handy, huh?"

"Gran taught me to be self-sufficient. And you can find tutorials for anything online now. What about you? Are you an adventurous DIYer?"

"To some extent. I won't touch plumbing or electrical, but I can operate basic power tools."

"Sure. But do you have your own tool belt?"

"You do?"

Kayla nodded.

"I'm going to need you to prove that to me someday."

Kayla grinned and pulled out her phone. After a couple of swipes, she turned it around to show Jo the picture of her wearing jeans and a tank top, with a tan leather tool belt secured around her hips. Jo widened her eyes, then snapped them up to meet hers. Her heated gaze set Kayla's heart thudding heavily right between her collarbones.

When Jo broke eye contact, Kayla had a micro-second of relief before she realized Jo was now staring at her mouth. Jo leaned forward, the tiniest fraction, just an angling of her shoulders, but Kayla knew that right then Jo was thinking about kissing her. And as crazy as it sounded sitting here among half the town, Kayla was ready for it.

A burst of loud laughter somewhere nearby startled Kayla from their bubble. As she swung her attention from Jo, she caught several pairs of eyes darting away from the two of them. She scooted back a couple of inches on the settee, regaining her composure. Jo found her attractive. That much was clear. But she seemed determined to ignore the connection between them, so maybe Kayla should as well.

♥

Jo made the first excuse she could think of, awkwardly asking Kayla which way the powder room was, then escaped, mentally kicking herself. She should have mentioned this morning's French-toast delivery. It couldn't possibly have been from anyone else. Instead, she'd just made things weird between them. And what was with the most intense session of eye contact she'd ever had?

She shouldn't have come tonight. She and Kayla would eventually have a conversation about the gifts. But Macy Tadd's childhood home couldn't be the place for it. She'd heard Macy's name already no less than a half dozen times, and she'd been here an hour.

She was about to turn the corner into the kitchen when she heard Kayla's name being said inside. She paused and stepped back from the doorway.

"Isn't it a little weird that she's dating another police officer?" She didn't recognize the voice and couldn't risk leaning around the door jamb to look.

"I don't think they're dating."

She shouldn't be eavesdropping, but they were clearly talking about Kayla and her.

"Please. Did you see how cozy they were in the corner?"

"Yeah. I've never even looked at my husband like that."

"It was kind of hot."

"I guess if you have to move on, it might be easier with someone just like your ex."

Not her ex. Jo wanted to correct them. Macy wasn't Kayla's ex. They hadn't broken up. But jumping out of the shadows to clarify the definition of Macy and Kayla's relationship would only make her seem crazy.

"Is she trying to replace Macy?"

"What? Like Macy 2.0?"

A round of laughter faded as the group moved farther away. Jo leaned out slowly, then slipped inside the now-empty kitchen. She braced her hands on the counter and hung her head. She'd made a mistake coming here. She slipped out the other door of the kitchen, the one leading to a family room. She suspected this was where the group she overheard had disappeared to but didn't know if they were still around. When she entered the room, a conversation in the corner stopped, and she thought she might have an answer. She hadn't recognized any of the voices, but judging by their guilty looks, these five women could be them. She thought for a second about confronting them, then decided she wouldn't ruin the Tadds' party like that.

Instead, she lifted her chin and strode through the room with her head high. She tracked down her coat on a rolling rack in a hallway between the family room and foyer, then slipped out the front door.

She made it to the end of the walkway leading to the driveway when someone called her name. Kayla hurried toward her.

"Hey. Is something wrong?" Kayla wrapped her arms around herself.

"Go back inside, Kayla. You'll freeze out here. I'm fine."

"You seemed upset when you went into the kitchen a bit ago."

"It was nothing."

"Didn't look like nothing."

"I overheard a conversation that I didn't like. It's fine. I'm over it." She tried to spin away, but Kayla caught hold of her arm.

Kayla glanced over her shoulder, where the din of voices and the sound of music could be heard through the closed door. She curled her hand around Jo's arm and steered her down the driveway. "I'll walk you to your car."

They made it most of the way in silence. But when, as they neared her car, she fished her keys out of her coat pocket, Kayla grabbed them from her hand.

"What did they say?" Kayla moved to stand practically toe-to-toe with Jo.

"Are you going to hold me hostage here until I tell you?"

"Maybe." She looked like she might do it.

Fine. If Kayla wanted to know so badly, she would reveal all the rumors about them. "There was some speculation about us—about if we are dating, or whatever."

"That's it?" Kayla chuckled.

"No—I—it's—what's so funny?"

"We're two lesbians in a small town. Some folks are always to going to talk. What else did they say?"

"I'm sure you can guess. We were in Macy's parents' house. Do you know how many conversations I've had tonight that started with how much she is missed?"

"Yeah. You're going to hear that. Why would that bother you so much?"

"Being called Macy 2.0?"

"Okay, ouch. But I can't help what people say. I can't erase Macy from their memory, nor would I want to. People haven't seen me with anyone for the past four years, so they might need time to get used to the idea that I want to date again."

"And if they never do?"

"It's possible some folks might not." Kayla flung her hands out in defeat. "Those aren't people who are close to me and want to see me happy. I really don't care what they think."

"Am I—is whoever you date supposed to just live in Macy's shadow forever?"

Kayla froze, and the implications of what Jo had almost said vibrated between them. So close. She'd been so close to just saying what she needed to say, what clawed at her, desperate to get out. *I want to give this a shot, but I'm afraid.*

Kayla moved forward, cradled Jo's face, and kissed her, tenderly, and in such contrast to the vicious arousal that rushed forward at the first touch of Kayla's lips against hers. But the kiss was over far too soon.

Kayla stepped back.

"No, Jo. *They're* not."

Kayla pressed Jo's keys into her hand and backed up, as if waiting for her to say something. And when she didn't, Kayla turned and walked back toward the house. Jo stood next to her car, her mind and body racing, but she couldn't pull together a request for Kayla to stay. Just stay.

S low it down going through town. Next time it's a ticket. And I know your mama wouldn't like that." Jo studied the teen driver behind the wheel of the beat-up Honda to make sure he seemed to be taking her seriously. She'd pulled him over in the middle of town, going ten mph over the limit. She'd met his mother, a dentist whose office was not more than a quarter mile from them right now, at the party last night.

"Yes, ma'am. She'd take my car away for a month. Thank you."

"Okay. Go on, then. And drive safely." She watched him leave, then turned back toward her cruiser to find Brianna leaning against the front of it.

"You should have given him a ticket."

"I'm trying to foster some goodwill."

"Eh." Brianna pushed off the car. "Do you want to walk?"

"Sure." As early March brought warm spring temperatures, they would patrol downtown on foot when they weren't busy on other calls. They'd keep their cars parked centrally so they could get back quick if they needed to respond outside of town.

"What's going on between you and Kayla?" Brianna didn't waste any time. Jo had barely taken two steps.

"Nothing." She slipped on her sunglasses, but they didn't provide an appropriate shield from Brianna's prying.

"Bullshit."

"I'm not sure you and I should be having this conversation."

"Who else are you going to have it with? Do you want to head back to the station and see if Freda will talk it through with you?"

"Who says I need to talk anything through?" She touched her own lips briefly. She'd been feeling the pressure of Kayla's there since that kiss last night. It had happened so quickly she didn't have a chance to participate.

"Kayla's expression when she came back into the party last night told me something was up. But she's a vault about it."

"And you think I'll be more forthcoming?"

"You need to be. You're screwing this up."

She stopped in the middle of the sidewalk, taking in Brianna's blunt assessment of the situation. Brianna took several more steps. Then she turned around.

"You warned me away from her when I first got here."

Brianna shrugged. "I changed my mind."

Jo tilted her head back and looked at the sky with a chuckle. "Oh, you changed your mind. Now it's okay for us to get involved. Have you surveyed the rest of the residents? Because I apparently need a majority approval around here before I can make a decision."

"Hey. Don't be bitchy about it. You chose to move here. What did you think small-town life was? Do you regret coming here?"

She sighed. "No."

"Great. Back to you and Kayla."

"There is no me and Kayla."

Brianna huffed. "Let's both work off the premise that I know you want there to be. And we both know Kayla does. What's the issue?"

She considered the question. There were so many, and none of them had gone away. But Kayla's kiss had somehow diminished the importance of most of them. A spotlight had shone on Kayla in that moment, leaving all her fears in the shadows. When she returned her attention to Brianna, she noticed she was staring at the diner across the street.

"Hey. Let's grab some lunch."

"Aren't you going home for lunch?"

"Not today."

Glad for the reprieve from talking about Kayla, Jo nodded.

As they stepped inside the diner, Jo immediately spotted Kayla in a booth about halfway down one wall. She rounded on Brianna, hoping she could see the accusation in her eyes, because she didn't want to say anything that could be overheard.

"Oh, you know what, I do need to go home for lunch. But you should stay. I'll cover the calls, then take my lunch break after."

"Brianna—"

Brianna backed through the door with a smug expression. Jo glanced down the row of booths, then at the door. She could still escape. Only a few people had noticed them entering, and it would just look like they'd changed their mind.

Kayla hadn't seen her yet. Her attention was on her phone, and even her fork seemed like an afterthought, resting limply in her other hand.

Still deciding what to do, she recalled the look on Kayla's face last night just before she kissed her. Her expression had been a mix of devastation and acceptance.

"*No, Jo. They're not.*"

Devastation and acceptance.

Had that been a good-bye kiss? Was Kayla letting go of the idea of a relationship? Did she think that was what Jo wanted? She wanted Kayla—so much it scared her. She'd been holding back from even trying, in part because of what she would feel if it didn't work out. But now, considering that it might be over before they even tried—that possibility hurt in a whole different way.

♥

"Are you my secret admirer?"

Startled, Kayla glanced up from her lunch to find Jo standing in front of her. She looked adorably nervous, shifting from one foot to the other. "Would you like to sit down?"

Jo glanced around, then sat. "Did you send me those gifts—and the notes?"

"Not really a secret, I guess." Kayla fidgeted with her napkin. She rubbed one hand on the back of her neck as the silence became awkward. When she met Jo's eyes, she saw her own uncertainty mirrored there.

Jo gave a small nod, as if having reached a decision. "The answer to your question is yes."

Confused, Kayla drew her brows together.

"That breakfast was most definitely the way to my heart." She rested her hand on the table next to Kayla's, fingertips barely touching hers. "You had reservations when we first met."

"I did." Kayla grinned. "I was attracted to you, but I didn't want to be."

"Because of my job."

Kayla nodded and inched her hand closer, toying lightly with Jo's fingers. "My fears aren't completely gone. I'd like to stay far away from that kind of pain again. But I didn't have the pain without my share of joy first. Maybe you can't have one without a chance of the other."

When the server stopped to refill Kayla's water glass, Jo made a move to pull her hand back, but Kayla captured her fingers and held on. She glanced up at the server and smiled, but didn't say anything until after the woman left.

"When I first asked you out, you said you wanted to be friends." Kayla tilted her head toward the server, now standing several tables away. "Is that why? You're worried what people will think?"

"You and Macy were—"

"I know what we were. The lesbian-couple mascot that folks around here could accept to prove to themselves that we aren't a backward Southern town." She rolled her eyes. "That sounds harsher than I meant it. Lots of good people live here, with no ulterior motives for acceptance. But we weren't some beloved symbol. We were a real couple, with real triumphs and plenty of disagreements as well." She eased her hand fully into Jo's and squeezed. "And I'm not looking to duplicate or replace that relationship. I'd like to spend some time with you and explore this connection I feel. One that I think you feel, too, yes?"

"Yes."

"Are you interested in that proposition?"

"No pressure to be the next shining queer example to the town?"

"Just Kayla and Jo."

"I am definitely interested in that."

♥

"I don't know why I assumed you could cook." Kayla stood on the opposite side of Jo's kitchen island while Jo floundered in the area between the stovetop and the wall oven. "Maybe it was this gorgeous kitchen." The gray vein in the otherwise white engineered-stone countertops matched the gray cabinets perfectly. Higher-end stainless appliances completed the look. Jo had even bragged that she could brew coffee in the Keurig built into the fridge via an app on her phone.

"It came with the house. Now, if you want me to salvage anything for dinner, get over here and help me."

Kayla laughed as she circled the island and moved closer to Jo.

She brushed her hand fleetingly against Jo's side when she got in range. Ever since she'd held Jo's hand at the diner—having been given permission—she found she liked touching Jo whenever they were close.

Jo had stayed and had lunch with her that day. When they parted, Jo issued the invitation to come over the next evening for dinner. Kayla had accepted, wishing she didn't have to wait another whole day to see her.

"What can I do?"

"Stir that." Jo pointed to a pot of bubbling tomato sauce on the stovetop. She grabbed another one that contained pasta in danger of boiling dry and dumped it into a colander in the sink. "I can cook. Sort of. I just have an issue with timing everything."

"Is something burning?"

"Shit." Jo snatched an oven mitt off the counter and jerked open the oven door. Light smoke rolled out, along with an acrid smell. Jo dropped a tray of blackened garlic bread onto the counter in disgust. "Well, that's it. My famous garlic toast is ruined."

Kayla looked pointedly at the box on the counter that she'd watched Jo take the frozen bread out of fifteen minutes before. Jo grinned and shoved her hair off her forehead.

"Any ideas for salvaging this mess?"

Kayla turned off the burner under the sauce. "Grab some plates. Let's see what we can put together."

Using a knife, she was able to scrape the char off a couple of the less burnt slices of bread. They prepared two plates and sat down next to each other at the counter. Jo picked up her fork but then waited, watching Kayla.

"Oh. I have to taste it first, huh?" She took a bite. "It's perfect."

Jo tried hers, then shook her head at Kayla. "Nice try."

The pasta was overcooked and starchy, and she evidently hadn't succeeding in ridding the bread of its bitter flavor. But none of that mattered. Jo had been trying to impress her with a nice meal.

"I hope you weren't famished." Jo set down her fork after pushing her food around on her plate for a while.

"I'm happy to be spending time with you."

"That's not a no. Do you want me to order something in?"

"No. I'm good, really." She stood and started to stack the dishes.

Jo took her hand and led her to the sofa. "I'll do that later."

♥

"Jo?" She could barely hear Kayla's soft entreaty over the sappy music accompanying the scroll of credits on the screen. Kayla had chosen a rom-com they'd both seen. Jo knew that meant Kayla wanted her to make a move, but an hour and a half later, she hadn't come up with one that felt smooth enough. She sat there, sneaking glances at Kayla and catching her looking back.

"Yeah?"

"Will you kiss me?"

The words made Jo's chest ache. "Are you sure?"

Kayla took Jo's face between her hands. "I'm so sure that if you don't kiss me, I might lose my mind. Anything beyond that, I promise to tell you if I want to stop. Okay?"

Jo nodded. "Ask me again."

Kayla held her gaze, her eyes shining. "Will you kiss me?"

"I will," Jo whispered just before pressing her mouth to Kayla's.

The kiss was everything she'd thought it would be—cartwheels in her belly, Kayla's hands in her hair, the sweet, responsive feel of Kayla's mouth against hers. When Kayla's tongue swept against her lower lip, Jo cupped Kayla's jaw and tilted her head to deepen the kiss.

After they eased apart, Kayla rested her forehead against Jo's. "Thanks."

Kayla's husky word caught Jo so off-guard that she laughed aloud. "You're welcome?"

"I didn't know what else to say."

"I would say—with regard to exploring this connection between us—that we've gotten off to a great start."

Kayla lifted one side of her lips in a lazy smile. "But it *is* just a start." She leaned in for another kiss.

Jo lost herself doing nothing more than kissing Kayla. Okay, maybe a little more than kissing. She slipped her hands under the edge of Kayla's shirt, skating over her abdomen. The ripple of her sensitive skin echoed in a tremble of arousal within Jo. When her fingers brushed the underside of Kayla's breast, Kayla put a hand on her arm, stopping her gently.

She held her hand there, against Kayla's warm skin, and met Kayla's eyes, waiting. Kayla guided her hand up a little more, letting her cup her breast, but she did nothing more than that. She wanted to explore but would wait for Kayla to indicate what was next.

"I want this. Believe me, I do. But I'd really like to be able to fall asleep in your arms and wake up together the next morning. Is that too cheesy? And if we take this any further tonight, I'll have to leave so I can open the shop early tomorrow."

"It's not cheesy. That sounds perfect. I can wait, if you can."

"You're making it pretty hard." Kayla squeezed her hand where it still rested over Jo's, catching her nipple between Jo's thumb and forefinger.

"I'm not sure I'm to blame for that." She rolled her thumb against Kayla's nipple, and when it hardened, Jo groaned, realizing she'd made the situation more difficult for herself as well.

"I should go." Kayla kissed her again.

"I'll get your coat." Jo leaned in, easing Kayla back against the couch.

"Mm. I can't seem to find my keys." Kayla buried her hands in Jo's hair, tugging lightly.

"You're looking in the wrong place."

"What if I think I'm in exactly the right place?"

Jo moaned and pulled back. She drew in a deep breath and slowly raised her hands in surrender. "I really want to respect your wishes."

Kayla's sexy smile threatened to pull her back in. So, she stood and held out her hand. She helped Kayla up and walked her to the door. After helping her put on her coat, she gave her the most chaste kiss she could manage. Tongues sliding together were chaste, right?

CHAPTER TEN

"Tonight's the night, huh?" Brianna turned from the counter at Beans to Brew and handed Jo her coffee.

"Shh." Jo glanced around, but none of the other patrons showed signs of having heard. "Really?"

Brianna rolled her eyes and headed for the door. "Okay, Casanova. Let's step outside where we can talk."

"What did Kayla tell you?" Jo asked when they'd gone a safe distance from the coffee shop.

"I'm her best friend. You think she doesn't talk to me?"

"Yeah, right?" This was another ploy by Brianna to get Jo to tell her something that Kayla hadn't.

"I know that you've been taking lunch to her at the store every day this week before your shift. With her working days and you on evenings, that doesn't leave a lot of alone time." Brianna raised her eyebrows suggestively. "Sundays she opens late, so it stands to reason, when you get off work tonight would be the perfect time for you two to—you know, get off."

"She didn't tell you anything."

Brianna paused with her coffee cup halfway to her mouth. "Nah. But when I asked her if she wanted to hang out tonight, she said she had plans. It wasn't hard to figure out with who. And she sounded nervous."

"Like nervous-excited, not nervous-apprehensive, right?"

Brianna laughed and tapped her hand on Jo's shoulder. "Jesus, yes. Don't be so worried. Hasn't she made it clear by now that she's into you?"

"Yeah, she has." Jo put a flirty twist on her words.

"Ew, okay. Too much innuendo." Brianna resumed walking toward her car.

Jo followed, her mind already wandering to when she would see Kayla later. This would be the longest shift ever.

♥

Kayla adjusted the pillows on the sofa for the third time, opting for a center crease in the top on this go-round. Did that look right? Damn. Why didn't she watch more HGTV? She turned on the lamp on the side table. Too dim? The overhead light felt less intimate. But wasn't intimate what she was going for here? Sure, but she didn't want the room to feel staged—like she had only one thing in mind.

She chuckled to herself. She'd seen Jo every day this week, sneaking kisses in the back room at McCall's while they ate lunch between customers. Neither of them had hidden the fact that they anticipated this day. It felt strange to have put a date and time on things, to not just let them happen organically. When she'd suggested waiting until the weekend, she'd thought that would take the pressure off. But, actually, she'd just given herself four more days to think about it.

As she passed through the living room again, she glanced at the pillows. Maybe they would look better if she—the doorbell interrupted her last chance to change those damn pillows. They were locked in, for better or worse.

She opened the door to Jo and stepped back to let her in. Jo had changed out of her uniform after shift, and they'd agreed to dress comfortably tonight, since it would be after eleven before Jo arrived.

Kayla kissed her, then drew back and touched the side of her face. "You look tired."

"Second half of the shift got busy. A bachelorette party got out of hand. Let me tell you, you haven't lived until you've witnessed a full-on bridesmaid bar brawl."

"If you're—we can just hang out tonight. No pressure if you're not feeling up to—anything else."

"No," Jo said quickly. "I'm still—unless you're not."

"I do. I am."

Jo laughed softly. "Well, we both sound like idiots."

They still stood awkwardly near the door. Kayla gestured to the living room. "Would you like anything to drink? Wine, beer, water?"

"No, thank you." Jo circled her arm around Kayla's waist and drew her close. She kissed the side of her neck. "If you need a transition, I'm happy to sit on the couch with you and talk. But if I'm being honest, I've been waiting all week to be close to you." She trailed kisses up the side of Kayla's neck and nipped lightly at her earlobe.

Kayla shivered and moved toward the bedroom, pulling Jo along with her. Every day had been foreplay—stolen moments between work and bedtime phone calls in the stillness of her room, wishing Jo were lying beside her.

In the bedroom, she'd left the light off and lit a mildly scented candle on her dresser. But the residual glow from the hallway allowed them to see each other clearly.

She pressed into Jo, aligning their bodies, and kissed her. She didn't hold back as she slipped her tongue against Jo's and deepened the kiss. Jo gave back the same passion, urgently grasping the back of Kayla's shirt.

"I want to give you everything you need," Jo said when they parted.

Kayla nodded, struck by the sincerity in Jo's rasp. She believed that Jo was as much in this moment as she was and that her sole intention was Kayla's satisfaction. A tiny moment of self-doubt wriggled through. No one had seen her naked in so long—no one new since she was in her twenties. She no longer had her youthful body.

"All good?"

She liked that Jo checked in. Arousal swirled in Jo's eyes, but if Kayla said it was too soon, Jo would slow down. She'd said it, that she would give Kayla everything. A burst of confidence rippled through her. She shouldn't be standing here doubting herself. She was a strong, capable woman. A business owner. A leader in the community. She'd even served a term on the board of the Chamber of Commerce.

What the hell was she doing? Mentally reciting her CV? This gorgeous woman standing in front of her wanted her, and damn it, good or bad, they were going to have sex. *Oh God, please be good.*

She gripped the hem of her T-shirt and pulled it over her head, then dropped it on the floor. She'd worn her favorite bra today, and in just a minute, Jo would discover the matching underwear.

Jo stepped closer, and Kayla shivered when Jo brushed her hands down Kayla's torso. The tickle of her fingertips grew firm when she reached her hips—and grasped. Jo bent her head and trailed a series of kisses over Kayla's shoulder and up the side of her neck.

Kayla grabbed her jaw and guided her until their lips met in a hurried kiss. Between them, Jo worked on the button, then the zipper, on Kayla's pants. As she pushed them down, she sank to her knees, leaning her cheek against Kayla's belly.

"You're so beautiful." She curled her fingers around the waistband of Kayla's underwear, pulled it down a half inch and kissed that spot.

Kayla moved her left foot out a half step. "Take them off." She registered the surprised flicker of Jo's eyes to hers at the same moment as she absorbed the thrill of giving the order.

When her underwear hit the floor, she stepped out of them and kept walking toward the bed. "Take off your—" She turned around to find Jo stripping off her own clothes as she followed her. "Eager?"

"Complaining?"

"Not at all." She took off her bra, then crawled backward onto the bed.

Naked, Jo followed.

Kayla's hands had been on Jo's body in various ways recently, but feeling the firmness under her clothes had not prepared Kayla for the beauty of Jo's bare form. Her abs were tight, with the slightest indentations defining her muscles. Her hips swelled into strong thighs. When she leaned forward and pressed her hands against the bed, her biceps flexed, and shoulder muscles bunched. She stalked toward Kayla on all fours, her hands and knees whispering against the comforter.

"You liked that control." Jo's eyes flashed, letting Kayla know she'd enjoyed it, too. "Do you want more? Or can I drive for a while?"

She wanted to dominate Jo; somehow she just knew that. The thought of that body under her, at her command, made her wet. But she hadn't done this in a while, and giving herself over to Jo appealed to her as well. She smiled, certain she would have many more chances to do whatever she wanted with Jo.

"Consider me your willing passenger." She lay back in submission.

Jo dropped kisses up her leg as she approached—over her hip—trailing a hand behind. When Jo ghosted her mouth past her hip to her lower belly, her clit tightened, demanding. She fisted her hands in the comforter in order to keep from grabbing Jo's head and guiding it where she wanted it.

Take a deep breath. Jesus. You don't want her to think you're so desperate you can't last ten minutes.

Just as she'd shored up her resolve, Jo looked up at her, a clear request for consent in her gaze. *Oh, yes, please.* She nodded, then gasped when Jo's mouth covered her. The first touch of Jo's tongue against her clit lifted her hips off the bed, the feeling so exquisite that inexplicably she writhed as if she needed to escape.

"Okay?" Jo's breath felt warm against her sensitive flesh.

"Don't stop."

Jo planted a hand on her stomach and lowered her head again. Kayla couldn't hold back a moan. Jo teased her lightly, then sucked her clit fully into her mouth, not letting Kayla's rapidly firing nerves adjust.

The pressure built, between her legs but also in her chest. The throbbing in her clit pounded in her head like relentless ocean waves. She was drowning and she loved it, gasping as pleasure rolled through her and the weight of Jo across her thighs pulled her under. She drew in deep, rasping breaths that fueled moaned encouragement for more.

When she felt Jo's fingers poised at her entrance, she froze, already clenching around the emptiness, desperate to be filled.

"Please." She panted, afraid Jo would stop.

Her back arched when Jo eased inside her, so carefully, so fully. Jo stroked slowly, giving her—everything—murmuring encouragement, calling her beautiful, asking her to let go. She cried out, her throat suddenly thick with emotion. She grasped Jo's other forearm and squeezed, grounding herself. She thrust against Jo's hand, simultaneously needing release and trying to hold on to the ascent for just a bit longer. But when Jo lowered her head again and raked her tongue against Kayla's clit, she tumbled into a pulsing orgasm.

Squeezing her eyes shut, she pressed her hand against the nape of Jo's neck, holding her there. It was too much—the pleasure wrapped around an ache in her chest she hadn't even known was there, pushing up into her throat until it escaped in a loud sob. Mortified, she covered her face with one hand.

Jo reacted immediately, tensing and lifting her shoulders. Though Kayla wasn't looking at her, she could feel Jo's eyes on her. She could sense the questions, but she couldn't answer, in the moment, without breaking down.

"Kayla?"

Jo eased her fingers free, and Kayla missed her right away. She pushed her own hand between her legs and whimpered, needing the pressure to step her down the back side of that incredible peak.

"I'm sorry. I'm so sorry. Did I push you into this?" Jo was beside her, desperate eyes flashing at Kayla's perceived pain.

Still splayed out on her back, hand between her legs, she shook her head, tears streaming out the corners of her eyes. She swiped at a line of them that ran into her hair. She captured Jo's hand and pressed it to her chest, covering it with hers.

"Please, talk to me. What happened?"

She fought her way through her own mixed-up emotions in order to ease the distress reflected in Jo's expression. "I'm—just overwhelmed." That was too simple a word for what swirled inside her, but she couldn't find a better definition just now.

"Was it—did you think about—"

"Hey." The idea that Jo would think she'd been thinking of Macy while they made love broke through. She slid a hand through Jo's hair and stroked down her jaw, resting her fingers on the side of her neck. "I was with *you*, the whole time. I'm sorry. Just give me a few minutes, and I'll try to explain this better, okay?"

Jo closed her eyes briefly, then nodded.

She rolled to her back, keeping an arm around Jo and drawing her close. She brought Jo's hand back to her chest and closed her eyes, enjoying both her post-orgasmic glow and the weight of Jo's body next to her. She drew in a deep breath, then released it.

"I've been with only one person in my life. And that was four years ago. I mean—I have—since then—by myself—" She stopped short, flooded with embarrassment at what she'd just admitted to.

A slow, sexy smile replaced the hesitant look on Jo's face. "Maybe you should tell me more about that. Or perhaps a demonstration?"

"You'd like that, wouldn't you?"

"Oh, very much." Jo caught her hand and drew it down her stomach to rest at the apex of her thighs, Jo's hand gently covering it.

"The point is, I was nervous and—it turns out, I didn't need to be. That was very nice."

"Very nice?" Jo lifted her head and narrowed her eyes at Kayla.

"Yes. *I* was incredible and you—it was a solid effort. Was there room for improvement?" She pursed her lips, faking consideration. "Probably, but if you—"

"Improvement?" Jo rolled her over, pressing her onto her stomach. "I'll show you improvement."

♥

Jo woke to the sunlight peeking through a gap in the curtain and the birds singing outside the window. What a sappy rom-com-esque way to describe it. But actual birds were in the tree just there. She lay on her side, and Kayla was curled up in front of her. Her arm rested around Kayla's waist, and Kayla's skin was so warm under her hand. In fact, Kayla was heated completely.

Kayla stirred and rolled over, burrowing into her. She kissed Jo's collarbone. "Good morning."

"Good God, woman. You are a heater."

"Mm. Does that mean you don't want to snuggle with me?" When Kayla would have moved away, Jo tightened her arms and held her close.

She flicked the comforter aside, leaving only the sheet. "It just means when we do, I use fewer covers."

"I don't have to open the store for a couple more hours. Interested in brunch? I'll treat you to French toast at Beans to Brew."

She thought about suggesting they stay in bed and pass the time in a much more pleasurable way. But French toast did sound good. And something in Kayla's invitation felt more serious than just a meal. Brunch at Beans to Brew was not a private affair. Kayla was asking her to go public—in Harbor Springs—with her, as a couple.

She didn't need long to consider her answer. Her heart swelled with pride that Kayla had made this offer. And, she found, she didn't give a single thought to what anyone who saw them would think. She was, it seemed, completely okay with letting the nosy residents of Harbor Springs know that she was dating their beloved Kayla McCall.

"That sounds perfect."

"Great. I'll grab a shower and get ready. I'll probably head to the store from there." Kayla rolled away from her and groaned as she sat up on the edge of the bed.

"Are you okay?"

Kayla chuckled. "Yep. Just some muscles I haven't used in a while."

Jo levered herself up and leaned against the headboard, one arm folded behind her head. "Can I ask you something?"

"Sure." Kayla twisted to look at her.

"The tears?"

Kayla drew her brows together and gave a bewildered shake of her head. "Endorphins?" She smiled. "I was feeling a lot. Pleasure, certainly. But also connected—you know? To you—to that moment. And also, somehow out of control—wonderfully so." She brushed a hand affectionately against Jo's cheek. "Give me a pass on the tears, babe. It was the most intense orgasm I'd had in a very, *very* long time."

"Yeah. Four years."

"Way longer."

Jo stared at her, letting the sad admission sink in. Kayla had assured her that she and Macy had ups and downs, like any other couple. Still, in her mind, she'd enshrined Kayla and Macy's relationship as the gold standard, then decided she couldn't measure up. Here was Kayla admitting, what? That, like any other couple, they'd had droughts—times when they didn't connect. Suddenly, Macy became more real, more fallible, and yet more distant from what they were building than she'd ever been.

♥

Kayla got out of the passenger side of Jo's car just as Jo circled to her. Jo closed the door, then paused, resting her hand against the car and giving Kayla a smoldering look.

"We could get back in this car and—"

"No deal, lady." Jo smiled and held out her hand. "You promised me French toast."

She grasped Jo's hand and followed her toward the front of Beans to Brew. She'd thought Jo would drop her hand when they got close, but instead she held on.

When they arrived at the hostess stand for the outdoor patio, Jo confidently asked for a table for two. And when they were led to a spot right in the center of the already crowded area, Jo never faltered. She pulled out Kayla's chair for her, and once she was seated, she lightly squeezed Kayla's shoulders before occupying her own chair.

She met Jo's eyes, a silent check-in, and Jo nodded. Her radiant smile didn't carry even a trace of tension. Kayla slipped on her sunglasses and discreetly checked the tables around them. They were getting some curious glances, to be sure. But most were accompanied by approving smiles. A couple of people even boldly made eye contact and nodded when she looked at them.

"Good morning, lovely ladies. I'll be your server today. Can I start you off with a beverage?"

As Kayla requested a mimosa, she caught a police officer one table over, shooting Jo a thumbs-up. Jo responded with a small wave, then turned back to her, absently giving her own drink order while not taking her eyes off her.

This was just the start of what she already suspected would be something serious and wonderful. She'd awakened this morning comfortable and safe in Jo's arms. *Don't rush.* But even as the thought passed through her mind, her heart beat strongly in anticipation of the life they could build together. And she couldn't be happier that she'd set aside her fears and risked caring for Jo.

CHAPTER ELEVEN

Valentine's Day, a year later

Kayla locked her Mini Cooper, holding on to her keys as she walked through the parking lot to McCall's. As she reached the sidewalk in front of the store, a florist van pulled up, and the passenger window rolled down.

"Delivery for Kayla McCall," the driver called out.

"Geez, Spencer. I've known you literally your whole life."

He grinned as he circled the front of the van and opened one of the side doors to the cargo area. He pulled out a large bouquet wrapped in tan parchment and tied with a piece of twine. "Mama says to be professional."

"I'll be sure to let her know you were just that." She dug a twenty out of her wallet for his tip, then took the bouquet. She could smell the roses even before she looked inside at the flawless red flowers.

"Those are the prettiest ones I've delivered all week. Someone must like you an awful lot." He slid her a knowing look and a wink while he climbed back into the van.

As he pulled off, she plucked the card from the plastic holder in the bunch.

I CAN'T "BEAR" TO BE WITHOUT YOU.

She smiled as she unlocked the door and shoved it open.

"Do you have a secret admirer?" Jo's voice from inside was unexpected.

"Shit. You startled me." Kayla took a breath to calm her racing heart.

"So, do you?"

She shook her head. "I've got an admirer. But it's no secret. The whole town knows about it."

Jo took a step forward. "Well, they are a gossipy bunch." She took Kayla's purse and the flowers and set them on the counter. "You know how some women say they're really not the red-roses type. Well, I guessed you were exactly that type."

Kayla smiled. "I really am." In the past year, Jo had sent her flowers a handful of times, and each bunch was bright and colorful. But this was the first time she'd selected red roses.

For the first time since she'd stepped inside, she noticed the outfit on her stuffed bear had been changed. He now wore a white cloth folded and wrapped around his lower body like a diaper, secured with a huge safety pin. Pink, glittery wings angled out from his back, and a crossbow balanced in one of his paws. She laughed as she moved closer to scrutinize him. The quotation marks in the note made sense now.

"What on earth happened to you, big guy?"

"He's really feeling the Cupid spirit for Valentine's Day."

"A crossbow isn't exactly traditional but would certainly be effective."

Jo moved behind her and wrapped an arm around her waist. "Look a little closer."

A red satin satchel had been placed in his other paw, and she removed it, glancing at Jo.

"Open it."

She untied the string, spread open the top, and withdrew a small velvet box. Her breath caught in her throat.

"Jo?" She met Jo's eyes, filled with adoration.

Smiling, Jo opened the lid of the box to reveal a diamond set in a band with smaller stones around it.

"When I moved here, I knew something was missing in my life, but I never could have imagined how amazing it would feel to find it. I love you, Kayla McCall. And I'd love nothing more than to marry you, even if it means I have to do it in front of every busybody in this damn town."

Kayla laughed around the lump in her throat. Her eyes welled until the ring began to blur. She swiped away tears and met Jo's eyes. "I want that, too. Minus the busybodies. Me and you and a small group of those closest to us?"

Jo wrapped her arms around Kayla's waist, sweeping her into a tight hug.

"I love you, too," she whispered into Jo's hair. "So much so that I'm going to forgive you for putting Gran's bear in such an embarrassing position."

"From what I've heard, your gran would have loved that." She jerked her thumb in the bear's direction.

"She would have. And she'd have adored you, too."

"You are going to sell so many crossbows this week. I am a genius at this marketing stuff."

Kayla laughed. "The lengths you'll go to in order to make me glad you're good at being a police officer."

Jo's face grew serious. "I promise to always be as careful as I can be."

"I know, love." A year ago, she'd been terrified of getting involved with another officer of the law. Now, the thought that she could have missed out on loving Jo diminished those fears. "I wouldn't change a thing about you."

Bouquet of Love

Anne Shade

Inspiration for Bouquet of Love

I was inspired to write *Bouquet of Love* because I don't think we have enough sweet, romantic stories featuring older female characters. Becoming middle-aged doesn't mean you stop wanting to be romanced and loved.

Like the main character Alyssa, too often women stop seeing themselves as desirable when they reach the age of fifty, especially when they find themselves reentering the dating pool after a long relationship has ended.

The fact that her secret admirer Collette is younger, appreciates Alyssa's age, finds her even more desirable than someone younger, and is willing to "woo" her in a way that shows Alyssa how worthy of love she is makes the story even sweeter. Who can resist something sweet on Valentine's Day?

Anne Shade

CHAPTER ONE

*A*lyssa heard the alarm clock's incessant beeping and sighed tiredly. *She had been up late grading essays and felt as if she'd barely slept.*

"Make it stop," a familiar voice groaned.

Confused, she turned over to find the outline of womanly curves beneath the covers beside her and a mass of red curls covering the pillow. "Shauna?" she asked in disbelief.

A pair of bright emerald-green eyes peeked out at her. "Of course. Who else would you be sharing a bed with?" Her eyebrows quirked in question.

Alyssa shook her head. "But you're dead."

Shauna, the love of her life, whose ashes she had flown to Ireland to spread across her mother's family's ancestral land five years ago, lay grinning beside her. "Yes, I am."

"Then I'm dreaming?" Alyssa asked.

"Yes, you are."

Alyssa reached over, smoothed a flaming lock of hair away from Shauna's face, and laid her hand on her soft cheek. "It's been so long since you visited me this way. I've missed you."

Shauna turned her head to place a kiss on Alyssa's palm. "I've missed you too, but it's time for you to move on."

Alyssa felt a tear run out the corner of her eye onto her pillow. "No. I'm not ready. Besides, who's going to want an old broad like me?"

"Any woman who's not blind or stupid. Besides, you're only as old as you feel."

Alyssa frowned. "I've felt really old lately. One of the kids in my class told me I reminded him of his grandmother. Not his mother, his grandmother."

Shauna laughed. "Then he must have a young grandmother. You're only fifty."

"Exactly. Too old and set in my ways to be trying to fall in love and start over."

"So, do you plan to spend the rest of your life puttering around this house lonely and horny?" Shauna said.

Alyssa shrugged as she trailed her fingers through Shauna's curls. "I have Max and Betty Blue."

Shauna looked at Alyssa skeptically. "Max may be good for a roll in the grass, but you know as soon as that pit bull from around the corner comes around, he won't give you a second glance until she's gone. And unless Betty Blue grew a heart, arms, and no longer needs batteries since I left, she's going to cause you more frustration than happiness."

"What if I don't know how to be happy without you?" Alyssa said, her chest aching from how much she missed Shauna.

Shauna grasped Alyssa's hand, kissed her knuckles, and held it between them. "What do you tell your students if they say they don't know how to do something?"

Alyssa always hated when Shauna used reasoning when all she wanted to do was pout. "The only way to know whether you can do something is to just do it. If you don't succeed, at least you can say you tried. That, in itself, is a success."

Shauna smiled. "Exactly. Besides, you promised me you wouldn't waste away alone in this house after I've been gone for a reasonable amount of time."

Alyssa shook her head. "Only you would hold me to a promise you badgered me to make while you were on your deathbed."

"Because I knew you would never do it unless I did. Now, turn off that annoying alarm and get up before you're late for work."

♥

Alyssa awoke with a start, and it took her a moment to realize she had been dreaming. She slammed the button on the alarm clock, then turned over and looked at the empty spot beside her on the bed. She ran her hand over the pillow that no longer held Shauna's scent or a stray strand of her red hair that she always left behind. Alyssa still had a lock of it in a small keepsake box with Shauna's wedding band, glasses, and love letters she had written to Alyssa just before she passed. Shauna had given them to her sister with instructions not to give them to Alyssa until after she was gone. She had left twelve letters, one to be read each month of that first year. They were filled with love, memories, and encouragement to keep going.

Alyssa knew they were Shauna's way of helping her grieve without completely losing herself in sorrow, which she had almost done that first year. She had stopped writing, given up her workshops at the community college, and almost stopped teaching, but the love her students showed her after her loss reminded her why she became a teacher in the first place. Those love letters and her students had kept her going when all she wanted to do was lie down and wallow in misery for the rest of her life.

Alyssa smiled as she remembered the first love letter Shauna had ever written her. It was after their first date. She'd had it delivered with a bouquet of flowers to Alyssa's classroom, and it brought such a blush to her face that her students had teased her for weeks afterward. After that Shauna would mail a handwritten note to Alyssa every month, even after they moved in together. Receiving a note never got old. If anything, it seemed to refresh what they felt for each other from the moment they'd met at a writers' retreat twenty years prior until the day Shauna passed.

Their relationship wasn't perfect. Shauna was bold, carefree, and outgoing, while Alyssa was cautious, quiet, and a homebody. They were complete opposites and had issues and arguments like most couples, but they always found a way to talk and forgive because, despite being such opposites, they balanced each other.

There was no one like Shauna, and Alyssa was now regretting having made that promise. If she knew one thing about Shauna, it was that when she had her mind set on something, she did whatever it took to make it happen. In this case, she would probably haunt Alyssa's dreams until she did what she had promised. But how did a shy, fifty-year-old lesbian who had only seriously dated five women since coming out at the age of twenty-five find dates?

Alyssa sought advice from the only other single person her age that she knew, her best friend Vicki, as they sat in the teachers' lounge during lunch.

"Only Shauna would still be trying to make sure you're happy from the beyond," Vicki said after Alyssa told her about her dream.

"Yeah, but who's going to want to date a middle-aged school-teacher who prefers to be home curled up with a glass of wine and a good book to partying in a club with a bunch of young, hip lesbians that I have nothing in common with," Alyssa asked.

"There's your first problem. You're generalizing. When is the last time you went to a club? I'm sure just as many women your age are there. Besides, you're the hottest middle-aged woman I know. If I weren't straight, I'd ask you out myself." Vicki gave Alyssa a wink.

Alyssa smiled. "Thanks, but you're too high maintenance for me."

"I'm not high maintenance. I just know what I want and haven't found the right man to provide me with the lifestyle that I deserve."

Alyssa looked at Vicki skeptically. "You've had two offers of marriage from men who gave you the world and would probably take you back in a minute if you asked."

Vicki waved dismissively. "Brandon had kids that wouldn't leave home, and Larry wanted his mother to move in with us. I need my own space and am not interested in playing second fiddle to some kids or parents."

Alyssa shook her head. "If only I had your confidence. You know I'm not the type of woman to approach or ask another woman out. It took forever for me to agree to go out with Shauna, and that was only after a month of phone calls because I couldn't believe a woman like her was interested in me. She was wild, beautiful, free, and made me brave enough to feel like I could do anything. Shauna didn't need technology to romance me. She did it with flowers, handwritten poems, and love letters. Nowadays everyone's on dating apps, sexting, and sending each other nude pics as introductions. What happened to wooing someone the old-fashioned way?"

Vicki chuckled. "Did you actually just say wooing?"

Alyssa smiled. "Yes, wooing. Unless I can find someone that will do that, I guess Max and I will live out our days together."

"Okay, as your best friend, I will not allow that to happen. Valentine's Day is in a little over a week. Let me play matchmaker and get you a date before the school's Sweetheart Dance?" Vicki asked.

Alyssa quirked an eyebrow. "No offense, Vicki, but do you know any other lesbians besides me?"

Vicki waved dismissively again. "A minor obstacle. Are you going to put yourself in my expensively manicured hands or not?"

Alyssa loved Vicki, but putting her romantic life in her hands sounded like a train wreck waiting to happen. She sighed in resignation. "What the heck. I don't have anything better to do."

♥

Collette sat nearby discreetly eavesdropping on Alyssa and Vicki's conversation. She kept her face buried in a book that she had lost all focus on the moment they walked into the teacher's lounge. Collette had briefly looked up upon their entrance and was gifted with a smile and nod from Alyssa. She returned the greeting, then quickly looked away to keep herself from staring at the beautiful woman.

Alyssa was fit but thick in all the right places. She was always dressed fashionably, today wearing a burnt-orange sweater dress that emphasized her curvaceous hourglass figure and made her golden skin glow. Her long, shapely legs were encased in a pair of soft chocolate-brown leather wedge-heel boots. Her thick, dark-brown hair was pulled back into a ponytail of soft curls that just reached her shoulders and brought attention to her bright, expressive brown eyes, softly sloping nose, and full lips that shone with a tinted gloss. As far as Collette could tell, Alyssa never wore any makeup except the lip gloss she'd seen her usually reapply after she'd eaten lunch.

Collette peeked up at the pair once again as they stood to leave. Vicki was a knockout, but Alyssa was beautiful in a natural, black-don't-crack kind of way. She moved in a slow, purposeful manner, as if every graceful reach of her hand, every sway in her hips, and every turn of her head on her long neck was done to a choreographed song only she could hear.

Collette had been entranced by Alyssa since the first time she'd met her six years ago when she took a writing workshop Alyssa taught at the community college. That workshop had changed Collette's life in more ways than improving her writing skills. It made her realize that muses and love at first sight both existed. The passion Alyssa displayed when she spoke of writing reignited the passion Collette had thought she'd lost. Writer's block had brought her to the workshop, and Alyssa had brought back Collette's creativity. She had also stolen and broken Collette's heart, all on the first day of class.

Before the class was even over, Collette had decided to ask Alyssa out for coffee, not caring that the beautiful woman was at least ten years her senior. Collette had waited until her other classmates were pretty much gone before approaching Alyssa's desk under the guise of asking her some inane question, when a gorgeous redhead had breezed into the room, swept Alyssa up in her arms, and planted a passionate kiss on her lips. Alyssa had blushed prettily and playfully swatted the woman off. After that, Collette had quickly changed direction toward the door.

She'd later learned from another classmate that the woman had been Alyssa's fiancée, and all of Collette's hopes of getting to know her were wrecked against the shores of disappointment. It wasn't until she started working at Forest Hill High School this semester as a history teacher and the new coach for the tennis team that she'd seen Alyssa again.

When Collette was recently introduced to Alyssa, she wasn't surprised that she didn't remember meeting her all those years ago. After Collette had found out Alyssa was unavailable, she had kept her head down until she finished the workshop, but she had never forgotten Alyssa. Taking that workshop had given her the courage to finally finish her first book in a mystery series she had started and submit it to a publisher, using the skills she had learned from Alyssa. Collette was currently working on the Rayne Edwards series under the pen name R. Cole. If anyone had seen Alyssa and read the description of her main character, Rayne Edwards, they would think Alyssa was the living embodiment of the fictional private investigator. Collette never told anyone that Alyssa had been the muse for Rayne and that she had completely overhauled the character to resemble Alyssa.

The books were her secret love letter to the woman she had carried in her heart from the moment she had walked into that classroom and smiled in Collette's direction six years ago. Now, watching that same woman laughing as she left the teacher's lounge, and remembering what Alyssa had said about wanting to be wooed, Collette smiled to herself. She had a week to get Alyssa to see how worthy she was of wooing and a second chance at love.

♥

"What about her?" Vicki asked Alyssa as they looked through the dating profiles of the women who had responded to the profile Vicki had set up for her on some dating app called Bumble Match or Matching Bee. She couldn't remember its name, but it was a complete waste of time.

"You do realize that none of these women is older than thirty?" Alyssa asked.

"And?" Vicki looked at her as if she didn't understand why that was so bad.

"And I'm not trying to be somebody's sugar momma."

"No one is asking you to be their sugar momma."

Alyssa looked at her skeptically. "Did you not see the one who asked if I'd let her call me Mommy while I spanked her?"

Vicki smirked. "Okay, that one was bad, but the others seem sweet."

Alyssa shook her head. "Vicki, this isn't going to work. Unless they make a dating app for lesbians over fifty, you're going to have to try something else."

"C'mon. It's only day one," Vicki said, pouting prettily.

Alyssa shrugged. "I guess you better get to work. You've only got a few more…"

Coach Roberts entered the teachers' lounge. A strikingly attractive woman at just about six feet, with a slim, muscular build; black dreadlocks that flowed just past her broad shoulders and framed her soft, oval face; a smooth, dark-brown complexion; even darker brown, almost black, eyes; and a wide, beautiful smile anchored by two deep dimples, she walked with a smooth, easy confidence that spoke of her years as a professional tennis player. Femmes were normally Alyssa's type, but something about Collette's androgyny intrigued her. Other than knowing a little about her tennis career, Alyssa found something else familiar about Collette Roberts when they were first introduced, but she couldn't place it.

"Hello…Earth to Alyssa," Vicki said, tapping her on the shoulder.

Alyssa turned around to find Vicki grinning knowingly and felt her face heat with embarrassment.

"I had no idea you were hot for the coach," Vicki whispered.

"And you will continue to have no idea," Alyssa said, unpacking her lunch.

"I hear she's single. Why don't you ask her out?"

"First, she's a decade younger than me. Second, even if she were my age, you know I'm not the type to pursue. I prefer to be pursued."

"How do you expect to be pursued if you don't show any interest?"

"Because if someone is interested in me, I would think they would express that interest whether they knew I was or not. That's how they would find out if I might be interested," Alyssa said, as if that made perfect sense.

Vicki chuckled. "That's a lot of guesswork. And you call me high maintenance."

"Excuse me, Ms. Harris and Ms. Ingram." Alyssa and Vicki looked up to find one of their students holding a bouquet of flowers.

"Yes, Shari?" Alyssa said.

The young lady handed her the flowers. "These came for you, and Mrs. Jay asked me to deliver them."

Alyssa looked at the flowers in confusion. "Are you sure they're not for Ms. Ingram?"

"Yes, ma'am. Your name is on the envelope," the young lady said, handing Alyssa a floral print envelope with her name written in fancy calligraphy.

"Thank you."

The young woman nodded with a smile and left.

"Is this your doing?" Alyssa asked Vicki suspiciously.

Vicki held up her hands. "Not me. Open the envelope."

Alyssa carefully slid her finger under the flap of the envelope to avoid tearing the beautiful stationery and pulled out a folded single page of paper with the same floral print from the envelope around the border of the paper and edged in gold.

"Wow, somebody went all out," Vicki said, wafting her hand over the paper. "The stationery even smells like flowers."

Alyssa was at a complete loss as to who would be sending her flowers. Her mother usually did on her birthday, but that was a month from now. Neither of her brothers would even think of sending their sister such a gift or a note written on frilly stationery. She unfolded the paper and read.

Dear Alyssa,

I hope this note finds you having a good day. You might not know this, but the carnation is a very underrated flower despite its various meanings equating to some of our strongest feelings. I've gifted you with this bouquet of red carnations symbolizing admiration and pink symbolizing gratitude to tell you how much I admire your beauty, strength, and kindness, and for how grateful I am to have met you.

Alyssa, you have become my muse. You've found the key to my soul, opened the door to my desires, and let loose a floodgate of creativity. You have provoked, teased, and intrigued me. You've made me see things in ways I never imagined and forced me to put words in writing for all to read. You are my desire...my creativity...my muse. I hope to soon have the pleasure of sharing what you have unknowingly helped me to create. Until then, a mystery I will remain.

> *With genuine affection,*
> *Your Secret Admirer*

Alyssa just stared at the beautiful words, inundated with a mix of emotions. If she didn't know any better, she would have sworn Shauna had written the letter, but Shauna wasn't here.

"Well, what does it say?" Vicki asked impatiently.

Alyssa handed her the letter, needing to process what had been written before speaking.

"Wow." Vicki fanned herself with the letter before handing it back to Alyssa. "You have a secret admirer. That is so hot."

Alyssa smiled uncertainly. "You don't think that's the slightest bit creepy?"

"No. Not at all. As old-school romantic as you are, I would think you'd love this."

Alyssa folded the letter and slid it back into the envelope. "I guess. It just seems convenient that I'd get a secret admirer the day after my dream of Shauna and you offering to fix me up." Alyssa looked at Vicki suspiciously.

Vicki shook her head. "I swear, it wasn't me. Besides, I would've just sent you roses and a nice little note. Not that bouquet of flowery words. Obviously, whoever it is knows you love that kind of stuff."

Alyssa leaned over and whispered conspiratorially, "Do you think it's someone here? Or, God forbid, a student?"

They both attempted to discreetly peer around the room. No one was paying them any attention. Most were caught up in their own conversations, or they had their faces buried in phones and laptops.

"If it is someone here, they're really good at hiding it. I seriously doubt it's a student. What teenager has money for flowers and writes like that?" Vicki asked.

Alyssa worried her bottom lip between her teeth. "Yeah. I guess you're right."

"Look. Don't worry yourself about it right now," Vicki said. "Whoever it is says they aren't ready to reveal themselves, which means they plan to do so at some point, so if they send you anything else, we'll see what clues we can pick from it," Vicki said.

Alyssa nodded but couldn't fight the strangest feeling that Shauna, wherever she might be, had a hand in this strange occurrence.

♥

Collette sat nearby wondering how she'd managed to stay low key after Alyssa received her flowers and letter. To keep herself anonymous, she'd gone to the nearest floral shop to set up the delivery instead of doing it herself and asked them to include the letter. She found it difficult to believe she'd written such sugary-sweet words of love outside of her novels, but something told her Alyssa would like them, especially if they had come from the heart, which they had. Collette had been dreaming of Alyssa since she'd met her on her first day at the beginning of the school year, waking up aching with missing her, as if Alyssa had really been there. Collette didn't know if it was the image that she had built up in her mind of Alyssa from the two months she'd spent in her writing workshop or how she'd managed to keep her crush on Alyssa alive through the fictional version of her Collette had created for her novels, but she felt as if she and Alyssa were meant to be together.

Collette was no stranger to love. As a matter of fact, her family and friends considered her a serial monogamist. Every relationship she'd had since coming out as a teenager had lasted two or more years. The longest had been her ex-wife, Lani, which had been four years. Collette was a romantic at heart, but she had always been drawn to women who were the complete opposite, leaving her feeling as if she did all the work in the relationship while her partners just sat back and enjoyed the benefits. She'd learned that Alyssa was also a romantic when the subject of writing romances came up during the workshop she'd led. Alyssa had truly lit up on that topic, telling the class that she was a frustrated romance author too afraid of putting herself out there, so she taught others how to do it and lived vicariously through them. Collette had struggled to provide romance for her character, and Alyssa had provided the tools she'd needed to give her character more depth by creating a love life for her. That was what sold her stories to the publisher who had originally said Rayne Edwards was a one-dimensional character who needed more depth and stories in addition to the mysteries she was solving.

Collette felt like that at times—one-dimensional, as if she needed someone to give her more depth and color. She gazed up from her book to look at Alyssa and smiled. Could she be the final piece of Collette's own story? She just hoped Alyssa would see the flowers and note today, as well as the ones that would be following, as the romantic gesture Collette hoped they would be. She was so lost in gazing at Alyssa, she hadn't realized Vicki had caught her staring and was looking at her suspiciously. Collette quickly glanced away, hoping Vicki hadn't figured out she was the secret admirer.

CHAPTER TWO

That night, Alyssa sat in bed staring teary-eyed down at beribboned stacks of love letters Shauna had composed over the years. Alyssa had kept every one of them. Two hundred and forty letters over twenty years, all in Shauna's rounded script. Then Alyssa picked up the letter she'd received this afternoon that she had laid off to the side. Although her name had been written in professional looking calligraphy, the letter itself was done in small, neat print. The style of the handwriting may have been different, but the tone and sentiment of the letter was so much like Shauna's it was scary.

Alyssa ran a finger over a stack of Shauna's letters. "I don't know how, or even if it's possible, but I know you had something to do with this, Shauna."

She brought the envelope from her secret admirer to her nose and inhaled the soft floral scent, smiling through the tears. Shauna probably would have wished she'd thought of that. Alyssa wracked her brain trying to figure out who her admirer could be. Most of her and Shauna's friends were in relationships, with families of their own. The single ones had never shown any interest in Alyssa before Shauna passed and checked in on her every now and then to try to get her out of the house, but offered nothing like a date or anything. Then she remembered one acquaintance they would see at every writers' retreat they went to, Jamil, who Shauna swore was crushing hard on Alyssa. She hadn't seen Jamil since Shauna's funeral because she stopped attending the retreats. Jamil called at least once a month to check on her and had even asked her out for coffee a few times, but Alyssa had politely turned her down, not wanting to encourage anything now that she was single.

Alyssa began to mentally sort through people she ran into daily, but she was so clueless, if anyone showed interest in her, she wouldn't have even noticed. Shauna had always teased Alyssa about how little she paid attention to others' view of her, how blind she was to her own natural beauty and sensuality. Even now, Alyssa chuckled and shook her head at the thought of someone thinking she was beautiful, let alone sensual. She grew up in a household where the importance of intelligence outweighed beauty. Her mother told her beauty only got you unwanted attention, that no one took beautiful women seriously, and that looks would only carry you so far in life. Now, a woman of intelligence, she could take on the world, could outsmart and outwit her way to the top and continue using her intelligence to stay there because, once beauty faded, so did the advantages it afforded.

Until she had seen herself through Shauna's eyes, Alyssa had spent her entire life believing she was pretty in an average way. Her looks hadn't been important, so makeup, fashionable clothes, and spending hours at a hairdresser were all unnecessary. She wore sensible clothing that complemented her figure but didn't draw attention to it. And she'd kept her hair in a natural, easily maintainable style. Shauna brought more fashionable and figure-flattering items to Alyssa's wardrobe, showed her how to wear makeup in a way that made her still look natural, and talked her into going to the hairdresser every other week for a blowout. Since Shauna's passing, Alyssa had reverted to not wearing makeup other than her lip glosses and keeping her hair natural. Her wardrobe still had Shauna's touch because Alyssa grudgingly admitted to herself that she liked the way she looked in styles Shauna had shown her looked good on her curvy frame. Finding out, after returning to her natural look, that someone still found her attractive enough to send her flowers and write her love letters made her feel things she hadn't felt in a long time.

Max, her eighty-pound rottweiler-pit bull mix, bounded into the room, laid his huge broad head on the end of the bed, and gazed expectantly at her with his big brown eyes.

"Hey, big boy. Did you finish your dinner?" she asked.

Max harrumphed.

"Okay. Let me just put these away, and we'll go for a walk."

He perked up and wagged his tail as he watched Alyssa carefully place Shauna's letters back in their boxes. As she followed him bounding through the house, she thought about the day he joined their little family. It was the day of Shauna's breast-cancer diagnosis, something Alyssa had no idea had been a concern. Not only had Shauna planned to break that bit of news to her but also tell her she had decided to get a mastectomy of both breasts instead of just the one affected by the cancer and thought to soften the blow by bringing home a puppy. Alyssa had been suggesting they get a dog for months, but Shauna thought caring for a dog would limit their ability to travel as much as they did. As soon as Shauna walked into the house carrying Max, Alyssa knew something was up. She assumed her wife had either done something wrong or was apologizing in advance for something she was about to do.

Alyssa had resented Max's presence for months after that, as if she blamed the innocent puppy for Shauna's cancer, but Max wouldn't hear of it. The more she ignored him, the more attention he wanted from her. Shauna ended up becoming Max's main source of entertainment until she became too weak from her treatments to do more than pet him. Alyssa became the main caretaker for Shauna and mother to their fur baby. The sicker Shauna grew, the more Alyssa and Max leaned on each other for comfort. When the treatments stopped and Shauna got stronger, Max was with them wherever they went. Their travel was limited but only because they chose it to be. If they couldn't drive to their destination and rent a pet-friendly vacation home instead of staying in a hotel, most of the time they didn't go. Max was perfectly fine on long car rides as long as he had his mommies with him. They were a happy little family until less than a year later, just months after they were married, the cancer came back and spread so quickly Shauna could do nothing but bide her time.

Alyssa and Max had to watch the love of their lives grow thinner and sicker once again by the day. Alyssa turned the guest bedroom into Shauna's hospice room and hired a full-time nurse for Shauna and a dog walker for Max while she was at work. She would come home every day to find Max sleeping beside Shauna's bed, barely acknowledging her with a look of greeting, and the scene broke her heart. The night Shauna passed, Max had woken Alyssa up by jumping on the bed and whining pitifully in her face until she finally got up, thinking he needed to go out. But instead of heading toward the front of the house, Max made a beeline back to Shauna's room, then looked back at her and yelped from the doorway. If Max hadn't woken her up, Alyssa wouldn't have had a chance to say good-bye before Shauna closed her eyes for the last time.

Both Alyssa and Max had refused to go back into that room for months. Max obviously took after his other mother and seemed to be the brave one of the two of them, so he was the first to take the steps toward closure. Alyssa came home from work one day to find that Max had taken the blanket Shauna had been using off the chair it had been placed on after they cleared out the hospital equipment and lay curled up on it in the middle of the empty room. She could only stand in the doorway, tears blurring her vision, too afraid to cross the threshold. Max gazed at her with such a human look of understanding that Alyssa would swear to this day that she could hear him in her head telling her, "It's okay. Shauna wouldn't want us to stop living." Locked into Max's bright, expressive eyes, Alyssa had crossed the threshold, lain down with him on the blanket, and cried. Max had stayed there, protectively and patiently waiting for her to finish before he licked away her tears and shoved his broad head into the crook of her neck. They had remained that way, with Alyssa running her fingers through Max's fur, until the house grew dark, and their stomachs grumbled in protest.

It had been the two of them ever since. Max always seemed to know when Alyssa was having a particularly emotional or bad day from missing Shauna. He never left her side on those days, whether it was curling up with her on the sofa or in bed, where she normally wasn't allowed but knew an exception would be made at that moment, for his presence and warmth always comforted her. It didn't take Alyssa long to figure out the real reason Shauna had gotten Max—to comfort her after she was gone. It was as if Shauna had known that her battle would be lost and couldn't bear the thought of leaving Alyssa completely alone. She couldn't imagine where she would have been without her fur baby. If, and when, she decided to start dating again, the person's first test would be to meet Max. If Max didn't like her, there would be no point in even continuing with the possibility of a relationship.

"You'll help Mommy out, won't you," Alyssa asked as she knelt in front of Max to put his harness on. He licked her face and gave a short bark.

Laughing, Alyssa kissed his nose. "That's my big boy."

She walked up the block, waving and nodding at neighbors in greeting, once again wondering who her secret admirer could be. She didn't think it would be any of them. They lived on a quiet residential street with other couples and families, most of which she had a neighborly friendship with. Even if it was one of the few single neighbors, wouldn't they send the flowers to her house instead of the school? They exited the residential block and strolled along a street of storefronts, and Max began pulling Alyssa toward one with a dog-bone-shaped sign that read *Gone to the Dogs Barkery*, an adorable dog bakery and pet boutique.

Alyssa stopped him, and he gazed back at her with a whine. "Don't you have enough treats at home?" she asked when he looked at her as if she had said something sacrilegious. "Okay, fine. One treat and that's it."

They walked into the shop, and Max was happily greeted by some of his neighbor friends in a cacophony of pants and tail wags that threatened to knock over displays.

"Alyssa, Max, I haven't seen you guys in ages!" An older woman with a platinum-gray Afro, big hoop earrings, wrists jangling with bracelets, dressed in jeans and a T-shirt with the shop's logo on it greeted them. She gave Alyssa a hug, then knelt before Max, who happily flopped onto his back to receive his allotted belly rubs.

"Hey, Claudine," Alyssa said.

"How's my vicious beast doing, huh? Are you taking good care of your mommy?" Claudine asked Max as she rubbed his belly. His tail swished and slapped the floor happily.

Alyssa couldn't help but laugh. "It's times like this that remind me he's a dog and not some wizened old man trapped in a dog's body."

"Hey, you never know. Cats aren't the only ones that are supposedly reincarnated souls," Claudine said as she gave one last belly rub and stood.

Max looked up at her and sighed in what could have been annoyance that she had stopped paying attention to him, then turned to his side to watch two of his buddies leave.

"How are you doing, honey?" Claudine asked.

"I'm good."

Claudine cocked her head to the side and looked at her curiously. "Are you?"

Alyssa gave her a reassuring smile. "Yes, I'm good. Really. Max just decided he wanted a treat, and I'm indulging him."

Claudine nodded. "Well, I have his favorite peanut-butter-and-banana cookies."

Max's ears perked up, and he looked at Alyssa expectantly. "You are so spoiled."

They followed Claudine to the counter, where she offered Max a large cookie, and he looked up at Alyssa, waiting for permission to take it. She nodded, and after handing the cookie to him, Claudine put three more in a bakery box.

"Oh, no. The vet already said he's put on a little weight," Alyssa said as Claudine placed the box on the counter in front of her.

Claudine waved dismissively. "He looks great. Anyway, he'd lost too much weight after…" Claudine paused as if realizing what she was about to say.

Alyssa gave her a smile. "It's okay."

Claudine reached over and gave her hand a squeeze. They watched Max enjoy his treat, then lie down contentedly with his head on his paws.

"Oh, my niece is working at your school now. I hadn't seen you since the school year started, so I haven't had a chance to tell you," Claudine said.

"Really? Who's your niece?"

"Collette Roberts. She's the new tennis coach and history teacher. I thought it might be nice to introduce you two. She just moved to town over the summer and hasn't really made any new friends yet."

"Coach Roberts is your niece?"

"Yes. Have you met her yet?"

"Uh, yes, briefly, but we haven't really talked since then." Because I'm a chicken, Alyssa thought.

"Oh, well, I told her I knew you. Maybe she's still getting adjusted. She's been living in California for the past four years."

"Wow. What brought her back to Arizona?"

Claudine frowned. "Divorce. Collette was too good for that woman, though no one asked my opinion. But listen to me, telling other people's business. Hopefully, you gals can connect soon. I think you'd get along great."

Alyssa smiled nervously. "Hopefully. Well, we better get home. I have papers to grade. C'mon, Max."

"It was good to see you, Alyssa. Feel free to stop by anytime. With or without my vicious beast." Claudine gave Max a wink as if he understood her.

If he could roll his eyes, he probably would have at that moment. Instead, he groaned and started heading for the door. Alyssa had just enough time to grab his cookies and follow him out.

♥

The next afternoon at lunch, Alyssa told Vicki about Collette being Claudine's niece.

"Well, isn't this a small world. There's your chance to at least start a conversation with her," Vicki said.

"She's recently divorced, so I can't imagine she's ready to start dating, and she hasn't shown any interest in me."

Vicki sighed. "That's why I suggested starting a conversation. That way you can get to know her and feel her out. How's anyone going to show interest in you if you don't put yourself out there? You're still wearing your wedding band."

Alyssa had thought all morning about approaching Collette until they ran into each other in the front office, and all she could get out was "Good morning" before her mouth went dry, and her mind went blank. She had never been good at talking to women she was attracted to. Trying to come up with witty banter or topics other than the weather always intimidated her. She was doubly intimidated by Collette because she was younger than Alyssa and carried herself with such self-confidence.

"And what happens if I do put myself out there and talk to her, only to find out she's not the least bit interested? Do you know how embarrassing it would be to spend the rest of the school year trying to avoid her?" Alyssa was the queen of excuses when it came to doing something that made her uncomfortable.

Vicki grinned knowingly. "Okay. Well, at least we still have hope with your secret admirer. Do you have any guesses who it might be?"

"No. I suppose we'll have to wait to see if I get another letter."

"Not if…when," Vicki said.

Their lunch break was almost over when Collette walked into the lounge. Alyssa gave her a quick glance, then looked down to concentrate on repacking her lunch bag.

"Coach Roberts," Vicki called.

"What are you doing?" Alyssa whispered frantically.

"What you're too afraid to."

Alyssa wanted to strangle her.

"Good afternoon, ladies," Collette said, her deep voice filled with warmth.

Alyssa slowly gazed up and met her bright smile. "Good afternoon."

"Do you have a moment to join us?" Vicki asked.

Collette looked nervously back toward the entrance, then smiled back at Alyssa and Vicki again. "Uh, yes, thank you, and please, call me Collette."

Vicki nodded. "So, Collette, how are you adjusting to Richmond High School?"

"It's going well. I'm looking forward to the start of the tennis season next month," Collette said.

"Alyssa, weren't you just telling me about the connection you and Collette have?" Vicki said, turning an expectant gaze on Alyssa.

Collette suddenly looked nervous. "Really?"

She was definitely going to strangle Vicki, Alyssa thought. "Yes. I frequent your Aunt Claudine's pet boutique."

Alyssa couldn't be sure, but she could've sworn she saw relief on Collette's face, but then Shari walked in with a cute wicker basket of flowers and headed straight toward their table.

Vicki clapped gleefully. "I told you there would be another one."

"Wow, Mrs. Harris. You seem to be really popular." Shari put the basket on the table. "There was another envelope as well."

"Thank you, Shari," Alyssa said with an embarrassed smile.

"These are simply gorgeous. Don't keep me in suspense. Read the note," Vicki said excitedly.

"Uh, I'll leave you ladies to the rest of your lunch," Collette said, standing to leave.

"Oh, sorry," Vicki said. "It seems Alyssa has a secret admirer, and it's brought so much excitement to our usually dull lunches."

"Dull? I'm not offended at all," Alyssa said sarcastically.

Vicki waved dismissively. "You know what I mean. Anyway, maybe you could join us for lunch tomorrow, Collette."

Collette nodded. "Maybe. Have a good day, ladies."

"You too," Alyssa said, forgetting about her flowers as she watched Collette stride to an empty table across the room.

"Unless you plan to grow some lady balls and ask her out, I suggest you stop torturing yourself by ogling her gorgeous backside," Vicki said, pulling out the envelope tucked into the basket.

Alyssa snatched it back. "Excuse me. Is your name Alyssa?" she asked, grinning.

Vicki held up her hands defensively. "Okay, okay."

Alyssa waved the envelope in front of her nose and detected that floral scent. Not overpowering, it was just enough to tease the senses. With a soft sigh and smile, she retrieved the note from inside.

Dear Alyssa,

Violets are a symbol of affection and considered the perfect gift for someone you may hope to pursue but don't want to seem too forward in doing so. I hope I don't sound too forward in admitting that I have admired you from afar for some time, but I'm not quite ready to reveal myself to you. I believe a little romance and mystery are good for the soul. For now, I will leave you with this thought:

When I close my eyes at night, your face appears before me in dreams so sweet they have me aching from the need of wanting you.

Then daylight filters through my windows, awakening me to the harsh reality that you're truly not here in my arms.

As I walk down the street, all I see is your lovely face, and I wonder how much longer it will be before I can hold you in my arms once again, whisper words in the darkness I so long to say but lack the courage to speak in the light of day.

Were reality but like my dreams, I would feast off your beauty to appease the insatiable hunger I feel at the very thought of you.

I would shed all my inhibitions, opening myself to you as willingly as a flower opens its petals at the gentle touch of the sun.

Why do you haunt my sleep so endlessly? You enter my dreams like a thief in the night to steal my heart, only to toss it aside when daylight arrives, leaving me bruised, battered, and wondering if I'll ever be able to call you mine.

You've barely spoken a word to me. Hardly gazed in my direction. Yet, once the moon begins making its way across the night sky, you become my heart, my soul, my mind, and I shall be forever patient, waiting for the day when you step out of my dreams into reality, and my arms, for there will be no other but you.

With genuine affection,
Your Secret Admirer

Alyssa was once again left speechless by her admirer's words. She handed the letter to Vicki.

"Another swoon-worthy letter. This person has mentioned in both letters that you're acquainted. You still can't figure out who it may be?" Vicki said.

Alyssa took the letter back and read it again. "No idea. I wracked my brain last night. The only person that came up as a possibility was Jamil."

Vicki furrowed her brow. "The chick that Shauna said followed you around like a sick puppy dog when you guys were on that last retreat?"

Alyssa looked at her in amusement. "She didn't follow me around. We just happened to end up in the same workshops. That's all."

"Girl, she was pretty much stalking you. Is she still calling to check up on you?"

"Yeah. When she called me a few weeks ago, she said she would be in town and asked if I wanted to meet for coffee. I politely declined, but I doubt it's her. She doesn't know where I work."

"I don't think you would need to be a super sleuth to find that out. Just do a search of the schools in the area, look up their faculty on the website, and there you are."

Alyssa frowned. "Well, if that didn't just freak me out."

Vicki chuckled. "Sorry. I didn't mean to imply she's a stalker. It's just with today's technology, you can find out pretty much anything on somebody."

Alyssa thought about Jamil and the letters she'd received. She really didn't know her well enough to be sure if she would do something like this. Maybe Jamil was shy like her, and this was the best way she could find to show her feelings, but something in her told her Jamil wasn't her admirer.

"I don't think it's her," Alyssa said, tucking the letter back into the envelope.

"Well, I guess we'll have to wait and see what other clues your admirer reveals. Whoever it is obviously knows something about flowers."

Alyssa smiled. "I think the little tidbits about the meaning of the flowers and connecting it to what she writes are charming."

"Look at you, all schoolgirl blushing over a secret admirer," Vicki said, teasing her.

CHAPTER THREE

Collette sat in her empty classroom trying to grade papers before her next class but couldn't focus. She'd almost given herself away when Alyssa's flowers arrived. She'd tried to be subtle in her escape and could only hope neither Vicki nor Alyssa had noticed the nervous sweat that broke out on her nose. When Vicki had called her over to sit with them, Collette had considered making some excuse like she was just there to grab some coffee. She knew the flowers and note would be delivered any minute but found the opportunity to sit and talk with Alyssa too tempting to decline. When the flowers arrived while she was there, she was almost ready to admit all, but the look of happy anticipation on Alyssa's face stopped her. Collette liked that she was the one that brought that expression on and wasn't ready to give up her secret just yet, especially if it brought Alyssa a spark of happiness. A knock on her classroom door interrupted her, and she was surprised to see Vicki waving at her through the window. Collette motioned her in.

"Hey. Am I interrupting?" Vicki asked.

"No. Just grading some papers. What can I do for you?" Collette offered Vicki her assistant teacher's chair.

Vicki sat down and crossed her long, bare legs, hiking up her moderately short skirt to mid-thigh. How could any of the boys in Vicki's class concentrate with their math teacher looking like a Black version of Kelly LeBrock's character from *Weird Science*?

"I want in," Vicki said, looking very smug.

"Excuse me?"

"You're Alyssa's secret admirer, and I want in for whatever you've got planned."

Collette tried to remain unfazed. Vicki couldn't really know she was Alyssa's secret admirer. "What makes you think it's me?"

"Let's see." Vicki stroked her chin as if she were stroking an invisible beard. "Both times the flowers showed up, you had just walked into the room and practically tripped over yourself trying to get away when they arrived today, and I see the way you look at Alyssa. I wasn't really sure until I watched your face as she read her letter. If you'd stared any harder, she would've burst into flames."

Collette thought about denying it, but Vicki would probably just watch her more carefully after this. She sat back in her chair with a sigh. "I guess I'm not as good at being a secret admirer as I thought."

Vicki chuckled. "You've been good so far. I'm just protective of my girl and was looking out to make sure somebody wasn't out to play games with her heart."

"Please know that isn't my intention. I genuinely have feelings for her."

Vicki nodded. "I can tell by the letters, and I want to help."

"Seriously? Why?"

"Like I said, Alyssa is my girl, and I want to see her find happiness. Shauna wouldn't want her closing herself away like she is. I see the way she looks at you, and since the feeling seems to be mutual, I want to help move things along."

Collette's eyes widened. "She has feelings for me?"

Vicki smirked. "She's at least hot for you, and that's a good start."

Collette couldn't believe it. Alyssa liked her, and her best friend was offering to help with her plan.

"So, will you let me?" Vicki asked.

"I guess so, but I'm not sure how you can."

Vicki sat forward in the chair, grinning happily. "Excellent. First, it's obvious from your notes that you knew Alyssa before. You have to tell me how."

Collette hesitated.

"You can trust me," Vicki said sincerely.

"I took one of her writing workshops six years ago."

Vicki's eyes widened in surprise. "Six years ago? You've been crushing on Alyssa for six years?"

Collette's face heated with embarrassment. "Not exactly. Yes, I was interested in her and was about to ask her out when I found out she was with Shauna. I continued in the workshop, staying in the background because I was afraid that if she noticed me, she'd see how, despite knowing she was engaged, my feelings grew during that couple of months."

It felt strange admitting her secret to Vicki. Collette had never told anyone about Alyssa and the effect she'd had on her. "In addition to Alyssa's natural beauty and the sexy, graceful way she carries herself, her joy of teaching and writing had a huge effect on me. I'd been struggling with my own writing at the time, and Alyssa helped free me of a lot of things that were holding me back."

"I understand why you couldn't admit your feelings for her then, but why didn't you ever tell her that? Alyssa loves to hear stuff like that from people who attended her workshops."

"I couldn't tell her how she helped me without admitting to so much more." Collette opened one of her desk drawers, pulled out a paperback book, and handed it to Vicki.

Vicki looked at it and back at Collette in confusion. "The Rayne Edwards Mysteries. I'm familiar with them. Ironically, they're Alyssa's favorite books. She always hoped she'd have a chance to meet R. Cole at one of the retreats she attended, but supposedly Cole likes to stay anonymous."

Collette grinned sheepishly. "R. Cole at your service."

Vicki seemed even more confused. Then a comical look of disbelief came across her face. "You're the anonymous R. Cole?" she practically shouted.

Collette gazed back toward the closed door, then pressed a finger to her lips. "I'd like to keep it that way."

"Of course. Sorry, but this is amazing!" Vickie gave her a mischievous grin. "Shauna used to tease Alyssa by telling her if they ever did meet the author, she could be Alyssa's hall pass."

Collette's face heated again. "I can't believe she's a fan."

Vicki gave an unladylike snort. "She's not a fan. She's a disciple. She once paid a hundred dollars at a charity silent auction for an autographed copy of your first novel."

"Seriously?"

Vicki nodded. "What do the novels have to do with Alyssa, besides her coincidentally being obsessed with them?"

Collette picked up her phone and opened a photo of a sketch someone had done of what they thought Rayne looked like from her description in the books and showed it to Vickie.

"That's a beautiful sketch of Alyssa. Did you do that?"

"It's fan art of Rayne based on the descriptions of her in the novels." Collette gazed down at the picture. It wasn't until she received the sketch that she had realized how much Alyssa had affected more than her writing skills.

"You modeled the main character of your entire series on Alyssa?" Vicki said in disbelief.

Collette nodded, unable to say it out loud. It sounded like such a stalkerish thing to do.

"Wow," Vicki said, looking back down at the book in her hand. Then she looked warily back up at Collette. "Please don't tell me you're one of those crazies that would take a job at the same place as the object of their desire to be near them. That's first-rate stalker shit there. I won't hesitate to turn you in."

Collette held up her hands. "No, I didn't. I swear! When I moved to town, my aunt told me she'd heard about the job from Principal Hart when he visited her store. He knew she had a niece that played tennis and told her they were looking for a coach. I had heard about Shauna's passing, but I didn't know Alyssa worked here until I told my aunt I had gotten the job."

Vicki looked relieved. "If you knew about Shauna and you obviously still have a thing for Alyssa, what made you wait until now, anonymously, to reveal your interest in her?"

Collette shrugged. "I knew when I saw them together while I was attending Alyssa's workshop that they had a strong love, so I can't imagine it having been easy for her to get over losing Shauna. I didn't want to intrude only to be shot down because she's still mourning her loss."

"What happened to change your mind?"

"I overheard your conversation about her dating again. I wasn't snooping, I swear," Collette said in response to Vicki's narrowed gaze. "Alyssa said she wanted to be wooed the old-fashioned way, so I saw that as the perfect opportunity to put myself out there, anonymously. If the flowers and note ended up in the trash, then I'd know she wasn't ready to move on and my feelings wouldn't be stomped on too much since she would never know it was me. Since they didn't end up in the trash and she seems genuinely happy to get them, I'll continue until Valentine's Day, when I'll reveal myself and hope she'll at least let me take her to dinner or something."

Vicki smiled. "Well, I can definitely tell you that you had her at the first note. Handwritten, special stationery, and poetic words. You hit all the check marks to woo her."

Collette couldn't help the happy grin that appeared. "You think so?"

"I know so. Now, what's the next move?"

"Like I said, continue with the flowers and note, and then reveal myself on Valentine's Day."

Vicki nodded. "Good. What's not broken doesn't need fixing. Besides, I'm not the poetry and love letter type, so I wouldn't be able to help you with that, but I could help you with the big reveal."

Collette was suddenly nervous. "I hadn't planned on anything big."

Vicki grinned. "Oh, honey. The only way to finish this is big, and I have the perfect idea."

♥

Later that night Collette sat at home wondering if pulling Vicki into her plans was such a good idea. She had to nix the first two suggestions Vicki had come up with. The first was to have Collette show up at the dance on horseback wearing a Prince Charming outfit spouting Shakespearean sonnets. The next was to set up a flash mob at the dance, with her and Alyssa's students performing the last dance scene from *Dirty Dancing*, Alyssa's favorite movie. It wasn't until Collette threatened to just tell Alyssa the next day that Vicki came up with an acceptable idea. It made Collette look forward to the day rather than quake in nervous fear.

She still found it weird that she was doing all of this when she could've just as easily walked up to Alyssa, reminded her of how they first met, and asked her out for coffee or lunch. After her debacle of a marriage, Collette had promised herself she would no longer go all out for another woman unless she had some guarantee that her feelings wouldn't be unrequited. Considering what little she knew about Alyssa, Collette didn't think that would be the case.

Vicki told her that Alyssa ate this stuff up. She also told her about Shauna writing Alyssa love notes on a regular basis. After hearing that detail, Collette worried she would bring up sad memories for Alyssa, but Vicki assured her everything was fine.

Collette also thought about Vicki telling her that Alyssa was attracted to her but had a hang-up about their age difference and was too shy to approach her. Collette didn't mind taking the initiative. She had always believed life was too short to waste time not going after something you wanted. She also didn't mind the age gap. She thought older women were sexy because they usually weren't about playing games. They knew what they wanted for themselves, what they wanted for their life, and what pleased them. Collette was the same way, and her ex had accused her of being set in her ways. Collette called it being self-assured. Alyssa might be shy, but Collette could tell she was self-aware and carried herself with an unconscious self-confidence that made her glow.

Collette smiled to herself. Even if it didn't turn out like she hoped, all this secret-admirer stuff would be worth the happiness she was able to bring to Alyssa's life.

Her phone rang, and she groaned as her ex-wife's name flashed on the screen.

"What can I do for you, Lani," Collette answered, not bothering to keep the annoyance from her tone.

"Wow? Is that how you greet your wife?" Lani said.

"Ex-wife."

"Damn, you're one cold woman, Collette."

"You should know. You made me that way." That was a low blow, but Collette couldn't help it. Lani pricked her anger like no one ever had.

The sound of Lani sighing on the other end told Collette her jab had landed squarely. "Look. I didn't call to pick a fight with you. I need your help."

Here it comes, Collette thought, secretly hoping this call would be different than all the others that had followed their divorce. "With what?"

"My next project is short on funds, and I was hoping you could, maybe, sign on as an investor. I'll even give you the executive producer title."

Collette could hear the desperation in Lani's voice. "No."

"No? Just like that? You don't even want to hear what the project is about?"

"No. I'm done funding projects that never see the light of day. I'm done funding the ability for you to do nothing all day but create works you never finish. I made my last spousal-support payment two months ago, and I don't plan to make any more of them or *investments*."

"This is the real thing, Cole, I promise. It's at the end and should be done within a month. I just need the funds to get there."

Hearing Lani say the nickname she'd given Collette when they first started dating grated on her nerves. "How many times do I need to say it, Lani? NO!"

"So, you're just going to leave a sister hanging like that? What happened to supporting one another? Building each other up?" Lani asked sarcastically.

"I supported you for three years—gave you most of my money, my love, and almost my freedom doing it. I'm done. If that's all you called for, then I have to go. I have papers to grade," Collette said tiredly.

"Papers to grade? You were serious about that teaching gig? You're, like, a former tennis star. I thought for sure you'd be teaching tennis at some bougie country club or desert resort."

"Yeah, well, I'm not. Bye, Lani." Collette hung up before Lani could say anything further to confirm that their divorce was the right decision.

She tossed her phone aside and buried her face in her hands. Lani Grayson was her burden to bear for following what was between her legs instead of her head when they met. Collette had become acquainted with Lani just a few short months after she moved to Los Angeles. She had gone to a mixer after a friend's play, of which Lani had been the star. The actress's exotic beauty awed her, much different than Alyssa's soft, natural beauty that had been the subject of her thoughts all those months. Lani's parents were gorgeous. Her mother was Nigerian, her father Samoan, and their daughter managed to inherit both of their good looks, which combined into one beautiful and sexy woman. They'd had a whirlwind romance and were living together within a few months after meeting. Collette was so enthralled with Lani and the circles she traveled in that it wasn't until too late that she discovered a vain, spoiled, selfish person under the pretty exterior.

Collette could look back and see the warning signs, but at the time she chose to ignore them, thinking love and marriage would change Lani. That belief was shot to hell when she took a red-eye home a day early from a meeting with her publisher to surprise Lani and found her and the director of an independent film she was starring in asleep in their bed. Collette hadn't even woken them up. She'd simply gone into the kitchen, made some coffee, and sat at the counter waiting for them. It only took a few moments for the director to come hurrying out of the room, barely giving Collette a nervous glance as he'd rushed past her and out the door. Lani had taken a little longer to make her appearance.

When she did, she looked refreshed and beautiful as always, pouring herself a cup of coffee and complaining about Collette not telling her she was coming home early. Like her wife hadn't just caught her in bed with a man. All the selfish, mean things Lani had said or done that she had ignored or let slide came back to Collette. Add what had just happened to the pile, and it all fell on her like a load of bricks. She'd walked right past Lani, grabbed her suitcase and backpack that had still been sitting by the front door, and told Lani she had a week to get out. When Lani had asked where she was supposed to go, Collette had told her she didn't care, but it wouldn't be pleasant if she was still there when she returned. Then she walked out.

Even though the apartment was leased in her name, Collette had left, because for the first time in her life, she was afraid of laying her hands on another woman in violence. If she had stayed and insisted Lani be the one to leave, the drama queen would have put on her best performance yet as the broken little girl whose parents' volatile relationship left her not knowing how to truly love someone until she'd met Collette.

It was a performance Lani had put on twice shortly after they moved in together. The first was when Collette found her backstage after a performance hemmed up in a corner with another actor. The other was when she had mistakenly sent Collette an intimate message meant for someone else. Lani had cried and begged Collette with huge crocodile tears to be patient with her. This was all new for her because she never saw a loving relationship from her parents, so she didn't know how to love someone back that way.

She should have gotten an Oscar for those performances because Collette had fallen for her lies despite her sister, her aunt, and her best friend telling her that she was too good for Lani. She had ignored them and reaped whatever heartache she sowed from it. Now, all Collette wanted to do was move on with her life, find a woman who would appreciate her for her and not for what she could do for them, and be happy.

That brought her back to thinking about Alyssa and her task at hand. Collette wasn't grading papers as she'd told Lani. She was writing her next letter to Alyssa, but she certainly wasn't going to tell her ex-wife that. She reread what she'd written, smiled in satisfaction, and placed it in the envelope. Tomorrow's flower was the peony. It was no coincidence that Vicki had told her it was Alyssa's favorite flower and that she had already planned to gift her with the bloom for the third letter. She wasn't usually superstitious or the type of person who believed in fate, but Collette was beginning to think that more than coincidence was bringing her and Alyssa together. Whatever it was, she was just going to go with it and hoped it turned out well.

♥

Alyssa had always looked forward to her lunch breaks. It wasn't just the time away from the kids but also the chance to socialize with her fellow teachers. Sadly, she didn't have much of a social life outside of work unless Vicki talked her into doing something, so this was the only time she conversed with other adults besides her neighbors. Now, since she'd been receiving the flowers and anonymous letters, her lunch break couldn't come fast enough. Word had spread about her mysterious secret admirer, and the teachers were making bets and whispering about who it might be. Another teacher? A student with a crush? Someone from her past? Alyssa couldn't imagine it being another teacher, considering she'd known most of them for years now, and they all pretty much knew she was gay. Only Vicki had read the letters, and they both determined that they weren't letters from a teenage crush. The last could be a possibility since she hadn't completely ruled out Jamil.

"So, who shall we eliminate today as your wooing admirer?" Vicki asked.

"You know, Phillip Randolph has had a bit of a crush on you for some time," Elizabeth, the school's advanced-biology teacher whispered conspiratorially. She and Frank Walcott, the senior choir director had joined Alyssa and Vicki for lunch.

"Good Lord, I hope not," Frank said. "One, he knows she's gay, and two, he's as dull as a rusty butter knife."

"And how would you know that?" Vicki asked with a quirked brow.

Frank snorted. "It's not even like that. We ended up at the same mixer during the teachers' conference back in November, and all he talked about was his cat and ex-wife."

"Well, it was just after his divorce became final after the wringer she'd put him through for almost a year," Alyssa said in sympathy.

"That's even more reason to rule him out. He's not over her yet," Frank said.

"Whoever it is, finding out makes me more nervous than receiving the flowers and letters. It's like anticipating the release of a book from your favorite author, and then when you finally read it, it doesn't live up to their usual reputation. You're disappointed and left wondering if they were really that good in the first place," Alyssa said.

Vicki chuckled. "Wow. You're not giving them much of a chance, are you?"

Alyssa shrugged. "Better to start with low expectations. That way I won't be too disappointed."

The others laughed, and then the room went quiet as Shari entered the lounge, grinning with her daily delivery in hand. Alyssa felt uncomfortable as all eyes turned toward her when Shari set the bouquet of huge red peonies in front of her.

"Mrs. Harris, I just want you to know that this has become the highlight of my day. I don't leave the office until the flowers arrive just so I can be the one to bring them to you. It's so romantic," Shari said dreamily.

Alyssa smiled at the young woman. "Thank you, Shari."

Shari nodded and left. Alyssa saw the usual floral envelope peeking from the wrapping and gently pulled it out. It seemed the whole room watched her with anticipation, and she suddenly felt nervous. Vicki must have seen her expression.

She stood, placing her hands on her hips, and looked around the room. "Can y'all at least give a girl some privacy?"

Everyone averted their gaze, trying to look busy, but Alyssa could still feel their discreet glances. Elizabeth and Frank didn't even bother to try. They grinned at her, waiting for her to open the envelope. With a sigh of resignation, she lifted the flap and pulled out the scented paper.

"Tell me that is not a handwritten note!" Frank said excitedly. "Who takes the time to write an entire letter by hand these days? Girl, whoever this is, they're a keeper."

"That is so romantic," Elizabeth said.

"Do I need to kick you two out of here?" Vicki asked.

Frank vigorously shook his head, and Elizabeth mimed locking her mouth closed.

"Go ahead and have your moment," Vicki said.

Alyssa smiled at her in appreciation and unfolded the letter.

Dear Alyssa,

The first day I laid eyes on you I thought of this flower. It's believed that in Greek mythology, the peony was created when a beautiful nymph named Paeonia attracted the attention of Apollo, who began to flirt with her. Paeonia real-

ized Aphrodite was watching them, and she became bashful and turned bright red. In anger, Aphrodite transformed the nymph into a red peony. Therefore, the peony is known to symbolize beauty and bashfulness.

I will not compare your beauty to a flower, for a flower's beauty eventually dulls and withers. Like Paeonia, your beauty rivals that of the goddess Aphrodite, but instead of causing anger and jealousy, it causes me to be the bashful one. I want to hide shyly away behind these letters until I have the courage to reveal all.

Like Apollo, I am enamored of you, my Paeonia, for no other's beauty compares to yours. And what makes you even more enchanting is that you are not even aware of the physical attributes you carry so freely because so much of the beauty within you rivals what's on the outside.

I dare to hope for the day when I will be able to show you in action, not just written word, how lovely you are to me. Until then, like Apollo, I shall worship you from afar, my Paeonia.

With genuine affection,
Your Secret Admirer

Like always, Alyssa handed the letter to Vicki as she tried to settle the butterflies taking flight in her belly and keep her heart from melting. She brought the bouquet of flowers to her face and inhaled deeply. The peony was her favorite flower. Did her secret admirer know that? Was that why the person said they thought of the peony when they first saw her?

"Wow," Vicki said.

Frank sighed dramatically. "Okay. Do we get to know what it says? Between the starry-eyed look on Miss Alyssa's face and your reaction, we're dying over here."

"That's completely up to Alyssa," Vicki said, holding the letter close as if she were afraid Frank would snatch it.

Alyssa didn't see any harm in letting them read it. She nodded, and Vicki handed the letter to Frank, who scooted his chair closer to Elizabeth so they could read it together. Alyssa gazed back down at the flowers. This was just too much to be a coincidence. Few people knew what her favorite flower was—her mother, Shauna, and Vicki.

She glanced at Vicki. "So, my secret admirer just happened to send and compare me to my favorite flower in my favorite color, and you still expect me to believe this isn't you playing with me after our conversation the other day?"

Vicki shook her head and held her hand up. "I will swear on a stack of Bibles that I had nothing to do with this. You know I am not romantic or a writer."

Alyssa still looked at her doubtfully, but Vicki was telling the truth. Her idea of romantic gestures was being taken to an expensive restaurant or gifted with a designer bag. With the money her family had, Vicki really didn't need a man to buy anything for her, but she still appreciated the thought.

"Well, it's obviously somebody you know," Elizabeth said. "They reference knowing how beautiful you are on the inside as well as the outside, and only someone close to you would know that."

"This is downright romance-novel stuff," Frank said, folding the letter and handing it back to Alyssa.

Alyssa tucked it back in the envelope. "Maybe it is Jamil?"

"You think?" Vicki said.

"Isn't that the woman Shauna told us was crushing on you?" Frank said.

Alyssa forgot Frank and Elizabeth knew about that. The fellow teachers and friends had come to a dinner party she and Shauna had hosted, and somehow the conversation had turned to crushes. Shauna had told everyone about Jamil.

"Yes, but she lives in Colorado," Alyssa said.

"And…" Vicki said with a quirked brow.

"And how would she get handwritten letters to the florist every day to send with the flowers?"

"She could've mailed a stack of them to a local florist with instructions about what to do," Elizabeth said.

"Ooh, I got it! We could talk to the florists in the area, find out which ones the flowers are coming from, and see if they'll tell you who's sending them," Frank said excitedly.

"Or we could just leave it alone, let my girl here continue to feel special, and wait for whatever big reveal her admirer has planned," Vicki said.

Alyssa narrowed her gaze at Vicki. "How do you know it's going to be big?"

"C'mon. Do you think someone that would do all this would let the build-up fizzle out without doing something awesome to reveal who they are? Let's just let things play out and see what happens on Valentine's Day," Vicki said.

Alyssa nodded, but she still suspected that Vicki was involved somehow. She just hoped it wasn't a prank because she was starting to think maybe Shauna was right about her being lonely. She missed having human companionship at home.

CHAPTER FOUR

Collette sat in the office she was assigned in the athletic department eating her lunch alone. She had avoided the teacher's lounge today, too paranoid about giving herself away when Alyssa's flowers and letter arrived. If Vicki had been able to read her reactions well enough to figure out what was going on, there was no telling who else would have and blown her cover. It was better just to keep a low profile until Valentine's Day.

The door opened, and Vicki rushed in, face flushed and breathing heavy. "I've been looking everywhere for you." She dropped into one of the guest chairs with a tired sigh.

"Have you been running?" Collette asked in amusement.

"No, but these shoes were only made for short spurts, not a full walk across the building. I thought you'd be in your classroom, and then I checked the office, the student cafeteria, and finally made my way here."

"What was so important you risked wearing down the heel on your Manolos for?"

"You know your designer shoes. I'm impressed."

"Ex-wife had a closet full of them. Anyway, what's up?"

"So, I just wanted to give you a heads-up. I almost blew it today, and Alyssa is now suspicious of me being involved. I managed to throw her off, but she's no dummy. We've been friends too long for her not to be able to read me like your books that she buries her nose in."

Collette sat back in her chair. "Maybe I should just confess. End this before it gets out of hand."

Vicki waved a hand dismissively. "No. Don't be silly. For the first time since Shauna passed away, Alyssa is genuinely looking forward to something not related to her students or her dog. She needs this, and

I think when it all comes together, you'll be happy with the outcome. Now, I have to make it back to my room before my next class, so this will be the last time I'll bug you in person until the big day. If somehow Alyssa found out we were meeting up she'll either figure it out or think I'm playing matchmaker, neither of which I want to happen. From now on, we'll text to finalize logistics."

"All right."

Vicki nodded, stood, and headed for the door but turned back. "Oh, and Collette."

"Yes?"

"What you're doing, I think it's wonderful, and I believe Shauna would approve," Vicki said with a wink before exiting the office.

Collette stared at the door long after Vicki was out of sight. She felt lighter after what Vicki had said about Shauna approving. The worry of whether all this was a waste of time because she didn't think she could ever live up to Shauna's image in Alyssa's life suddenly lifted. Collette had met Shauna once during the last night of the writers' workshop she attended. Alyssa had allowed everyone to invite someone to attend a sort of graduation she'd planned, where everyone would perform readings from the work they had been doing during the workshop. Shauna had attended, which had been a thrill for many of the students because she was a best-selling fantasy and sci-fi author in her own right. She had helped Alyssa choose winners for special awards they had given out, then hosted a mixer at a nearby restaurant for the class and their guests.

Collette had won one of the awards that night for a mystery short story with a bit of sci-fi elements she had added to challenge herself. Shauna had approached her to tell her how much she not only enjoyed her reading but the whole story in general. It seemed Alyssa had let her read some of the stories she thought were particularly good, and Collette's was one of them. She was ashamed to admit that she hadn't wanted to like Shauna, but the fiancée of the woman she was secretly in love with was nothing but charming and cordial, chatting and giving helpful advice in her melodic Irish brogue. It was also obvious that she absolutely adored Alyssa, watching her as she made her rounds speaking with each of her students and their guests.

Collette's aunt, who had come as her guest, and Shauna were talking when Alyssa had made her way over to them. Collette almost melted into a puddle as Alyssa told her that her story had entertained her, that she had real talent, and that she wouldn't be surprised if Collette didn't get picked up quickly by an agent or publisher. She must not have been too good at hiding her feelings because, as Alyssa and Shauna were walking away, she'd caught a knowing grin on Shauna's face and wished the floor had opened and swallowed her. Collette had left shortly after that, and it had been the last time she'd seen either one of them until she took the job here.

Collette had heard from her agent about Shauna's death, which, surprisingly, hit her harder than she would've expected it to. Shauna was a talented author, and her passing was a sad loss to the lesbian fiction community, but also, she knew Alyssa had to have been devastated. She'd donated to the cancer charity Alyssa had asked people to give to in Shauna's memory and wished she could do more, but Alyssa didn't know her from Adam, so she didn't intend to reach out to her. Even after finding out Alyssa worked at the same school, the thought of asking her out didn't cross Collette's mind. Alyssa could've still been grieving, and Collette couldn't imagine trying to take Shauna's bold, beautiful place in Alyssa's life until she overheard Alyssa and Vicki's conversation. To have Vicki say she thought Shauna would approve meant more to Collette than Vicki could've imagined.

♥

Alyssa awoke the next morning a little disappointed that it was Saturday. Since she had received the flowers and letters from her secret admirer only while she was at work, she assumed she wouldn't get anything on the weekends. It had been only three days, but she looked forward to the daily dose of romance. She hadn't realized how much it meant to her until yesterday's delivery that came with her favorite flower. She figured that part was a coincidence and doubted the person knew it was her favorite, but the letter made it feel special just the same.

"Are you ready for our morning run, Max?" Alyssa asked as she threw her covers aside and stepped into her slippers.

She looked over the end of the bed, surprised not to find him curled up in his doggy bed. "Max?" she called as she made her way toward the front of the house. Max yipped in response, and Alyssa found him lying at the door with his tail happily slapping the floor.

"Got tired of waiting for me, huh?" she asked as she bent over and gave him a scratch behind the ears. "Let me just grab a protein bar to eat while I get dressed, and then we can head out," she said, turning toward the kitchen.

Max yipped again, and when Alyssa turned back around, he was staring at the door.

"What is it?" Alyssa walked over to the window beside the door and peeked out. She could see a bag on her porch.

Hoping it was from who she thought it was, Alyssa rushed to open the door to find a floral decorated gift bag with a bottle of wine, a box of chocolates, and the signature stationery. Her secret admirer knew where she lived. Alyssa couldn't decide whether to be creeped out or to wonder if this was the person's way of throwing her off that it was someone at school. She looked up and down the street but didn't see anyone at that hour on a Saturday morning except her fellow early rising neighbors, who waved in passing. She waved and hurried back into the house with an excited Max hot on her heels. His tail wagged as he looked at her expectantly.

"Sorry, buddy. There's nothing for you. Did you see anyone?" Alyssa asked him.

He cocked his big head to the side and looked at her as if to say, "If I did, I couldn't tell you. I don't talk, remember?"

Alyssa shook her head with a chuckle, grabbed the last cookie from the box Claudine had given her the other day, and gave it to him. He happily took it, lay down, and slowly ate it piece by piece, as if he knew it was the last one and needed to savor it. Alyssa felt nervous as she took the envelope from the bag. Seeing her name written in the now-familiar script made her heart skip a beat. She hadn't had this feeling of excited anticipation in a long time. For just a moment she felt guilty about it being for someone else, especially someone she might not even know. Then she remembered her dream and her promise to Shauna. She had nothing to feel guilty about. She had actively shut herself away and mourned for the past five years. Deep within her heart she would always mourn the loss of Shauna, but it was time to move on. With trembling fingers, she pulled the paper from the envelope.

Dear Alyssa,

Just a little something to enjoy this weekend. I believe wine is just as beautiful an expression of admiration as flowers. It takes passion, creativity, and respect to carefully bring the fruit of the vine to the bottle. It is very much like building a loving relationship, and just like love, sharing wine is an intimate and special experience that I hope we can share soon.

There's no special meaning for the truffles. I just think they go well with the wine (winking smiley face). Enjoy!

Have a wonderful weekend.

With genuine affection,

Your Secret Admirer

Alyssa pulled out the rest of the contents in the bag—a twelve-piece box of Godiva dark-chocolate truffles. The wine surprised her. She wasn't an expert. Vicki was the enthusiast, but she knew this wasn't your run-of-the-mill, off-the-shelf wine. It was a Vin Santo Italian wine, which could average forty dollars a bottle. Whoever her secret admirer was, they had good and expensive tastes. She ruled out the possibility of it being one of her fellow teachers just from the expense of the wine. Besides, the attention to detail, the romance of it all, and the handwritten letters felt to her like things a woman would do. Besides herself, the only other gay teachers she knew of at the school were Frank and Collette. Obviously, it wasn't Frank, and Alyssa immediately ruled out Collette because she believed if Collette were interested in her, she wouldn't go through all this. She would probably ask her out directly. That left only one person, Jamil.

The nervous anticipation Alyssa had felt earlier dissipated. Jamil was nice, and she could see her as a friend, but nothing about her attracted Alyssa to her romantically. Alyssa liked strong, independent, self-aware women. Jamil always came off as a bit needy and insecure. Could this secret-admirer role be her way of being bold? She was an author of regency-style romances, so this very well could be something she would do since Alyssa had turned down her invitations to meet up when she was in town. Romance her from afar to get her interest piqued, then show up on Valentine's Day to reveal herself. Alyssa sighed in frustration. She would hate to have to face Jamil that way. A stranger wouldn't be hard to turn away, but having to shoot down someone she knew already would be heartbreaking. Max whined and bumped her hip with his head.

"Oh, sorry, buddy. Let me go change, and we'll get going." She ruffled his head and jogged to the bedroom to change into her running gear.

♥

Collette restocked the packaged dog treats on a shelf at her aunt's pet boutique, grinning at her own ingenuity. When her aunt had asked her last night if she could cover for her at the shop today while she took care of some business, Collette decided it would be the perfect opportunity to drop off an unexpected gift to Alyssa from her secret admirer. She had texted Vicki to make sure it wouldn't feel a little creepy having her secret admirer know where she lived, but Vicki thought it would be a great way to throw Alyssa off, not that she was thinking Collette was her admirer, but it wouldn't hurt to have her thinking it may be someone outside the workplace. Vicki had even given her Alyssa's Saturday morning routine. She got up at six a.m. for her morning run with her dog, Max, stopped at her favorite café for coffee, stopped back at home to freshen up to go grocery shopping or run errands, took Max to the dog park, and then spent the rest of the day being antisocial unless Vicki got her back out of the house.

Since Collette couldn't leave the shop until closing, she had to drop her gift off at five a.m. to avoid possibly running into Alyssa or being seen by one of her neighbors. That meant she was at the shop early, trying to find a way to stay busy for almost three hours until it opened. It made for a longer day than she normally had on a Saturday, but it was worth it. Or at least she'd know if it was worth it when Vicki texted her later to tell her if her gift was well-received or not.

The sound of the oven timer beeping had Collette rushing to the back of the shop to take her aunt's homemade dog treats out of the oven. She placed them on the cooling rack, trayed the ones she'd left cooling on another rack, and headed back toward the front when the bell over the door jingled, letting her know she had a customer. She almost dropped the tray of treats when she saw Alyssa looking at a rack of dog collars. It took Collette a moment to notice the huge black-and-tan dog sitting obediently beside Alyssa but eyeing Collette curiously. She smiled at him and could swear he smiled back as his mouth opened and his tongue lolled out, but he didn't move an inch from his spot. She slid the tray into the display case, smoothed her *Gone to the Dogs* T-shirt, and softly cleared her throat.

"Good morning," Collette said in greeting.

Alyssa looked up at Collette in confusion, then wide-eyed surprise. "Uh…Good morning."

"My aunt had some business to take care of and asked me to cover for her today." Collette answered Alyssa's unasked question.

Alyssa gave her a bashful smile. "Oh…uh…okay, well, I was just looking for a new collar. It seems my procrastination in replacing the very worn-out one Max was wearing until a few minutes ago has caught up with me."

Collette was surprised. "He's sitting there so obediently to not have a collar on."

Alyssa scratched behind Max's ear. "My big boy graduated top of the class at obedience, behavioral, and agility training, didn't you, buddy?"

Max's tail slapped the floor happily at the love and praise. Collette came around the counter and slowly walked toward the pair. Max might have a master's in training, but he was still a dog, and Collette knew to approach carefully so as not to seem threatening.

"May I pet him?" she asked.

"Yes. Thank you for asking first. People that aren't intimidated by his size usually just walk up and start petting him, which makes him skittish."

Collette stopped a few steps away and offered her fist to Max, who looked at it, then up at Alyssa for permission.

Alyssa smiled lovingly down at him. "Go ahead. Say hello."

Max walked up to Collette, sniffed her fist, licked it, then flopped down at her feet onto his back.

"He only does that for one other person—your aunt," Alyssa said in surprise.

Collette knelt and rubbed Max's belly. "Maybe I have a similar smell. Or it's the dog treats I just took out of the oven." She smiled up at Alyssa.

Alyssa's face darkened in a blush as she smiled shyly. "Maybe."

Collette gave Max one last pat, then stood. "Do you think your mom would mind if I gave you a treat?"

At the word *treat*, Max scrambled up on all fours, almost knocking over the display Alyssa was looking at, and stared expectantly at Collette.

Alyssa chuckled. "That's a dangerous word to mention around him."

Collette smiled. "I guess so."

"Well, since he was such a good boy the last bit of our walk without a collar, I guess he deserves a reward," Alyssa said, giving Max a firm pat. "C'mon, fella."

Max waited for Alyssa to come alongside him and walked with her to the counter before sitting obediently, watching her with pure adoration.

Collette walked back behind the counter, grabbed one of the fresh large dog biscuits she'd just brought out, and handed it to Max, who waited for Alyssa to tell him he could have it. Alyssa nodded, and Max gently took the biscuit from Collette's outstretched hand and lay down to enjoy his treat.

"Wow. He really is well-behaved," Collette said.

"When Shauna brought him home from the shelter, they warned her that he would probably get big, but we had no idea how big. When he started outgrowing his collars in a matter of months, she insisted we take training classes to learn how to handle him. After we lost Shauna…" Alyssa looked down at Max with a sad smile, "training and agility classes kind of became our weekly activity to keep us occupied. Max is the reason I started running. The trainer suggested it might be a good way to help keep his energy level down and to help us bond."

"It's good that you have each other," Collette said sympathetically.

"Yeah," Alyssa said, looking sad again.

Collette hated that her comment might have brought that sadness on. "So, I hear you're one of the chaperones for the Sweetheart Dance," she said, hoping to pull Alyssa out of her sadness.

"Yes. I've avoided it the past few years. Vicki usually takes my spot, but she says she has a date, so I guess it's my turn."

"Well, I'll be chaperoning as well. Will you be joining the teachers' after-party with drinks at Lido's? I hear it can get pretty wild."

"Probably not. I'm not much of an after-party kind of girl. I'll probably just head home and watch a movie or something." She slid the collar she'd decided on and her credit card across the counter. "I'll just take this. I've gotta get out of these sweaty clothes and shower."

Collette grinned, and Alyssa blushed and looked away as if she'd realized the sexy image that statement suggested.

Collette took her out of her obvious misery by ringing up her purchase, cutting the tag off the collar, and handing everything back to her. Their fingers brushed, and Collette felt as if she'd had a jolt of electricity from the contact. Alyssa must have felt it also, because her face darkened further, and she quickly turned away to place the new collar around Max's neck.

"Please tell your aunt I said hello, and I guess I'll see you Monday," Alyssa said before quickly turning and hurrying out of the shop.

Collette watched her go with a shake of her head. She thought Vicki had been exaggerating when she told her Alyssa was hopeless when it came to flirting. Collette had the feeling that if she had just come right out and asked Alyssa for a date, she probably would've still run in the other direction. Hopefully, her secret-admirer plan was warming Alyssa up enough to accept Collette openly expressing her interest when reveal time came.

♥

"I feel like such an idiot," Alyssa said to Vicki, who had come over for their annual Valentine's Movie Night, although they had currently forgotten the movie they were watching.

They usually did it on Valentine's Day so Alyssa wouldn't have to spend it alone, and Vicki thought the holiday was too contrived, which was why it surprised her that Vicki had accepted a date for that night.

"Why? You didn't do anything but mention to another sexy lesbian that you were all sweaty and needed to take off your clothes and shower." Vicki winked teasingly.

With a heavy sigh, Alyssa refilled her glass with the wine she had received that morning from her admirer. "Do you think she read anything into it?"

Vicki waved dismissively. "I doubt it. She knew you'd just come back from a run. I'm sure she considered it an innocent comment."

"I guess. I ran out of there so fast I barely said good-bye."

Vicki narrowed her gaze at Alyssa. "You sound like you want her to be interested after you made all these excuses as to why you couldn't date if she was."

Alyssa's face heated. "No. I just don't want to give her the wrong idea, that's all. Like I was flirting or something."

Vicki grinned. "I can't imagine her thinking you running away was flirting."

"Shut up," Alyssa said, trying to hold back her own grin.

"This wine is wonderful. Slide that box of chocolates over," Vicki said.

Alyssa shoved the box across the coffee table to Vicki. "Did I tell you how good she was introducing herself to Max and how he reacted to her?"

"Are we still discussing Collette Roberts? Your secret admirer drops off this delicious, and expensive, bottle of wine, and you want to talk about someone you supposedly don't want to date?" Vicki asked, her brow quirked in question.

Alyssa shrugged and sipped at her wine. "What if it's someone I'm not the least bit attracted to?" she asked worriedly.

"You won't know that until you meet them." Vicki frowned. "Unless you've already figured out who it is and know for sure that you're not interested."

"I'm really beginning to believe it's Jamil. Especially after this morning's delivery. Whoever it is knows where I live and has mentioned being already acquainted with me. Very few people at work know where I live, no one else in our social circle has ever expressed interest in me before, and I don't want to even imagine it being a stranger. That would just be too creepy," she said with a shiver.

"What if it is Jamil?" Vicki asked.

Alyssa worried her bottom lip between her teeth. "I'll tell her I'm flattered but not interested. Hopefully, she'll finally take no for an answer."

"Okay, then what's the obsession with running into your school crush this morning?" Vicki asked, teasing.

Alyssa tossed a piece of popcorn at her, which landed perfectly down her open cleavage. They both laughed as Vicki dug the kernel out and popped it into her mouth.

"I don't know. I've just been thinking maybe I need to learn to be a little bolder, like Shauna was always trying to get me to be."

"Are you going to ask Collette out?" Vicki said in surprise.

Alyssa snorted. "Let's not get crazy. I'm just thinking of maybe feeling her out. Seeing if she is interested. I don't know. You don't think I should?"

Vicki shrugged. "I think you should wait and see who your secret admirer is. I honestly don't think it's Jamil. As many times as you've turned down meeting up when she's in town and the fact that you haven't heard from her in a while make me think she finally got the hint. Besides, aren't you the least bit curious to find out who would go to all this trouble to get your attention?"

Vicki handed her a chocolate. She really was curious and flattered. Then a thought occurred to her. "You don't think Shauna would have set this all up, like she did that final year of love letters?"

Vicki gave her a sympathetic smile. "Okay, I know she was good at surprises, but I think even this would be a bit much. Arranging for you to have a secret admirer five years after her death. Do you think she's going to come back from the grave to reveal herself?"

"I know that sounded crazy, but this was such a Shauna thing to do, and I had that dream about her the day before all this started. It just feels connected somehow." Alyssa's eyes began to burn with the start of tears.

Vicki set her bowl of popcorn and glass of wine on the coffee table, scooted closer to Alyssa, then did the same with hers and grasped her hands. "Look, I know you still miss her very much, and anyone with a heart would understand if you weren't ready to move on. Maybe we could do what Frank suggested and find out who the florist is that the flowers are coming from, then leave a message for your admirer telling them thank you but no thank you."

Alyssa shook her head. "No. I'm tired of being locked away in this house alone. Max is a great companion, and you're a wonderful friend to spend so much time with me, but I'm sure both of you are going to get sick of me sooner or later."

Vicki reached up and wiped a tear from Alyssa's cheek. "Never. You were the only one that talked to my nerdy, Coke-bottle-glasses, crooked-pigtail-wearing behind when we were kids. I'm here for you no matter what."

Alyssa placed an affectionate kiss on Vicki's hand that she still held. "Thanks."

"Now, if you want me to repeat my opinion, which I'm going to do whether you ask or not, I think you should wait to see who your secret admirer is. If it turns out to be someone you don't think you'll be interested in, then politely kick them to the curb and feel out Coach Roberts. The worst that could happen is that you gain another friend and get free tennis lessons," Vicki said with a wink.

Alyssa chuckled and pulled Vicki into her arms. "I love you."

Vicki gave her a tight squeeze. "I love you, too, girl."

CHAPTER FIVE

Alyssa woke up the next morning slightly hung over after she and Vicki finished the entire bottle of wine and box of chocolates. Vicki was asleep in the guest room, so Alyssa tried to be as quiet as possible as she got up to let Max out into the yard to take care of his business. She just didn't have the energy for their morning run. She put real coffee on instead of popping a pod into her Keurig. She needed something fresh and strong to get through going to church with her mother, then brunch after. Alyssa usually didn't go to church—not because she wasn't a believer, but she just never received any comfort from attending. She felt like she always had to be in character as Deacon Crain's daughter. Except for a short time after Shauna passed, when grief and anger had her faith at an all-time low, she did prayer meditation at the end of each day. It helped to make her day feel complete and her sleep peaceful.

After a strong cup of black coffee with lots of sugar instead of her usual flavored creamer and a piece of buttered toast, Alyssa left the doggy door open for Max to come in whenever he finished enjoying his morning sunbathing, then went and got ready for her day. When she came out Max was eating his breakfast and Vicki was still dressed in a pair of Alyssa's pajamas nursing a cup of coffee.

"Morning," she groaned.

Alyssa smiled. "Morning. Since when does wine give you a hangover?"

"Since I didn't eat anything yesterday except a bagel while I was grading papers."

"Why didn't you tell me? You know I would've fixed something or at least ordered pizza."

"I honestly didn't think about it. After I raid your refrigerator to fix myself breakfast, I'll be fine. I figured Max wanted to eat since he was waiting patiently by his bowl when I got up."

"Thanks. He's already been out in the yard, so he should be fine until I get back. Just leave the doggy door open for him when you leave."

"Will do. Tell Mama and Papa Crain hi for me."

"I will. I'll see you at work tomorrow."

After an affectionate embrace, Alyssa left Vicki to her own devices since she had a key to the house. She arrived at the church she had practically grown up in just before services were scheduled to start and found her mother at her desk in the church office. Vivica Crain was the church's secretary and bookkeeper. Dressed in what Alyssa liked to call her uniform—a white blouse buttoned up to the neck ensuring there wasn't the slightest bit of cleavage showing, a solid-colored skirt that brushed along the tops of her flesh-toned stocking-covered calves, sensible matching low-heeled pumps, and the only pop of color she ever allowed herself, a pastel cardigan—her mother sat with her reading glasses perched on the edge of her nose as she ran her finger along a column of numbers in an account book.

"Good morning, daughter," Alyssa's mother said without even looking up from her task.

Alyssa used to swear her mother really did have eyes in the back of her head.

"Good morning, Mommy." Alyssa bent and kissed the offered cheek her mother angled her way. "Is Daddy with Pastor Lewis?"

"Yes. You'll see some programs on the table there, if you'd like to set them out for me. I should be finished shortly," her mother said.

Alyssa smiled. *"If you'd like to…"* in Mom-speak really meant *"I'm not asking, but it sounds more polite."*

"Okay," Alyssa said and headed out of the office toward the chapel.

Ten minutes later Alyssa had finished her task, and shortly after, her father entered the chapel from the deacon's office at the side of the stage where the pulpit, deacons, and choir sat.

"Hey, Pumpkin. I didn't know you were here," her father said, walking toward her with open arms.

She allowed herself to be enveloped in his warmth. "Hey, Daddy. Mommy said you were with Pastor, so I didn't want to bother you."

"You know you aren't a bother. Besides, Pastor would've loved to chat with you before service."

Alyssa looked at her father knowingly. "You mean he would've loved trying to convince me to come back."

He grinned. "Well, you can't blame him for wanting his star attraction here. 'Amazing Grace' just hasn't sounded quite the same since you left."

"That's sweet, but I've heard Linda Johnson sing it. You all are just fine without me."

"But are you fine without God?" Alyssa heard her mother say behind her.

"Now, Viv, was that necessary?" Alyssa's father asked with a slight frown.

"Leonard, you know we did not raise her to be a part-time Christian. Coming to service once a month will not secure your place in heaven."

Alyssa's father shook his head, and Alyssa just smiled. She was used to this, ever since she stopped going to service because Pastor Lewis refused to officiate at her and Shauna's wedding. It seemed he was fine with having gays in his congregation and directing and singing in his choir, but marrying them was a step too far. When he told her that gay marriage went against God's word, that it should be only between a man and a woman, Alyssa had walked away from the only church home she had ever known and didn't return until after Shauna passed. She'd started coming back only to alleviate her parents' concern that she hadn't completely drowned in her grief, and she showed up only once a month. Despite knowing the reason Alyssa left, her mother kept trying to get her to come back full-time.

Alyssa placed an arm around her mother's waist. "I'm sure God knows where my heart is and has at least a little corner of Heaven waiting for me when that time comes, which I hope is a long way off," she said, then placed an affectionate kiss on her mother's cheek.

"See, Viv. Our baby girl is just fine," Alyssa's father said. "I have to get Pastor Lewis's robe from his office. I'll see you after the service." He gave Alyssa a peck on the cheek and her mother a prolonged kiss on the lips before walking up the aisle.

Alyssa held back a grin as she watched her mother watch her father as if he were the only person that existed in the world. Once her father was out of sight, her mother turned to her and must have realized she'd been caught because her complexion darkened with a blush.

She cleared her throat and adjusted the collar of her blouse. "Why don't you come help me set up the snacks in the nursery."

"Yes, ma'am." Alyssa followed her out.

She thought about the deep love her parents still shared after sixty-five years of marriage, the kind of love she had always wanted and finally found with Shauna. Unfortunately, it was snatched away from her too soon. The thought of trying to rebuild something like that from scratch at her age was daunting. She focused on helping her mother, trying not to think about her situation because it would only bring on sadness. By the time she and her mother finished, people were arriving for the service. Alyssa took a seat in a middle pew, not too far back for her mother to complain that she was hiding and not close enough for Pastor Lewis to feel tempted to call her up to *"give us a little taste of your blessed voice,"* as he was so fond of doing sometimes. Alyssa sat through the entire three-hour service, an hour of it trying to be polite by not covering her ears as Pastor Lewis shouted his fiery sermon at the congregation, feeling just as disconnected from it all as she always did.

After the service, she let her mother lead her around by the hand to catch up with people she hadn't seen since last month, then to Pastor Lewis for the usual spiel of how she was missed and how he hoped her visits would become more frequent. Thankfully, her mother also hadn't been too pleased with how Pastor Lewis had turned down Alyssa's request to officiate at her wedding and wouldn't allow her to be subjected to conversing with him longer than what she considered a respectable five minutes.

After that, her mother left the accounting of the tithes and offerings in her assistant's capable hands and said their good-byes to Alyssa's father before heading out for their monthly brunch date. Since her mother had come to church with her father, Alyssa drove them to her mother's favorite brunch spot, Snooze Town & Country. She ordered her usual shrimp and grits and their signature Morning Marg, and Alyssa ordered hers—sweet-potato hash, and a vanilla almond matcha tea latte.

She loved these brunch dates, not just because she liked spending time with her mother, but it was the only time Alyssa ever really saw her loosen up. Especially when the Morning Marg kicked in. As far as Alyssa knew, her mother never drank more than a couple glasses of wine during social occasions, so this was her way of treating herself. After their drinks were brought out, her mother took a large sip of hers and sighed contentedly.

"Rough day?" Alyssa asked, grinning.

Her mother gave an unladylike snort. "Try rough month. With

Pastor Lewis's retirement coming up, many of the older members are jumping ship. They're not too crazy about the young liberal preacher replacing him. They're worried that Pastor Wilson will bring in too much change."

"What about you and Daddy? You've been a major part of the church since we were kids."

"I think it's time for a change. Pastor Lewis showed his unwillingness to bend and be more inclusive when he refused to marry you and Shauna. But the last straw, at least for your father and me, was when he refused to baptize Shelly Carson's son a few months ago."

"Why? Isn't he only like ten? What could he have possibly done to warrant not being baptized?"

"He confessed to Shelly that he liked boys and worried that he might go to hell, so he asked if he could get baptized. Shelly told him he wasn't going to hell for being gay, but he insisted on the baptism anyway. She talked to Pastor to get his advice, and he refused to baptize him until she sent him to some conversion group," her mother said in disgust, taking another long sip of her drink.

Alyssa was shocked. "Is that why the Carson family left?"

"Yes. It's also why the board suggested Pastor consider retiring. Despite most of them agreeing with his views on sexuality, refusing to baptize a member took things too far even for them."

"Wow. I thought he'd chosen to retire on his own. He is almost ninety."

"Yeah, but enough about that. What's going on with you, and how's my grandpuppy doing?"

Alyssa smiled. Her brothers had given their mother five grandchildren, but Max was her youngest and favorite because he was less needy than the human ones, she'd said.

"He's doing good. We've both dropped some weight since we started running."

"I noticed you looked a little thinner. I was sort of hoping it was because you'd met someone." Her mother grinned.

"Have you been talking to Vicki?"

Her mother quirked a brow. "No. Why? Does she know something I should know?"

Alyssa looked guiltily down into her drink.

"Out with it."

"I'm not seeing anyone, but I do seem to have a secret admirer."

Alyssa suddenly felt embarrassed, as if she were a preteen instead of a fifty-year-old grown woman, telling her mother about a crush.

Her mother looked at her in surprise. "Really? When did that start?"

Alyssa told her mother about her dream and all that followed. She left out the details of the letters but gave her the general gist of them. Their food arrived, and her mother ordered another margarita before responding.

"Did I ever tell you that your great-grandmother saw spirits?" her mother said as she began eating.

Alyssa looked at her in confusion. "Maybe you should slow down on the margaritas, Mommy."

Her mother looked amused. "I'm not that much of a lightweight. It'll take a couple more of these for me to start not making sense."

"So, what does Grandma Ella seeing dead people have to do with my secret admirer?"

"Grandma Ella believed that loved ones returned sometimes to deliver an important message. Sometimes it's cryptic and takes a bit to figure out, and others are direct and to the point. Shauna was never one to hold back, so I'm not surprised she came back to push you along. Or that she might've directed this admirer your way."

Alyssa chuckled. "Mommy, you can't really believe Shauna came back from the dead to give me a secret admirer."

"Of course not, but if God thinks it's time for you to move on, then there's no telling what He can do. For all you know, He could've given Shauna's spirit the ability to visit your admirer in their dreams to put thoughts in their heart about you. Possibly thoughts they already had."

"I guess."

"Besides, you're not getting any younger, and most women like Shauna are probably already taken."

Alyssa frowned. "Wow, thanks."

Her mother waved her hand dismissively. "That's not what I meant. You've got a lot of love in you that was meant to be shared with someone special. I thought Shauna was going to be that person, but I guess God had other plans for her. You're not meant to waste away with only Max as company, so I'm sure whoever has been sent to you must be just as worthy and need that love even more than Shauna did."

Alyssa looked at her and smiled. It had taken a long time for them to reach the point in their relationship where they could talk about her in a relationship with any woman, let alone so acceptingly about Shauna. Fortunately, by the time Shauna came into her life, Alyssa's mother had decided her religious beliefs weren't worth losing her daughter over. She'd accepted Shauna into the family with open arms. They had gotten along so well that Alyssa's mother would call the house sometimes to talk to Shauna instead of her.

Alyssa's mother reached across the table and took her hand. "Look, baby, don't think too hard on this admirer thing, which I know you're doing. Just enjoy the attention. It was difficult watching you shut yourself away after Shauna passed. We worried that you wouldn't pull yourself out of that dark hole you had crawled in, but when you did, your dad, brothers, and I were thankful. Besides, if it doesn't get creepy, there's nothing to worry about until the day they reveal themselves. Even then, you may find yourself pleasantly surprised."

Alyssa gave her mother's hand a gentle squeeze. "Thanks, Mommy."

"Now, I need something sweet and one last margarita. Your daddy may even get lucky this afternoon." Her mother winked as she waved their server over.

Alyssa could only laugh as her usually sedate mother cut loose.

♥

Collette sat in her room at her Aunt Claudine's house, where she was staying until she got her own place, carefully writing her next letter to Alyssa. A knock on her door had her discreetly laying a blank sheet of paper over what she had written and turning toward her aunt, who stood in the doorway.

"I'm heading to the grocery store. Do you need anything?" Claudine asked.

"No. I'm good. Just finishing some grading."

Claudine cocked her head to the side and looked toward Collette's desk. "Students writing history papers on scented stationery now?"

Collette opened her mouth to respond but couldn't come up with a possible explanation other than the truth. Claudine had raised her and her sister after their parents were taken from them by a drunk driver when they were just kids. She taught them that before opening their mouths to tell any lie, they better have a damn good reason for it, because she would find out the truth sooner or later, and she always did. As kids, Collette and her sister Jackie believed their aunt must've been psychic. But they were just really bad liars. That was why she found it difficult to be in the teacher's lounge when her flowers to Alyssa arrived and why Vicki was able to get her to confess so easily. If Alyssa had brought up the flowers and letters while she was shopping in the boutique the other day, Collette probably would've confessed all right then and there, just to avoid having to act like she didn't know what was going on.

Collette looked at her aunt, who watched her curiously. "No. I'm writing a letter." There. She didn't lie, but she also didn't admit to anything.

Claudine grinned. "Must be someone special to have you pulling out the calligraphy set and special stationery."

Collette chewed on her bottom lip, debating whether to tell her aunt what was going on. After all, Alyssa shopped at the pet boutique often. Collette didn't want Claudine to let something slip in conversation. In the end, she did what she'd always done, confided in Claudine and told her everything—about how she'd met Alyssa previously, the connection to her book's character, and what started her on her secret-admirer journey.

When Collette finished, Claudine nodded with a smile. "All this time I've been thinking Rayne was someone you imagined, and it turns out I've known her for years. I love it. You two are great for each other, and I'd hoped you'd connect at some point."

"We haven't exactly connected yet, except when she came in the store Saturday."

Claudine's gaze narrowed. "You didn't tell me about that."

Collette's face heated with a blush. "Yeah. I didn't want to accidentally let it slip what I've been doing. I'm sure I don't need to tell you not to mention this if she comes in before the end of the week."

"Your secret is safe with me." Claudine gave her a conspiratorial wink. "I'm just glad you've moved on from that life-sucking leech you mistakenly married."

Collette chuckled. "Wow, Auntie. Tell me how you really feel."

Claudine sat on Collette's bed. "Child, you knew how Jackie and I both felt about that girl from the jump, but you married her anyway. You can't fault me for throwing a jab upside your head every now and then to remind you not to make that mistake again."

"All right. I'll give you that. I grudgingly appreciate the reminder, especially since she called me the other day."

Claudine frowned. "Let me guess, asking for something."

Collette nodded.

"I'm assuming you had sense enough to tell her to kiss your ass?"

Collette laughed. "Not in those exact words, but yes."

"Good. I knew my sister and I raised you with some sense. Speaking of sisters, Jackie called me to check up on you."

"Why didn't she just call me herself?"

"Because she wasn't sure she'd get a genuine answer. I told her you were fine, and obviously I was right." Claudine looked toward Collette's unfinished letter.

"Thanks. I'll call her after all this is over. She'll make a big deal out of it, and I don't even know if it's working."

"Is she throwing the flowers and letters away? How do you know she isn't?"

"Her friend Vicki is helping me. She told me I've piqued Alyssa's interest and that without knowing I'm her secret admirer she's already attracted to me. Unfortunately, our age difference and the fact that she's almost painfully awkward when it comes to dating is keeping her from acting on her feelings. I'm a little nervous that once she finds out I'm her admirer, she may shut me down completely if she already has those doubts."

"That just means you're going to have to put on that Roberts charm and convince her that age is just a number. Maybe tell her about Rayne's connection to her. That might get the juices flowing," Claudine said, grinning.

Collette scrunched her face in distaste. "Ugh, Auntie. Juices flowing? Really?"

"What? Just because I'm a woman of a certain age doesn't mean I've forgotten what passion is. Don't let this gray Afro fool you. I can put it down." She smoothed her hands along her still-fit and shapely body.

Collette held up her hands in surrender. "Enough, please. I don't need that image in my mind, thank you."

Claudine chuckled. "Okay. I'll go and let you finish your letter." She stood to leave. "Text me if you think of anything you need."

"I will."

"I'm happy you've connected with your Rayne." She gave Collette a wink over her shoulder as she walked out of the room.

CHAPTER SIX

A lyssa tried not to gaze up at the clock on the wall again as the parent of one of her students reprimanded her for giving their precious child a C on their last paper, which Alyssa had explained she was lucky to have gotten, since she had plagiarized most of it. Alyssa had given her the grade because what the student hadn't copied from a paper a previous student from her class had written to try to make it her own was quite good. Unfortunately, her mother didn't understand why her daughter doing the work alone didn't warrant a perfect grade, and Alyssa was losing patience with the woman, who had insisted on meeting with Alyssa today, and this was the only time she could fit her in.

Alyssa discreetly peeked down at her watch and swallowed a sigh of frustration. She already knew she wouldn't have time for her usual forty-five-minute lunch break. At this point she would be lucky to have enough time to run to the lounge and grab her lunch to eat at her desk before her next class. She would also miss sharing the daily delivery from her admirer with Vicki. That would mean they would either hold it in the office or deliver it here to her classroom.

"Mrs. Stanford, as I've explained, plagiarizing from someone else's work is dishonest and would normally warrant a failure, but Kate usually does wonderful work, so I took that into account when grading this last assignment."

Mrs. Stanford pursed her lips disapprovingly. "And as I have explained, Kate is under a lot of pressure right now with studying for her SATs and preparing for the upcoming tennis season. You can't cut her a little slack? After all, it was her sister's paper that she got the story idea from. This grade could affect her GPA and her chances of getting into Columbia."

"It doesn't matter where Kate got the idea. She didn't do the work required of her, which was to come up with an original story and write it in her own words. I appreciate your concern for your child's education, but Kate has been on the honor roll her entire school career. I seriously doubt this one grade will affect her current standing or future educational goals. Now, I have a class in twenty minutes that I have to prepare for. If you would like to schedule more time to discuss this further after school, I would be more than happy to do so."

Alyssa stood, an indication that the meeting was over. Mrs. Stanford sat for a moment longer, giving her an angry glare.

She finally stood to leave. "I will be speaking with Principal Hart about this."

Alyssa gave her an encouraging smile. "Please do. Have a nice day, Mrs. Stanford."

As Mrs. Stanford opened the door, Vicki stepped into the doorway, then quickly shuffled aside at the sight of the angry mother.

"Ms. Ingram," Mrs. Stanford said, looking distastefully at Vicki's short skirt as she passed.

Vicki smiled smugly. "Mrs. Stanford."

Mrs. Stanford huffed and practically stomped away. Vicki, arms filled with a bouquet of small sunflowers and Alyssa's lunch bag hanging from her fingers, chuckled and walked into the room, throwing her butt out to shut the door behind her.

"Special delivery." She placed the bouquet and lunch bag on Alyssa's desk. "I figured since you probably wouldn't make it to lunch, I would just deliver everything to you here."

"You didn't have to do that. Thank you."

"How else would I find out what was in the letter today?"

Alyssa chuckled. "How am I not surprised you had an ulterior motive?"

"Because you know me so well. Now," Vicki waved her hand over the flowers impatiently, "let's see what poetic words await us. Since it's just the two us, you can read it out loud." She sat in the chair Mrs. Stanford had just vacated and looked at Alyssa expectantly.

Alyssa shook her head in amusement and pulled out the envelope peeking from the flower wrapping. She loved the light floral scent she'd come to expect when opening the letter. It made her sigh in contentment as she waved the paper under her nose before reading its contents.

> *Dear Alyssa,*
> *I know sunflowers aren't usually considered romantic,*

but I believe they are one of the most romantic flowers of all. Sunflowers symbolize adoration, loyalty, and longevity. Aren't those three traits anyone would want in a romantic relationship?

I'm sure you'll find this hard to believe since we barely know each other, but I truly adore you. Like the sun draws the sunflower, your passion, creativity, and inner beauty drew me to you. I felt a connection so deep it was as if I'd found a piece of me I never knew was missing. You became my muse and a ray of sunshine in a lonely, dark place.

I hope that doesn't seem too much, that it doesn't push you away. I'm telling you this because I hope, when I reveal myself, that you'll understand why I feel you are worth, and deserve, all this love and attention. I also hope you understand, before we meet (again), that these feelings are more than a crush, more than a simple Valentine's stunt. I would like for this to be the beginning of something beautiful and long-lasting. You are to me as the sweet summer sun is to these flowers. Your inner glow provides me with creative nourishment and vibrancy, your bright rays reach out and fill my heart with joy, and the depth of feelings I have for you lifts me up in the hopes of one day basking in your love.

If this is all too much for you, if I'm only making a fool of myself by continuing to reach for something that may lead to nothing because you aren't the least bit interested, then I will give you an opportunity to put a stop to this, here and now. If you are interested in this continuing until I reveal myself to you in just a matter of days, please leave two sunflowers in a vase in your classroom window. If you aren't interested, which I will completely understand, please leave a single flower in a vase, and I will no longer send you flowers or these letters.

I leave my heart in your beautiful hands, Alyssa.
With genuine affection,
Your Secret Admirer

Alyssa looked up wide-eyed at Vicki, who seemed speechless for the first time ever. "That was unexpected."

"They're giving you an out," Vicki said.

Alyssa gazed back down at the letter and read the last part again, to herself. "Yeah."

"How do you feel about that?"

"I honestly don't know." Alyssa was too surprised to really absorb what she was feeling.

"Well, let's talk this through. First, they confirmed you've met before, so it isn't a total stranger. Second, they've obviously cared for you for some time. More than likely, it was someone you met that didn't know you were married right away, and when they found out they managed to keep their feelings for you to themselves. Lastly, they're obviously serious about pursuing more than just a fling with a crush. They want to pursue the possibility of more but don't want you to feel pressured into doing so. That sounds like someone who's very mature."

Alyssa looked at Vicki curiously. "If I didn't know any better, I'd think you knew who it is."

Vicki quirked an eyebrow. "Now how would I know that? I'm just trying to help you figure out what to do next. Of course, I can ignore the fact that this could be the second woman of your dreams who seems to fit one major requirement—someone to woo you. I can also point out the negatives if you like." Vicki lifted a finger to tick off each point she made. "First, it could be a man you know but never showed the least bit of interest in, who is completely clueless to what being gay means. Second, it could be Jamil. Lastly, it could be a crazy stalker. Have I hit all the major possibilities?"

Alyssa sat down at her desk. "There's one last one. Someone is just being nice because they know how lonely I am."

"Alyssa, besides me, who's aware of that? You know I wouldn't tell anyone, and I wouldn't be so cruel to play with your heart that way. I know it's difficult not to read too much into the creep factor of this whole thing, but you're a woman of words. What feelings or vibes do you get from reading the letters?"

Alyssa looked back down at the letter, drawn to the first paragraph. "*Sunflowers symbolize adoration, loyalty, and longevity. Aren't those three traits anyone would want in a romantic relationship?*" Those were definitely three traits she believed were important in a relationship, whether it was friendship or romance. Her admirer sounded mature, like they knew what they wanted, and Alyssa's gut told her they were a woman. Wasn't that what she would be looking for if she were actively trying to date? A mature, confident woman? That was usually her type, which, ironically, also scared her because she never believed she would be their type—until Shauna. Alyssa's dream conversation with Shauna came back to her.

"It's time for you to move on."

"What if I don't know how to be happy without you?"

Alyssa now realized that Shauna had made her promise to move on because she knew how afraid Alyssa would be of starting over. She would have to face her own insecurities and fears of dating and open herself up for rejection if she attempted to date someone out of her league. No matter how much she had changed during her time with Shauna...her hair, her clothes, being less introverted...after Shauna's death, she had returned to feeling like the quiet, bookish, church mouse she had been before Shauna came into her life. That was until her secret admirer entered the picture. Alyssa felt things she thought she'd never feel again: excited anticipation, intrigued, and desired. She ached to be held, to be kissed and touched with passion, to fall asleep talking about any and everything, to wake up with and fix breakfast for someone. She ached to be loved by another woman again.

Alyssa opened one of her desk drawers and pulled out a slim glass vase, poured water from her water bottle into it, and pulled two stems from the bouquet to place in it.

"That's my girl," Vicki said with a grin as Alyssa walked over and placed the vase on a stack of books right in the center, and largest, window. Fortunately, her classroom was on the first floor, so the flowers would be easy to spot.

♥

Collette made her way across the campus with her assistant coaches toward the tennis courts to strategize about the upcoming season. The path took her right past the windows to Alyssa's classroom. She'd placed herself to the right of the coach she was walking with.

"To have the opportunity to work with an NCAA Women's Tennis Championship player like you, Coach Roberts, is a real honor." The young man was talking as Collette gazed in his direction while discreetly looking over his head toward the picture window in Alyssa's classroom.

It took everything she had not to whoop for joy when she saw the vase with two long-necked flowers prominently displayed in it.

Collette directed her wide grin of happiness at the coach. "Well, it's an honor to coach such a great team."

Her smile must have beamed brighter than she thought, because he looked up at her with a bright blush. "We had a great head coach last year, but with you I think we'll be even better."

Collette schooled her smile and thanked him as they continued.

After her meeting with her coaching staff, Collette stopped by her office to pick up her work before heading to the gym. She had just gotten in her car when her phone buzzed. She dug it out of her bag, and Vicki's name flashed on the screen. She hit the speaker button and placed it on the holder.

"Hey, Vicki. I was going to call you tonight to finalize our plans," Collette said.

"Hey. I just thought we could do it now. I have a friend coming in from out of town who'll be here for only one night, so I may be too preoccupied for a phone call."

Collette grinned knowingly at the phone. "Uh, okay, well, my agent has set up an impromptu meet and greet with a select group of my fans for tomorrow, for which Alyssa should be receiving an invitation. I've made all the other arrangements involved, so we should be good to go if you can convince her to attend."

Vicki laughed. "It won't take much convincing. I told you she's not so secretly in love with R. Cole. Offering her the opportunity to attend an event where Cole plans to finally reveal her identity is like offering me the chance to raid Beyoncé's closet."

Collette smiled. "I take it that's good."

"Girl, they would have to get about six security guards that all looked like Michael B. Jordan to get me out of there."

"So, you're saying R. Cole is Alyssa's version of Michael B. Jordan and Ivy Park rolled into one. No pressure," Collette said nervously.

"You'll be fine. Like I told you, she's already into you, Collette Roberts. Finding out you're R. Cole, her favorite lesfic author, will be icing on the cake. I'll make sure she attends the meet and greet. You just do what you do best. Be you. I'll text you if there are any hiccups."

"Okay. Thanks."

After the call Collette wasn't feeling as confident as she had when she saw the flowers in the window. It was easy to ignore that the letters were leading to her revealing herself and her feelings to Alyssa in person because she hadn't made any set plans on the actual reveal. Now that she had, it was becoming all too real.

♥

So anxious about the outcome of leaving the two sunflowers in the window the previous day, Alyssa ended her last class before lunch five minutes early. When she'd left the flowers, she'd been tempted to hide out in the classroom at the end of the day, leering from the shadows to see who would stop to look toward the window but realized that would've seemed creepier than what some would consider a secret admirer to be. So, after her last class she shut the lights off and left before she could change her mind. Now she sat in the teachers' lounge, jumping every time the door opened. After several minutes of this behavior, she was relieved to see Vicki walk in and stop short at seeing her already sitting there. Vicki's classroom was just steps from the teachers' lounge, while Alyssa's was in another wing, so Vicki was usually the first to arrive.

Vicki grinned knowingly. "Well, isn't somebody early?"

"Everyone finished their tests ahead of time, so I dismissed them," Alyssa said, trying to sound nonchalant.

Vicki snorted. "Okay."

Alyssa didn't even try to hide her smile as they stood in line to use one of the lounge's three microwaves. Once they were seated and chatting about Vicki catching up with an old friend the previous night, Alyssa's anxiety lessened. She probably would've had a nervous breakdown if Vicki hadn't been there to distract her until Shari arrived at her usual time to drop off her delivery.

"Ms. Harris, if you get tired of receiving these, let me know, and I'll take them home. Maybe it'll make my boyfriend jealous enough to start buying me flowers," Shari said as she laid a huge bouquet of bright-red, burgundy, and white roses on the table.

"Shari, if you don't have a boyfriend who gives you at least a rose on special occasions, you need to find yourself a new one, not try to change the one you have," Vicki said.

Shari frowned. "You sound like my mother."

Vicki looked horrified. "I know she did not just compare me to a woman old enough to be her mother."

Alyssa chuckled. "Thank you, Shari. You are old enough to be her mother."

"True, but there was no need to point it out. That's just rude," Vicki said with a pout directed at Shari's retreating figure.

Alyssa didn't respond as she was too busy unfolding the note that came with the flowers.

Dear Alyssa,

As is fitting, I've saved the best for last. Roses, the flower of love. Did you know that each color of rose has its own individual meaning? I've chosen these three, as their meaning best represents what I hope will happen once we come face-to-face.

The bright-red rose symbolizes romance, which I hope I have brought to you with these gifts and letters.

The burgundy rose symbolizes enduring love and unconscious beauty, which I believe represents what's in your heart. Your ability to love openly and fully is such a gift, one I hope to receive in the future. Regarding unconscious beauty, I don't even think you realize how beautiful you are, not just physically but the beauty that glows from your personality. I've had the pleasure of being gifted with that presence in the past and hope that I will do so again.

The white rose symbolizes a new start and hope for the future, which I hope our meeting will be for both of us. A new start at a friendship, love, or whatever else may follow.

Just so you know, I'm not looking to tie you down or pressure you to make any decisions about us. All I want is what I think we both want—a companion to sit and have long talks about how much we have in common, the connection of our shared creativity, and a partner who understands what we feel without having to put it into words. That's what I'm at least hoping happens. Only time will tell.

Until then, I look forward to revealing all to you with my final note on Valentine's Day.

With genuine affection,
Your Secret Admirer

Nervous butterflies took flight in Alyssa's belly as she absentmindedly handed the letter to Vicki. This was it. The last letter before her secret admirer revealed her identity and everything became real. This weekend she would connect the actual person with the one she'd unsuccessfully tried to imagine. She only knew for sure that even though Shauna and her admirer were incredibly good at writing love letters, that's where the similarities ended. While Shauna's letters were sweet, romantic, and loving, Alyssa's admirer's letters were filled with passion and desire. She also had the feeling that the person, who she still strongly believed, and hoped, was a woman, didn't seem to hesitate to say what she wanted or express her feelings. She was the opposite of Alyssa, who tended to be guarded when it came to romantic feelings for someone. If she really had met her admirer before, Alyssa hoped it was at least someone she liked. It would be awkward enough to meet the woman who'd managed to soften a place in her heart with her letters if it was someone Alyssa really didn't know or like.

"Are you okay?" Vicki interrupted her thoughts.

Alyssa shook her head. "I don't know. It's starting to become real, and I don't know if I'm ready for that."

"Did you expect to maintain this like a pen-pal relationship? You knew all this was leading up to meeting them. Have you changed your mind?"

"No. I'm just nervous. I never did well with blind dates, and this is sort of feeling like one."

Vicki placed the letter back in the floral wrapping. "Well, you have until Saturday to figure it out. When they send the note mentioned, you could always not show up."

"That would be cruel, especially after she gave me a chance to change my mind, and I didn't. I feel obligated now."

"She?"

Alyssa shrugged. "I think only a woman would take the time to handwrite such passionate letters using scented stationery. I know that sounds sexist, but it's just the feeling I get from the letters."

"Sounds about right to me. You know now we're going to have to go shopping for a new outfit."

"No. I have plenty of clothes."

Vicki snorted. "You haven't gotten new clothes since that last vacation you and Shauna took. And that was only because you needed a Western outfit for some theme night at the resort. C'mon. Indulge me. Let's go shopping like we used to when we were teens cruising the mall."

"All right." Alyssa only agreed because she knew Vicki would bug her until she gave in. She also thought that maybe a new outfit would make her feel braver, because at that moment her nerves were getting the best of her, and she was seriously thinking about Vicki's suggestion of not showing up at the reveal.

♥

Alyssa arrived home to find a shoebox-sized package on her doorstep. She didn't recall ordering anything recently. She looked at the return address in confusion. It was from a literary agency in New York, addressed to her. She hadn't submitted anything in years. Even if she had finally gotten up enough nerve to, she'd promised Shauna she would go through the independent publishing house her books went through. Alyssa set it aside to walk Max, fix them dinner, and then grade the tests she had given her classes that day. It was almost eleven o'clock before she finished and decided to head to bed after letting Max out. As she walked into the foyer to turn on the alarm, she noticed the package sitting forgotten on the credenza and took it with her to her bedroom.

She opened the table on what used to be Shauna's side of the bed and pulled out a pocketknife Shauna had kept there in case of intruders. Alyssa smiled at the memory of teasing Shauna about watching her favorite musical *West Side Story* one too many times. She carefully opened the box to find another slightly smaller gold box wrapped in purple ribbon, held together with a beautiful vintage crystal butterfly hair clip.

"What in the world?" Alyssa said to Max, who blinked lazily from his bed with his head resting on his paws.

She gently unclipped the ribbon and opened the box. The first thing to catch her eye among purple and gold confetti paper was a book. When she picked it up and opened the cover, she widened her eyes in surprise. Then she squealed in delight, causing Max to pop his head up and stare at her.

"It's a personally autographed copy of R. Cole's upcoming release, *The Butterfly Murders!*"

She showed it to Max as if he knew what he was looking at. Alyssa couldn't imagine who would send her something like this as she set the book aside to examine the rest of the contents. She found a bag of miniature Snickers, the main character Rayne Edwards's favorite candy, and an oversized envelope. She opened it to find an invitation.

Alyssa Harris
As an avid fan of R. Cole
You are Cordially Invited

To Attend an
Exclusive Meet & Greet with
The Author of The Rayne Edwards Mystery Series
R. Cole
On
Friday, February 13
Quiessence at the Farm
6016 S. 32nd St
Phoenix, AZ
Cocktail Attire Required

"WHAT!" Alyssa shot up off the bed and did a little dance.

Max stood up and whined.

"Oh. I'm sorry, buddy." Alyssa rubbed behind his ear to calm him. "Mommy is just excited. Nothing to worry about."

Max looked at her doubtfully but huffed and lay back down, watching Alyssa.

"How is this possible? Why am I getting this?"

She looked at the label on the outer box again and realized R. Cole's agent had probably sent it to her, but she had no idea why. She hadn't entered any contests or done anything that she was aware of to draw attention to herself. Not only that, but R. Cole was supposedly a recluse, choosing to keep her identity a secret, although Alyssa did recall reading an interview with the author where she mentioned the possibility of revealing her identity with her next series. This had to be some joke.

Alyssa walked over to the wall of books Shauna had built for them and took down the autographed copy of R. Cole's first book, which she had paid an arm and a leg for at a silent auction. She compared the autographs and had no doubt that the one in the copy of *The Butterfly Murders* did look genuine. Neither her birthday or any other special occasion was coming up except Valentine's Day. She had a sudden thought. Could this be her secret admirer? Was this where they were revealing themselves? She laughed off the crazy thought. Only a few people knew she was practically obsessed with R. Cole. Maybe one of them submitted her name to some contest? Alyssa picked up her phone and called Vicki.

"Hey girl. I thought you'd be in bed by now."

"Hey. So, something weird happened. I came home to find a package on my doorstep from a literary agency in New York."

"Okay. How's that weird? Wait. Did you submit one of your novels and didn't tell me?"

"No." Alyssa described what was in the box. "Did you have anything to do with this? Maybe submit my name to some contest or something?"

"No. Are you sure you didn't and forgot?"

"I think I'd remember if I entered a contest to meet R. Cole. You don't think this has anything to do with my secret admirer, do you?"

"I don't see how. Unless your admirer is R. Cole. Wouldn't that be something?"

"Funny. I seriously doubt R. Cole even knows I exist."

"I believe that invitation says she does. Wait. What about all the mailing lists you're on for all her new releases? Maybe they got your name from that list. Since this is a new release, they're doing something special. Didn't you tell me about an article you recently read about Cole talking about possibly revealing her identity after her next novel?"

"I guess that all could make sense. Normally when I get an early release it's usually not sent with such fanfare. It's usually in a brown padded envelope with the standard greeting and best wishes and that's it."

"Like I said, maybe they're doing something different. I guess this means we're getting two new outfits when we go to the mall tomorrow."

Alyssa chuckled. "You're just spending all my money."

"If we find something too fabulous for your budget, it'll be my treat. After all, your birthday is next month."

"We'll see. Catch you tomorrow."

"G'nite, girl."

After she hung up, Alyssa placed everything back in the gift box and set it on her dresser. The excitement had worn off, and now she was too tired to try to figure this mystery out.

CHAPTER SEVEN

That Friday, Alyssa stood looking at her reflection in her mirror wondering if she suddenly had become the luckiest woman she knew, or someone was playing a cruel joke on her. In a couple of weeks, she had acquired a secret admirer and an invitation to meet her favorite mysterious, mystery author.

"You look so hot," Vicki said as she placed a necklace she had chosen from Alyssa's jewelry around her neck to go with her new burgundy pleated midi dress with kimono sleeves and tie waist.

Alyssa tried adjusting the daringly low-cut neckline to show less skin. "I still think it's too much. I had a nice black cocktail dress I could've worn."

"Yeah, it is nice. That's the problem. You're about to meet a woman you've been crushing on for a few years now, you're single, and you're ready to mingle. You needed a dress that could say all of that in one look."

Alyssa laughed. "Single and ready to mingle?"

"Well, ready to dip your toes in the dating pool at least. Also, I said I would get you a date by Valentine's, and this is my way of moving things along."

"You do know it's a meet and greet. I won't be the only person there."

"Probably, but that doesn't mean you won't catch Ms. Cole's eye. Especially the way that dress is showing off your girls." Vicki gave Alyssa's breasts a little lift.

Alyssa chuckled and playfully slapped her hands away. "You know, for a straight woman, you sure are obsessed with my boobs."

"That's because you were naturally gifted with them, and I had to pay for them, so it's an obsession based on jealousy. Now, I got you a car service in case you decide to imbibe, so call me when you get there and when you're on your way home."

"You didn't have to do that."

Vicki shrugged. "I know, but I'm hoping it'll encourage you to relax and enjoy yourself without worrying about driving."

Alyssa grinned. "I guess this makes up for you not holding up your promise to find me a date by Valentine's."

"Girl, please, I tried. I can't help it if you're picky."

"I'm not picky. I'm choosy," Alyssa said, pouting.

Vicki snorted. "That's fancy for picky." Her phone buzzed, and she pulled it out of her pants pocket. "Your car is here."

Alyssa's heart began beating frantically. "Wow. I'm suddenly really nervous."

Vicki pulled her in for a quick embrace, then took her hands. "There's nothing to be nervous about. You've met tons of famous authors. R. Cole is no different from them, or you. She puts her pants on one leg at a time just like everyone else."

"I sit on the bed and put both my legs in at the same time."

Vicki rolled her eyes. "Once again, you call me high maintenance." She began pulling Alyssa toward the door, grabbing the clutch she had picked out with the dress on the way out.

When they stepped out onto the porch, Alyssa was surprised to see a limo, not a standard town car, waiting for her. She turned toward Vicki. "A limo? Really? This is too much."

Vicki waved dismissively. "It's a big night for you. I thought you should arrive in style."

She pulled her best friend into a hug and planted a lip-smacking kiss on her cheek. "Thank you. You know I love you, right?"

"I know. Make sure you fix your lipstick when you get in the car."

Alyssa looked down at Max, who sat serenely by Vicki's side on the porch. "What do you think, buddy?" She did a little spin. "Do you think this outfit will impress R. Cole?"

Max gave a bark of approval, and Alyssa gave him an ear scratch in return. "Be good for Auntie Vicki. I shouldn't be out too late."

"Let's hope that's not true. Now stop procrastinating and go," Vick said, shooing her away.

Within a half hour the limo pulled up in front of the Farm at South Mountain where Quiessence, a popular farm-to-table restaurant known for their seasonal tasting menus and multi-course dinners, was located. Alyssa had been here once a couple of years ago for a friend's wedding reception and had wanted to come back but never found a reason to treat herself to such an expensive night out. She checked her lipstick and hair, which Vicki had insisted on blowing out and curling and then clipping back on one side with the butterfly hair clip that came with the invitation, one last time before the driver opened the door and assisted her out of the car. He told her he wouldn't go far and gave her his card so she could text him when she was ready to leave. Alyssa made the lengthy but beautiful walk from the parking lot, past the breakfast café and garden where they grew their own food, to the restaurant on shaking legs, wishing she had worn flats instead of the strappy heels Vicki had talked her into wearing.

"You can't have a slit in a dress like that with legs like yours and not wear a strappy heel to show them off," she'd told Alyssa when she started to argue.

Seeing her image reflected in the window as she entered, Alyssa had to admit, in a not-so-conceited way, that she did look good. It had been a long time since she had taken such care with her appearance. She gave the hostess a smile at her greeting.

"Hi. I'm here for the R. Cole gathering?"

The hostess looked confused for a moment as she ran her finger down the list on the stand in front of her and then smiled. "Yes, of course. If you'll follow me, please."

They walked through the main dining room, out onto the patio, and just past it to a walkway that led to a cabana with the curtains tied back to reveal a table set for two in front of a stone fireplace.

"Here you are," the hostess said.

Alyssa looked from the table to her, confused. "There must be some mistake. I was told there was a private reception for R. Cole... the author."

The hostess continued to smile, but Alyssa could see a bit of humor in her eyes. "Yes. This is it. Reservation for R. Cole. Your server should be by shortly. Enjoy, Ms. Harris."

Alyssa continued to watch in confusion as the young woman walked away. She looked back at the table and noticed a familiar floral envelope propped against a floral centerpiece. It took her a second to realize that the centerpiece was a bouquet of all the flowers she had received from her secret admirer. Her brain bounced from one question to another. Why would she be invited to a private dinner with R. Cole when she didn't even know the woman? Why were there signs of her secret admirer at her dinner with R. Cole? How would her secret admirer know of her love of R. Cole novels? And the most far-fetched question…Could R. Cole be her secret admirer? That one got a quiet chuckle out of her.

Alyssa walked up to the table and, with trembling fingers, picked up the envelope. She didn't even need to lift it to her nose to recognize the subtle floral scent. She took a seat as she opened the envelope, suspecting she would need to sit down for this one.

Dear Alyssa,

I thought it would be fitting to end these mysterious correspondences with a real mystery and a double reveal. At the time I began my endeavor to woo you, I had no idea that you were an avid R. Cole fan, which seems to make all of this feel as if it were meant to be. Or maybe it's just the romantic in me. Either way, I first laid eyes on you six years ago as you stood in front of a classroom full of eager writers-to-be and recited a quote from Maya Angelou that has stuck with me ever since:

"I've learned that people will forget what you said, people will forget what you did, but people will never forget how you made them feel."

I felt a pull toward you that I never had experienced with anyone before. Ms. Angelou was right about never forgetting how you make people feel. Your love and passion for the craft of writing and the power of words shone brightly through every class that summer. Your joy and willingness to take the time to nurture that same passion in others was something I don't think anyone that attended your writing sessions would forget. I know I didn't. But that wasn't all that drew me to you. I eagerly looked forward to the way your beautiful, honest smile would light up the room. I loved watching the way you encouraged every attendee as if each one was your star pupil. How nurturing you were when an attendee's story turned out to be more personal and emotional than expected as she broke down reading it in front of the class. Then there's the light touch you place on someone's shoulder or arm as you speak with them, the way you cock your head as you listen attentively to what someone is saying.

And finally, there's your beauty, so pure and natural. You aren't obvious about it and don't even seem to believe it when others tell you how beautiful you are. It's as if you don't see what is so obvious to others. So many times I wished I could tell you all of this, but I envied what I couldn't have from afar. Your heart belonged to another, so I had to accept that what I felt for you would never be requited. Then, whether it was fate or coincidence, our paths crossed again, giving me the opportunity to reveal my feelings for you in the hopes that you would at least have dinner and conversation with me to see if you could possibly be interested in me. I would also, at least, like to show you my appreciation, for if it weren't for you, there would be no R. Cole or Rayne Edwards novels. If you haven't guessed by now, I'm R. Cole.

Now, Alyssa, I'm going to give you the same opportunity I did with the bouquet of sunflowers I sent. If this is all too much, if you want to walk away, you're welcome to do so. Once again, I'll completely understand. But, if you're interested in spending an evening having a nice dinner and conversation, nothing more, then please signal the server standing nearby, and I will be joining you shortly.

With genuine affection,
Your no longer Secret Admirer,
R. Cole

Alyssa stared at the same signature in the two autographed books she had and thought, just for a second, that maybe she was dreaming. She brought her hand to her other forearm and pinched it, just to be sure.

"This is crazy," she said to herself. R. Cole was her secret admirer, but how? Alyssa thought back to her previous letters when her admirer mentioned they had met before. Could she have met R. Cole at one of the many conferences and retreats she had attended? Then she looked back at the letter in her hand.

...when I first laid eyes on you six years ago as you stood in front of a classroom full of eager writers-to-be and recited a quote from Maya Angelou...

Alyssa remembered what she was referring to. Six years ago, she'd worked as an editor for Shauna's publisher for about a year before they suggested she start doing writers' workshops. The one R. Cole was referring to had been her first one of three before she'd stopped to care for Shauna. R. Cole had attended that workshop? Alyssa racked her brain trying to place the faces of the thirty people who had attended that session, but it was difficult. Then it hit her again, where she was, who she was there to meet and how her letters had made her feel. R. Cole was her secret admirer! Alyssa folded the letter, put it back in the envelope, took a deep breath, and gazed up at a young man standing expectantly nearby. She waved him over, her heart beating a mile a minute as she did so.

"Will you be staying for dinner, Ms. Harris?" he asked.

"Yes."

He nodded with a smile. "Excellent. My name is Alan, and I will be your server tonight. May I pour you a glass of wine?" he asked, indicating a wine bucket Alyssa hadn't even noticed sitting near the table. In it was the same brand of wine she had received from her admirer…or should she say R. Cole.

A giggle almost bubbled up before Alyssa cleared her throat and nodded. "Yes, please."

Alan smiled knowingly, opened the bottle, and poured wine in her glass and the one across from her. R. Cole's glass, she thought, not able to hold back the goofy grin she knew must be on her face.

"Ms. Cole will join you shortly," Alan said, giving her a slight bow before departing.

Alyssa looked around nervously, waiting for her mysterious dinner companion to jump out of a nearby bush. She picked up her wine and took a long drink to calm her nerves. When that didn't work, she closed her eyes and took a few deep, calming breaths. When she opened her eyes, she saw someone walking up the pathway toward her and furrowed her brow in confusion. It was Collette Roberts, carrying a single red rose and looking sexy as hell in black slacks, white dinner jacket, white open-collar, button-down shirt, and her locks hanging loose around her face. She looked just as nervous as Alyssa had been feeling since she'd arrived.

"Collette?" Alyssa stood as Collette reached the table.

"Yes. You look beautiful," Collette said as she handed Alyssa the rose. "I'm so glad you decided to stay."

Alyssa absently accepted the rose, still staring at Collette in bewilderment. "You're my secret admirer?"

"Yes."

"I'm so confused. The letter said that R. Cole was…" Then it dawned on her why Collette had seemed familiar to her when they first met. She must have been in that workshop, and her being here now meant she was R. Cole. Her legs felt like rubber, and she gripped the table for support.

"Here. Why don't you sit down," Collette said worriedly as she grasped Alyssa's other arm to steady her and ease her back into her chair.

♥

Collette had been out of sight nervously watching everything from a window inside the restaurant. She'd been whispering a prayer as Alyssa read her letter that she would decide to stay instead of taking her up on her offer to leave. She'd almost collapsed with relief when Alyssa signaled the server over and settled back in her seat. As eager as she was to run out and just get the reveal over with, she had chosen to give Alyssa time to let everything sink in. After all, she'd just learned that her favorite author was her secret admirer, which meant a double reveal. She couldn't imagine what was going through Alyssa's head right now, but it had to be a little overwhelming.

Collette had watched Alyssa close her eyes and take a couple of deep breaths. That was as good a time as any to get this over with. She'd taken a deep breath of her own and headed up the path toward the private cabana she'd booked. Alyssa's confused reaction was pretty much what she'd expected, but not her legs practically going out from under her. She was currently kneeling in front of Alyssa, handing her a glass of water that had been sitting on the table.

"Are you all right?" Collette asked in concern.

Alyssa sipped the water and nodded. "I was too nervous to eat much today and probably drank the wine too fast."

"It probably didn't help finding out your secret admirer is not only R. Cole but also one of your coworkers," she said guiltily.

Alyssa gave her a small smile. "There is that. So, you're really R. Cole?"

She suddenly felt shy. "At your service."

Alyssa cocked her head to the side as she furrowed her brow and studied Collette's face. "Are you the young woman who wrote the mystery sci-fi short that Shauna liked so much?"

Collette nodded. "My hair was a lot shorter then, and I used to wear makeup and more feminine clothing."

"I see. Please, sit down. I wouldn't want you getting grass stains on your pants," Alyssa said.

"Are you sure you're all right? I can give Wes a call to come take you home if you like."

"I'm fine, really."

She nodded and stood to take the seat across from Alyssa.

"Wait. How do you know who my driver is?" Alyssa asked.

Collette realized she'd probably just outed Vicki's involvement. "Uh…Well…I'm actually the one that set up the car service."

Alyssa shook her head. "I knew Vicki was involved in this somehow. I can't believe she lied."

"Technically, she didn't. She had nothing to do with this until after your second bouquet, when she figured out I was the secret admirer. I sort of gave myself away trying to discreetly watch you when the flowers and letters arrived. She confronted me to make sure I wasn't out to play games with you or hurt you. Once I proved to her that I had genuine intentions toward you, she insisted on helping me to at least plan the reveal. That's the only part she was involved in."

"So, she knew you were R. Cole all this time?"

"Yes."

"Okay. I need a minute to let this sink in." Alyssa picked up her glass of wine and began to take another sip but then reached for a roll from the breadbasket in the middle of the table.

"Why don't I get them to bring out the first course, so you can get something a little more substantial in your stomach." Collette nodded toward the server standing nearby, who nodded and headed back toward the main restaurant.

Alyssa gave her an appreciative smile. Collette's stomach was in a ball of knots as she quietly sipped her wine and gave Alyssa the minute she needed.

"So," Alyssa said, as if she'd counted exactly one minute. "If I'm understanding the situation, you attended one of my classes six years ago, developed feelings that you kept to yourself because I was in a relationship, moved on with your life until you started working at Richmond, where I just happened to be working as well, never mentioned us meeting before when we were introduced, and realized you were still interested in me. But instead of asking me out, you waited five months to tell me as a secret admirer through a series of letters, and now here we are. Is that about right?"

The look Alyssa gave her was that of a student trying to make sense of their teacher's explanation but not quite getting it. Collette smiled in understanding.

"I know that seems a little far-fetched, maybe even crazy if you look at it on the surface, but it's not quite that straightforward. Well, at least not the last part. Yes, I was in your workshop and felt a connection to you that developed into something more than a simple physical attraction. I was a bit lost back then. A few years out of college, I had a devastating injury that brought my professional tennis career to an end before it even really began, and I was relegated to giving private tennis lessons to privileged kids and their parents who didn't take it seriously." Collette frowned at the memory.

"I wasn't happy. Of course, you know the saying, *those who can, do. Those who can't, teach.* I realized that I couldn't do what I loved, what I'd been doing since my mother put a racket in my hand at five years old." Collette had to take a moment of her own because she still felt the loss of that part of her life—the part that kept her connected to her mother after her parents' car accident when she was just thirteen.

Alyssa reached across the table and laid her hand on Collette's. When she gazed up at Alyssa, she saw a sympathetic smile. She didn't know if Alyssa knew about the loss of her parents, but the warmth of her hand and her caring smile eased some of the pain, especially since she knew about Alyssa's own devastating loss.

Collette took a deep breath. "My aunt and sister saw how unhappy I was and talked me into trying to pursue my other love, writing. I had started and stopped several novellas and one full novel, but it was just a way to relieve stress. I'd never considered trying to get anything published, but I needed to find something else before I ended up in a pretty dark place. I finished the novel, connected with an agent through one of my tennis clients, and she loved the story and series concept but thought it could use just as much feeling as it did mystery and action. That's how I ended up in your workshop. As I said in my letters, your passion and love for writing was infectious, and the way you nurtured all of us inspired me." She turned her hand over to gently grasp Alyssa's hand, still lying on hers. "You became my muse."

She confessed how much of an effect Alyssa had on her writing Rayne Edward's story. As she explained, she realized it might sound as if she had become obsessed with Alyssa and hoped that wasn't what Alyssa was thinking as she listened with a furrowed brow and frown.

"I hope that doesn't sound too crazy," Collette said when she finished.

Alyssa's frown turned up into a soft smile. "Not too crazy, but I'm thinking that Shauna must have known you were R. Cole. After the party to celebrate completion of the workshop, she told me she thought one of my students had a crush on me, and when she went to point out who, you had already left. Then when we started reading the Rayne Edwards mysteries, she jokingly said maybe R. Cole was that mystery student because she recognized the style of writing and that Rayne's description sounded like me. I always waved her off as being silly, but maybe she wasn't so far off after all."

Collette's face heated with embarrassment. "I may have seemed obsessed with you, but I swear, that's not it. I just felt like I wanted to acknowledge the woman who brought my passion for writing back."

"It's okay. I'm flattered. It lets me know I made an impact."

Collette smiled. "You definitely did. Just to assure you, I expressed my obsession only through Rayne. Without you, there wouldn't have been a Rayne Edwards series. Just so you know, I didn't stalk you or anything after that. Ending up at Richmond High was pure coincidence. After publishing my first novel, I moved to California to take a job at a country club as a tennis instructor, but since I had my writing, I no longer looked at teaching tennis as settling. Long story short, I met and married the wrong woman, got divorced, and ended up here living with my aunt, who helped me get the job at Richmond."

"When I met you, I knew something was familiar about you, but I guess since you look so different now, I couldn't place what it was. Why didn't you say anything?"

Collette shrugged. "When I saw you, I had all those feelings again, but you didn't seem to remember, and I was afraid that if I mentioned meeting you before, I would end up telling you everything. I thought you were probably still mourning Shauna and wouldn't be too happy to have some woman you barely know tell you she's been secretly crushing on you for six years."

Alyssa grinned. "Yeah. I guess that wouldn't have been the best thing to do. I'm assuming that's also why you've never asked me out for coffee or anything."

She nodded.

"What changed your mind, and why as a secret admirer?"

Collette hesitated to answer because she was starting to see the creep factor of her plan that she hadn't considered. "I sort of overheard you and Vicki talking about how you loved being wooed in a romantic, old-fashioned way and remembered that feeling I got around Valentine's

Day when I was in high school, and the student council sold roses for people to send to their boyfriend, girlfriend, or secret crush. I received one from a secret admirer who happened to be a girl I had also been crushing on and thought it would be sweet and unique to do something like that for you, but in a mature way to make you feel special."

Alyssa reached across the table again to take her hand. "Well, you succeeded. It was sweet, romantic, and made me feel special. Thank you."

She gave Alyssa's hand a gentle squeeze. "It's been my pleasure. So, you're not creeped out or disappointed to find out that your secret admirer and favorite author is just an average high school sports coach and teacher?"

Alyssa smiled shyly. "Honestly, no. I've imagined R. Cole would be this bigger-than-life character I would be lucky enough to just make eye contact with and that my secret admirer would be someone I didn't know or wouldn't be the least bit interested in knowing."

"And now?"

Alyssa's face darkened with a blush, and she looked bashfully down at their clasped hands. "And now I'm overwhelmed knowing that I was R. Cole's muse and that I'm very interested in getting to know both the mysterious author and the admirer."

Collette felt like she could finally breathe a full breath for the first time in days. She lifted Alyssa's hand and placed a soft kiss on the back of it. "Then why don't we spend the evening getting acquainted with both?"

♥

Three hours later, Alyssa arrived home feeling as if she were walking on air and living a dream come true. Both Max and Vicki were waiting for her. Max greeted her in his usual boisterous and happy manner, but Vicki looked as if she were afraid to approach her.

Alyssa gave Max a sturdy pat while grinning at Vicki knowingly. "Don't worry. You're safe, but not completely out of hot water."

Vicki sighed loudly and acted as if she were wiping sweat from her brow. "I'll grab the bottle of wine I have chilling in the fridge, and you can tell me all about it."

She followed Vicki into the kitchen. "I can't believe you managed to keep that secret for a week."

Vicki chuckled. "Girl, I almost blew it a couple of times. You know I don't like keeping things from you. Hopefully, judging by the grin that hasn't left your face since you walked in, it was worth it."

She accepted the glass Vicki poured, and they headed into the living room.

"Okay. Tell me everything," Vicki said excitedly.

She chuckled and told Vicki about her night with Collette. She still couldn't believe Collette Roberts was her admirer, let alone R. Cole. What were the chances that she would ever get to meet the mysterious author, then find out that she had been her muse and secret crush?

"So, you're happy with the outcome?" Vicki asked.

She smiled more broadly. "Very. I still can't believe it and would never have imagined it turning out this way, but I'm not disappointed."

Vicki raised her glass. "Let's toast to old-fashioned wooing for the win."

She chuckled and touched her glass to Vicki's.

"What's next?" Vicki asked.

"Well, we're both chaperoning the dance tomorrow night, so we're going to hang out together after. Maybe go to the teachers' after-party."

Vicki looked disappointed. "That's it?"

"What did you expect? That we'd run off into the sunset and get married?"

"Funny. No, but I thought something more exciting than chaperoning hormonal teens and hanging out with your coworkers."

Alyssa laughed. "Sorry to disappoint you, but it turns out Collette is just as much a homebody as I am. Tonight was enough excitement for both of us. She's letting me set the pace, and although she's had feelings for me for some time, she still wants to take time for us to get to know each other."

Vicki smiled. "You really like her, don't you?"

She nodded. "She's down-to-earth, romantic, funny, and smart. Did you know she has a BA in American History and an MA in Afro-American Studies, fluently speaks Spanish and French, and left a high-paying tennis-instructor position to teach kids because she thought they would benefit from it more than the rich adults she was instructing?"

Vicki gave her a knowing smirk. "Oh, you are definitely hooked. She sounds as wonderful as I'd hoped she'd be."

Her face heated. "Yeah. Me too."

♥

Alyssa peeked out her front window for the third time in the past five minutes. Collette was picking her up so they could go to the dance and after-party together. It would, sort of, be their first official date, and she was just as nervous now as she'd been last night. She checked herself out in the large mirror in the foyer. Fortunately, her blow-out still held, so she just freshened up the curls. The dance's color theme was red, pink, and white, so she wore a red wrap dress with a pleated skirt that brushed just above her knees, a pair of wedge-heeled red pumps with an ankle strap, and a gold heart necklace with matching earrings. She loved theme parties, so she always dressed the part any chance she got. Looking down at her watch, she realized she'd gotten dressed a little too early in her eagerness about the evening. Collette wasn't due to arrive for another fifteen minutes.

She was headed back toward the living room when Max suddenly got up from his pillow where he'd been watching Animal Planet and trotted past her to stand staring at the door. Seconds later the doorbell rang, and he gazed back at her expectantly. Alyssa met his gaze with confusion. He only did that when someone he knew had arrived, like her parents or Vicki. She wasn't expecting either of them. She walked up to the door and looked out the window beside it, then down at Max in surprise.

"How did you know?"

His tongue lolled out of his mouth in his doggy smile, and his tail wagged happily. She shook her head in disbelief and opened the door.

"Hey," she said to Collette.

"Hey. I know I'm a little early, but I had to stop and get you this, and it took me less time than I expected." Collette offered her a small plastic container with a pink-and-red sweetheart-rose wrist corsage.

"That is so sweet," Alyssa said, accepting it.

Collette grinned. "Well, it is a sweetheart dance. Can't have my date show up without a corsage. By the way, you look beautiful, as always."

"I see you also took the theme to heart." Collette wore white pants and shirt, a pink blazer, a pink bow tie with red and white hearts, Xs, and Os, and red Converse sneakers. She looked adorable.

Collette did a little spin. "You like? These were the only red shoes I had, but since it's a high school dance I didn't think anyone would really notice."

Alyssa smiled. "They're perfect. Why don't you come in? I just have to let Max out one last time and grab a sweater."

"Speaking of Max." Collette walked into the foyer and knelt in front of Max, who stood beside Alyssa watching Collette expectantly. "I have a Valentine treat for him, if Mommy doesn't mind him having it."

The word *treat* had Max's tail wagging and tongue lolling.

"Of course, he can have it. Max, sit," she said. He did as he was told.

Collette waited for her to nod before she reached inside her blazer and pulled out a plastic bag with a heart-shaped dog biscuit. "I hear peanut butter and banana is his favorite."

She was speechless. For her to think of Max was a surprise. Well, she did say whoever she dated would have to pass the Max test, and Collette seemed to be doing that with flying colors.

"Uh, yes, it is. You can have it, Max," she told him as he looked from the biscuit to her.

Max gently took the biscuit from Collette and trotted back to his pillow.

"That was very thoughtful," she said as she led Collette into the living room.

"It was my pleasure. Besides the fact that I love dogs, I figured it was only right to bring the man of the house a peace offering, since I'm hoping to visit more often. That is, if his mom is okay with that." Collette gave her a sexy grin that made her heart skip a beat.

"I think his mom would enjoy that."

Their gazes held for a moment before she managed to pull herself up from the depths of Collette's beautiful dark eyes. "I guess while Max is enjoying his treat, I'll go grab my sweater and be right back to let him out after he's finished."

"Take your time. I can let him out. I assume the door to the backyard is through the kitchen?"

"Yes. Thank you."

Alyssa turned and headed back to her bedroom to grab the pink cardigan she'd planned to wear but forgotten. She took a moment to let the feelings she hadn't experienced in a long time sink in. She had already been attracted to Collette, but now that she knew Collette felt the same, her attraction seemed to have grown stronger overnight. She'd been so starved without physical human contact that the urge to reach up, pull Collette's face down toward hers, and kiss her full, soft lips was overwhelming.

"Pull it together, girl," she said to herself before taking a deep breath and heading back out to Collette.

Neither Max nor Collette was there. The "beep" of the back door told her where they had gone. She went into the kitchen, refilled Max's water bowl, and set her coffeemaker timer in case she got back late and forgot. By the time she finished her tasks, Max was trotting in and went straight to his water bowl, and Collette followed, closing and locking the door behind her.

"Thank you again," Alyssa said.

Collette nodded. "You're welcome. Nice setup you have out there. A full outdoor kitchen and firepit."

Alyssa looked wistfully out the kitchen window. "That became Shauna's pet project as soon as we moved in. She liked to entertain and wanted an outdoor space that rivaled the ones on those backyard-makeover shows. I haven't used the kitchen since she's been gone, but the firepit gets quite a bit of use when Vicki or my family comes over."

Collette walked over and took one of her hands. "I'm sorry if I've made you sad."

She looked back at Collette and smiled to reassure her. "You haven't. I'm just realizing how much I've shut myself away since she passed and how it's time for me to start living again."

"Well, let me be the first to say welcome back to the land of the living. It would be my honor to help escort you on your journey." Collette raised her hand and placed a soft kiss on her knuckles.

A surge of heat traveled from the point of contact of Collette's lips and spread quickly throughout Alyssa. *"Down, girl,"* she said to herself.

"I guess we better go," she said aloud.

Collette grinned knowingly and released her hand. "I guess so."

CHAPTER EIGHT

Alyssa and Max stood on the front porch as Collette backed out of the driveway, blowing them both a kiss. She had just dropped them off after spending an afternoon at the dog park with them. It had been three months since they had officially started dating about a week after Collette revealed she had been her secret admirer, and she felt even more like a blushing, wistfully sighing schoolgirl than she did then. Gazing down at Max's besotted tongue-wagging face as Collette drove off, she knew he felt the same.

"C'mon, big boy. I don't know about you, but I need a nap."

Max yawned, as if on cue, and she chuckled.

They headed into the house, she kicked off her shoes, found her cozy corner of the sofa, turned the TV on to Animal Planet, Max curled up on his pillow, and they were both out within minutes.

♥

Alyssa awoke to the feeling of someone watching her. She peeked an eye open to find Shauna sitting cross-legged at the other end of the sofa looking at her with a soft smile. Alyssa sat up, scooted closer to Shauna, and mirrored her sitting position.

"Hi," Alyssa said.

"Hi. You don't seem surprised to see me this time."

Alyssa shrugged. "I had a feeling you'd visit sooner or later."

Shauna quirked a ginger brow. "Did ya now?"

She reached up and smoothed a wayward curl back behind Shauna's ear. "I figured you would want to check in."

"Sort of. I have a pretty good idea of how you've been doing."

Shauna took her hand and pressed a kiss to her palm before grasping her other hand and holding them both gently between hers.

"This is probably going to sound like a crazy question, especially since this is only a dream, but did you have anything to do with Collette?"

Shauna grinned. "No, love. That was all you. You inspired something in her. The same something you inspired in me, my sweet Erato."

She felt like someone caressed her heart as Shauna called her by the nickname she had addressed Alyssa by in her love letters. Shauna had nicknamed her after Erato, the mythological muse of love poetry, after she admitted that she wasn't one to write love poems until she met her. Alyssa had never imagined herself as someone who could inspire such sentiment, but she loved that Shauna thought she was.

"I like her. I think she's good for you. She even got you to do what I'd been bugging you to do for years. I would've been happy if you'd at least submitted a short story for someone to publish, but you finally finished that manuscript and sent it in. I'm proud of you."

Her face flared with heat. "Thank you. I probably would've submitted it if you were still here. I just didn't have the heart to finish it after you passed away."

"I know. I'm sorry I broke your heart. I fought as hard as I could, but I guess, like your mother always says, God must've had other plans." Shauna smiled wistfully and reached up to caress her cheek. "Like being your guardian angel."

Her eyes clouded with tears. "I would've rather you still be here as my wife."

Shauna wiped away a tear. "I know, but I'm content knowing I've left you in excellent hands—your family, Vicki, and Collette. She's brought back that love in your eyes, and I love her for that."

"Who said anything about love?"

Shauna chuckled. "No one has said it, but I can see it. In both of you. Even in Max." She turned to look over at him as he snored loudly and slept peacefully.

She smiled. "Sometimes I think he likes her better than me."

"No. I think he's happy to have a full pack again. He probably also senses how happy Collette makes his mommy."

She grinned so hard at the thought of how happy she was with Collette that her cheeks ached. They were going away for Memorial Day weekend, just the two of them. Collette had been so patient with

Alyssa needing time before she consummated their relationship, and that was going to be the weekend it happened.

Shauna smiled knowingly. "It's about time."

Her face heated with embarrassment that Shauna knew what she was thinking about.

"Love, all I want is for you to be happy. That's all I've ever wanted. If I can't be here to make you happy, I can't imagine anyone better than Collette to do it."

"What now?" she asked, feeling a bittersweet sadness instead of the heartbreaking one she'd endured for so long.

"It's time for me to move on, but you know I'll always be here." Shauna placed her hand over Alyssa's heart.

A loving warmth that left behind a sense of peace enveloped her heart. She placed her hand over Shauna's. "Thank you for loving me. For helping me love myself."

Shauna's emerald eyes sparkled like jewels with unshed tears. "It was my pleasure, love."

♥

Alyssa truly awoke this time with that sense of peace still warming her heart. She looked at the end of the sofa where Shauna had been sitting to find Max curled up asleep in her place. As if he'd sensed her watching him, his eyes blinked open and looked so sad.

"C'mere, buddy."

She held her arms open, and Max scrambled across the sofa to her, lying on his side with his big head in her lap.

She lovingly stroked his wiry fur. "She'll always be here," she said, patting Max's chest above his heart.

He looked up at her with a heavy sigh but with less sadness in his eyes. She knew how he felt. Shauna would always be her first true love and would hold a large part of her heart for as long as she lived, but she had learned with Collette's bouquets of love, which she still received weekly, that her heart was big enough to chance making room for another.

About the Authors

JULIE CANNON divides her time by being a corporate suit, a wife, mom, sister, friend, and writer. Julie and her wife have lived in at least a half a dozen states, traveled around the world, and have an unending supply of dedicated friends. And of course, the most important people in their lives are their three kids, #1, Dude, and the Divine Miss Em.

Julie's novel *I Remember* won the Golden Crown Literary Society's Best Lesbian Romance in 2014. Visit her website: JulieCannon.com

ERIN DUTTON resides near Nashville, TN, with her wife. They enjoy traveling with their much doted-on dog. In 2007 she published her first book, *Sequestered Hearts*, and has kept writing since. She's a proud recipient of the 2011 Alice B. Readers Appreciation Medal for her body of work.

When not working or writing, she enjoys playing golf, photography, and spending time with friends and family.

ANNE SHADE writes from the idyllic suburb of West Orange, New Jersey, and is the author of *Femme Tales*, queered retellings of three classic fairytales short-listed for a 2021 Lambda Literary Award; *Masquerade*, a Roaring 20s romance; and *Love and Lotus Blossoms*, a coming-of-age and coming out story listed as a Publishers Weekly Best of 2021 novel. She is currently preparing for the release of her next novel, *Her Heart's Desire*, a contemporary romance set for release February 2022.

Books Available From Bold Strokes Books

Deadly Secrets by VK Powell. Corporate criminals want whistleblower Jana Elliott permanently silenced, but Rafe Silva will risk everything to keep the woman she loves safe. (978-1-63679-087-9)

Enchanted Autumn by Ursula Klein. When Elizabeth comes to Salem, Massachusetts, to study the witch trials, she never expects to find love—or an actual witch…and Hazel might just turn out to be both. (978-1-63679-104-3)

Escorted by Renee Roman. When fantasy meets reality, will escort Ryan Lewis be able to walk away from a chance at forever with her new client Dani? (978-1-63679-039-8)

Her Heart's Desire by Anne Shade. Two women. One choice. Will Eve and Lynette be able to overcome their doubts and fears to embrace their deepest desire? (978-1-63679-102-9)

My Secret Valentine by Julie Cannon, Erin Dutton & Anne Shade. Winning the heart of your secret Valentine? These award-winning authors agree, there is no better way to fall in love. (978-1-63679-071-8)

Perilous Obsession by Carsen Taite. When reporter Macy Moran becomes consumed with solving a cold case, will her quest for the truth bring her closer to Detective Beck Ramsey or will her obsession with finding a murderer rob her of a chance at true love? (978-1-63679-009-1)

Reading Her by Amanda Radley. Lauren and Allegra learn love and happiness are right where they least expect it. There's just one problem: Lauren has a secret she cannot tell anyone, and Allegra knows she's hiding something. (978-1-63679-075-6)

The Willing by Lyn Hemphill. Kitty Wilson doesn't know how, but she can bring people back from the dead as long as someone is willing to take their place and keep the universe in balance. (978-1-63679-083-1)

Watching Over Her by Ronica Black. As they face the snowstorm of the century, and the looming threat of a stalker, Riley and Zoey just might find love in the most unexpected of places. (978-1-63679-100-5)

Always by Kris Bryant. When a pushy American private investigator shows up demanding to meet the woman in Camila's artwork, instead of introducing her to her great-grandmother, Camila decides to lead her on a wild goose chase all over Italy. (978-1-63679-027-5)

Exes and O's by Joy Argento. Ali and Madison really only have one thing in common. The girl who broke their heart may be the only one who can put it back together. (978-1-63679-017-6)

Paris Rules by Jaime Maddox. Carly Becker has been searching for the perfect woman all her life, but no one ever seems to be just right until Paige Waterford checks all her boxes, except the most important one—she's married. (978-1-63679-077-0)

Shadow Dancers by Suzie Clarke. In this third and final book in the Moon Shadow series, Rachel must find a way to become the hunter and not the hunted, and this time she will meet Eshee Yumiko head-on. (978-1-63555-829-6)

The Kiss by C.A. Popovich. When her wife refuses their divorce and begins to stalk her, threatening her life, Kate realizes to protect her new love, Leslie, she has to let her go, even if it breaks her heart. (978-1-63679-079-4)

The Wedding Setup by Charlotte Greene. When Ryann, a big-time New York executive, goes to Colorado to help out with her best friend's wedding, she never expects to fall for the maid of honor. (978-1-63679-033-6)

Velocity by Gun Brooke. Holly and Claire work toward an uncertain future preparing for an alien space mission, and only one thing is certain—they will have to risk their lives, and their hearts, to discover the truth. (978-1-63555-983-5)

Wildflower Words by Sam Ledel. Lida Jones treks west with her father in search of a better life on the rapidly developing American frontier, but finds home when she meets Hazel Thompson. (978-1-63679-055-8)

A Fairer Tomorrow by Kathleen Knowles. For Maddie Weeks and Gerry Stern, the Second World War brought them together, but the end of the war might rip them apart. (978-1-63555-874-6)

Changing Majors by Ana Hartnett Reichardt. Beyond a love, beyond a coming-out, Bailey Sullivan discovers what lies beyond the shame and self-doubt imposed on her by traditional Southern ideals. (978-1-63679-081-7)

Highland Whirl by Anna Larner. Opposites attract in the Scottish Highlands, when feisty Alice Campbell falls for city girl about town Roxanne Barns. (978-1-63555-892-0)

Holiday Hearts by Diana Day-Admire and Lyn Cole. Opposites attract during Christmastime chaos in Kansas City. (978-1-63679-128-9)

Humbug by Amanda Radley. With the corporate Christmas party in jeopardy, CEO Rosalind Caldwell hires Christmas Girl Ellie Pearce as her personal assistant. The only problem is, Ellie isn't a PA, has never planned a party, and develops a ridiculous crush on her totally intimidating new boss. (978-1-63555-965-1)

On the Rocks by Georgia Beers. Schoolteacher Vanessa Martini makes no apologies for her dating checklist, and newly single mom Grace Chapman ticks all Vanessa's Do Not Date boxes. Of course, they're never going to fall in love. (978-1-63555-989-7)

Song of Serenity by Brey Willows. Arguing with the Muse of music and justice is complicated, falling in love with her even more so. (978-1-63679-015-2)

The Christmas Proposal by Lisa Moreau. Stranded together in a Christmas village on a snowy mountain, Grace and Bridget face their past and question their dreams for the future. (978-1-63555-648-3)

The Infinite Summer by Morgan Lee Miller. While spending the summer with her dad in a small beach town, Remi Brenner falls for Harper Hebert and accidentally finds herself tangled up in an intense restaurant rivalry between her famous stepmom and her first love. (978-1-63555-969-9)

Wisdom by Jesse J. Thoma. When Sophia and Reggie are chosen for the governor's new community design team and tasked with tackling substance abuse and mental health issues, battle lines are drawn even as sparks fly. (978-1-63555-886-9)

A Convenient Arrangement by Aurora Rey and Jaime Clevenger. Cuffing season has come for lesbians, and for Jess Archer and Cody Dawson, their convenient arrangement becomes anything but. (978-1-63555-818-0)

An Alaskan Wedding by Nance Sparks. The last thing either Andrea or Riley expects is to bump into the one who broke her heart fifteen years ago, but when they meet at the welcome party, their feelings come rushing back. (978-1-63679-053-4)

Beulah Lodge by Cathy Dunnell. It's 1874, and newly betrothed Ruth Mallowes is set on marriage and life as a missionary…until she falls in love with the housemaid at Beulah Lodge. (978-1-63679-007-7)

Gia's Gems by Toni Logan. When Lindsey Speyer discovers that popular travel columnist Gia Williams is a complete fake and threatens to expose her, blackmail has never been so sexy. (978-1-63555-917-0)

Holiday Wishes & Mistletoe Kisses by M. Ullrich. Four holidays, four couples, four chances to make their wishes come true. (978-1-63555-760-2)

Love By Proxy by Dena Blake. Tess has a secret crush on her best friend, Sophie, so the last thing she wants is to help Sophie fall in love with someone else, but how can she stand in the way of her happiness? (978-1-63555-973-6)

Marry Me by Melissa Brayden. Allison Hale attempts to plan the wedding of the century to a man who could save her family's business, if only she wasn't falling for her wedding planner, Megan Kinkaid. (978-1-63555-932-3)

Pathway to Love by Radclyffe. Courtney Valentine is looking for a woman exactly like Ben—smart, sexy, and not in the market for anything serious. All she has to do is convince Ben that sex-without-strings is the perfect pathway to pleasure. (978-1-63679-110-4)